Irvine Welsh

ECSTASY

Three Tales of
Chemical Romance

V
VINTAGE

Published by Vintage 1997

2 4 6 8 10 9 7 5 3 1

First published in Great Britain by
Jonathan Cape Ltd, 1996

Vintage
Random House, 20 Vauxhall Bridge Road,
London SW1V 2SA

Random House Australia (Pty) Limited
20 Alfred Street, Milsons Point, Sydney
New South Wales 2061, Australia

Random House New Zealand Limited
18 Poland Road, Glenfield,
Auckland 10, New Zealand

Random House South Africa (Pty) Limited
Endulini, 5A Jubilee Road, Parktown 2193, South Africa

Random House UK Limited Reg. No. 954009

A CIP catalogue record for this book
is available from the British Library

ISBN 0 09 959091 3

Printed and bound in Great Britain by
Cox & Wyman, Reading, Berkshire

To Sandy MacNair

They say that death kills you, but death doesn't kill you. Boredom and indifference kill you.

I Need More, Iggy Pop

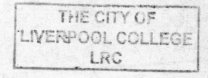

Ecstatic love and more to Anne, my friends and family, and all the good people – you know who you are.

Thanks to Robin at the publishers for his diligence and support.

Thanks to Paolo for the Marv rarities, especially Piece of Clay; Toni for the eurotechno; Janet and Tracy for the happy house; and Dino and Frank for the gabber. Nice one to Antoinette for the stereo and Bernard for the gaff.

Love to all the posses in Edinburgh, Glasgow, Amsterdam, London, Manchester, Newcastle, New York, San Francisco and Munich.

Glory to the Hibees.

Take care.

Contents

Lorraine Goes To Livingston

*A Rave and
Regency Romance*

For Debbie Donovan and Gary Dunn

1 Rebecca's Chocolates

Rebecca Navarro sat in her spacious conservatory and looked out across the bright, fresh garden. Perky was down at the bottom end by the old stone wall, pruning the rose-bushes. She could just about make out the suggestion of that familiar pre-occupied frown on his brow, her view distorted by the sun shining strongly into her face through the glass. She felt floaty, drowsy and dislocated in the heat. Succumbing to it, she allowed the heavy typescript to slip through her hands and fall onto the glass coffee table with a fat thump. The first page bore the heading:

UNTITLED – WORK IN PROGRESS
(Miss May Regency Romance No. 14.)

A dark cloud hovered ominously in front of the sun, breaking its spell on Rebecca. She took the opportunity to steal a brief glance at her reflection in the now-darkened glass of the partition door. This triggered a brief spasm of self-loathing before she altered her position from profile to face-on and sucked in her cheeks. The new image obliterated the one of sagging-flesh-hanging-from-the-jawline to the extent that Rebecca felt justified in giving herself a little reward.

Perky was engrossed in his gardening, or pretending to be. The Navarros employed a man to do the gardening and he undertook his duties thoroughly and professionally, but Perky would always find a pretext to go out and do some pottering. He claimed it helped him to think. Rebecca could never, for the life of her, imagine what her husband had to think about.

Despite Perky's preoccupation however, Rebecca was still swift and furtive as her hand reached across to the box. She pulled up the top layer and quickly removed two rum truffles from the bottom section. She crammed them into her mouth, the sickly sensation almost making her faint, and started to chew violently. The trick was to consume as quickly as possible; in doing it this way there was a sense that the body could be cheated, conned into processing the calories as a block lot, letting them go through as two little items.

This self-delusion could not be sustained as the vile, sweet sickness hit her stomach. She could *feel* her body slowly and agonisingly breaking down those ugly poisons, conducting a meticulous inventory of calories and toxins present before distributing them to the parts of the body where they would do the most damage.

So at first Rebecca thought that she was experiencing one of her familiar anxiety attacks when it hit her: that slow, burning pain. It took a couple of seconds before the possibility, then the actuality, dawned on her, that it was more than that. She couldn't breathe as her ears began to ring and the world around her started to spin. Rebecca fell heavily from her chair to the floor of the conservatory, gripping her throat, her face twisting to one side, chocolate and saliva spilling from her mouth.

A few yards away, Perky chopped at the rose-bushes. Buggers want spraying, he thought, as he stood back to assess his work. Out of the corner of his eye he saw something twitching on the conservatory floor ...

2 Yasmin Goes
To Yeovil

Yvonne Croft picked up the copy of the book *Yasmin Goes To Yeovil* by Rebecca Navarro. She had scoffed at her mother's addiction to this series of pulp romantic fiction known as the *Miss May Regency Romances*, but she just couldn't leave this book alone. There seemed, times, she considered, when its hold on her reached fearsome levels. Yvonne sat up in the lotus position in her large wicker basket chair, one of the few items of furniture alongside the single bed, the wooden wardrobe, the chest of drawers and the miniature sink in her small rectangular room in the nurses' home of St Hubbin's Hospital in London.

She was greedily devouring the last two pages of the book, the climax to this particular romance. Yvonne Croft knew what would happen. She knew that the wily match-maker Miss May (who turned up in every Rebecca Navarro novel in various incarnations) would expose Sir Rodney de Mourney as an unspeakable cad and that the sensuous, tempestuous and untameable Yasmin Delacourt would be united with her true love, the dashing Tom Resnick, just as in Rebecca Navarro's previous work *Lucy Goes To Liverpool*, where the lovely heroine was saved from kidnap, the smuggler ship and a life of white slavery at the hands of the evil Milburn D'Arcy, by dashing East India Company official Quentin Hammond.

Yvonne nonetheless read with enthusiasm, and was transported into a world of romance, a world free from the reality of eight-hour backshifts on geriatric wards, looking after decaying, incontinent people who had degenerated into sagging, wheezing, brittle, twisted parodies of themselves as they prepared to die.

*

Page 224

Tom Resnick rode like the wind. He knew that his steadfast mare was in great pain and that he risked Midnight's lameness by pushing the loyal and noble beast with such savage determination. And for what? His heart heavy, Tom knew that he would never reach Brondy Hall before Yasmin was joined in marriage to the despicable Sir Rodney de Mourney, that trickster who, unbeknown to his beautiful angel, was preparing to swindle her out of her fortune and reduce that lovely creature to the role of imprisoned concubine.

At the ball, Sir Rodney was relaxed and cheerful. Yasmin had never looked so beautiful. Her virtue would be his tonight, and how Sir Rodney would savour the final surrender of this headstrong filly. Lord Beaumont stood by his friend's side. — Your bride-to-be is indeed a treasure. To be frank with you, Rodney, my dear friend, I thought that you would never win her heart, convinced as I was that she had seen us both as frippery fellows indeed.

— Never underestimate a huntsman, my friend, Sir Rodney smiled. — I am far too experienced a sportsman to pursue my quarry too closely. I simply held back and waited for the ideal opportunity to arise before administering the coup de grâce.

— Despatching the troublesome Resnick overseas, I'll wager.

Sir Rodney raised an eyebrow and lowered his voice. — Please be a little more discreet, my friend, he looked around shiftily and, convinced that nobody had heard them over the noise of the band that played the waltz, continued — yes, I arranged for Resnick's unexpected commission with the Sussex Rangers and his posting to Belgium. Hopefully Boney's marksmen have delivered the knave to hell even as we speak!

— A good thing too, Beaumont smiled, — for the lady Yasmin had sadly not conducted herself in the manner appropriate to a delicately nurtured female. She seemed to know little discomfiture on that occasion when you and I visited her; finding her embroiled in the concerns of someone no more than an urchin — certainly far beneath the notice of any aspirant to social heights!

— Yes, Beaumont, the wanton streak, though, has appeal in a filly, though that streak must be broken if the woman is to become a dutiful wife. It is this streak that I shall break tonight!

Sir Rodney was unaware that a tall spinster was standing behind the velvet curtain. Miss May had heard everything. She moved off, into the body of the party, leaving him with his thoughts of Yasmin. Tonight would be

Yvonne was distracted by a knock on the door. It was her friend Lorraine Gillespie. – Ye on a late, Yvonne? Lorraine smiled at her. It was an unusual smile, Yvonne thought, one which always seemed to be directed at something beyond its recipient. Sometimes when she looked at you like that, it was as if it wasn't even Lorraine at all.

– Yeah, worst bleedin luck. That fucking Sister Bruce; proper old bag she is.

– Ye want tae see that Sister Patel ... her fuckin patter, Lorraine winced. – You will go-ooh and change the bedclothes, and when you have done this, you will go-ooh and do the drug round, and when you have done this you will go-oh-oh and do the temperatures and then when you have done this go-oh-oh ...

– Yeah ... Sister Patel. She's damaged goods, that one.

– Yvonne, is it cool for me tae make a brew, aye?

– Yeah, sorry ... you stick on the kettle, will ya, Lorraine? – I'm sorry to be such an anti-social cow, I just gotta finish this book.

Lorraine went over to the sink behind Yvonne and filled the kettle and put it on. On her way past her friend she bent over her chair and filled her nostrils with the fragrance of Yvonne's perfume and shampoo. She caught herself rubbing some of Yvonne's shining blonde hair between her thumb and forefinger. – God, Yvonne, your hair's gone really lovely. What shampoo is that you've been using?

– It's just that Schwartzkopf stuff, she said, – you like it?

– Yeah, said Lorraine, feeling a funny dryness in her throat, – I do. She went back over to the sink and unplugged the kettle.

– So you going clubbing tonight? Yvonne asked.

– Aw aye, I'm always up for clubbing, Lorraine smiled.

3 Freddy's Bodies

There was nothing like the sight of a stiff to give Freddy Royle a stiffie.

— Bit bashed about this one, Glen, the path lab technician explained, as he wheeled the body into the hospital mortuary.

Freddy was finding it hard to maintain steady breathing. He examined the corpse. — She's bain a roight pretty un n arl, he rasped in his Somerset drawl, — caar accident oi presumes?

— Yeah, poor cow. M25. Lost too much blood by the time they cut her out of the pile-up, Glen mumbled uncomfortably. He was feeling a bit sick. Usually a stiff was just a stiff to him, and he had seen them in all conditions. Sometimes though, when it was someone young, or someone whose beauty could still be evidenced from the three-dimensional photograph of flesh they had left behind, the sense of the waste and futility of it all just fazed him. This was such an occasion.

One of the dead girl's legs was lacerated to the bone. Freddy ran his hand up the perfect one. It felt smooth. — Still a bit wahrm n arl, he observed, — bit too waarm for moi tastes if the truth be told.

— Eh, Freddy, Glen began.

— Oh zorry, me ol moite, Freddy smiled, reaching into his wallet and peeling off some notes which he handed over to Glen.

— Cheers, Glen said, pocketing the money and hastily exiting.

Glen fingered the notes in his pocket as he walked briskly down the hospital corridor and took the lift to the canteen. This part of the ritual, the exchange of cash, left him elated and debased at the same time. He could never tell which emotion was the strongest. Why though, he reasoned, should he deny himself a cut if the rest of them were in on it? Those arseholes who had more than he ever would: the hospital trustees.

Yes, the trustees knew all about Freddy Royle, Glen reflected bitterly. They knew the real secrets of the chat-show host, the presenter of the lonely hearts television show, *From Fred With Love*, the author of several books, including *Howzat! – Freddy Royle On Cricket, Freddy Royle's Somerset, Somerset With a Z: The Wit Of The West Country, West Country Walks With Freddy Royle* and *Freddy Royle's 101 Magic Party Tricks*. Yes, those trustee bastards knew what this distinguished friend, this favourite caring, laconic uncle to the nation did with the stiffs they got in here. The thing was, Freddy brought millions of pounds into the place with his fund-raising activities. This brought kudos to the trustees, and made St Hubbin's Hospital a flagship for the arm's-length trusts from the NHS. All they had to do was keep *shtumm* and indulge Sir Freddy with the odd body.

Glen thought about Sir Freddy, thrusting his way to a loveless paradise with a piece of dead meat. In the canteen, he joined the line and examined the food on display. Glen decided against a bacon roll and had processed cheese instead. He thought of Freddy and the old necrophiliac joke: someday some rotten cunt will split on him. It wouldn't be Glen though: Freddy paid too well for that. Thinking of the cash and what it could buy, Glen's thoughts turned to AWOL at the SW1 Club tonight. She would be there – she often was on a Saturday – or at Garage City in Shaftesbury Avenue. Ray Harrow, one of the theatre technicians, had told him. Ray was into jungle; he had the same *modus operandi* as Lorraine. Ray was okay, he had lent Glen tapes. Glen couldn't get into jungle, but he'd try for Lorraine. Lorraine Gillespie. Beautiful Lorraine. Student Nurse Lorraine Gillespie. He knew she worked hard: conscientious, dedicated on the ward. He knew she raved hard: AWOL, The Gallery, Garage City. What he wanted to know was how she loved.

When he came to the end of the line with his tray and paid the cashier, he saw the blonde nurse sitting at one of the tables. He didn't know her name, all he knew of her was that she was Lorraine's friend. By the look of things she was just starting her shift. Glen thought about sitting beside her, talking to her, perhaps even finding out about Lorraine through her. He moved over towards her, and then obeying a sudden nervous impulse, half-slipped and half-collapsed into a seat a couple of tables away. As he ate his roll he cursed his weakness. Lorraine. If he couldn't work up the bottle to talk to her friend, how was he ever going to work up the bottle to talk to *her*?

Then she rose and smiled over at him as she passed him. His spirits lifted. The next time he'd talk to her, then the time after that he'd talk to her when she was *with Lorraine*.

When Glen returned to the ante-room, he heard Freddy next door in the mortuary. He couldn't bear to look, but he listened at the swing doors. He heard Freddy's gasps, – Wor, wor, wor, looks like a good un!

4 Admission

The ambulance arrived quickly, but it seemed a long time for Perky. He watched Rebecca gasp and groan on the conservatory floor. Self-consciously, he grabbed her hand. − Chin up, old girl, they're on their way, he said once or twice.

− You'll be right as rain, he told her, as the ambulance men loaded her into a chair, placed an oxygen mask over her face, and wheeled her into the back of the van. It was as if he was watching a silent film in which his own sounds of encouragement seemed like a badly imposed voice-over. Then Perky was aware of Wilma and Alan Fosley, watching the scene from over their hedge. − Everything's fine, he assured them, − just fine.

The ambulancemen, in turn, gave Perky a similar reassurance that this would indeed be the case, intimating that the stroke looked a mild one. This contention carried a conviction that he found unsettling and it served to lower his spirits. Perky found himself hoping fervently that they were wrong and that a doctor would come up with a more negative evaluation.

He started to perspire heavily as he turned the options over in his mind:

The best scenario: she dies and I am minted in the will.

Next best: she is okay and continues to write, and promptly completes the latest regency romance novel.

He shuddered as he realised that he was in fact flirting with the worse-case scenario: Rebecca is incapacitated in some way, perhaps even reduced to a vegetable, incapable of writing but a drain on our resources.

− Aren't you coming with us, Mr Navarro? one of the ambulancemen asked, his tone quite accusatory.

— You chaps go ahead, I'll follow in the car, Perky replied sharply. He was used, in social situations, to giving orders to people from such a class, and was therefore riled by their presumption that he should do as *they* think appropriate. He looked over at the rose-bushes. Yes, they could do with a spraying. At the hospital there would be all the fuss and palaver of checking the old girl in. Yes, time for a spraying, surely.

Perky's attention was arrested by the manuscript which lay on the coffee table. There was chocolatey vomit on the front page. With some distaste, he brushed the worst off with a handkerchief, exposing the bubbled, wet paper.

He opened its pages and started to read.

5 Untitled – Work In Progress (Miss May Regency Romance No. 14.)

It only required the most modest of fires to heat the small, compact schoolroom in the old manse at Selkirk. This was considered a particularly advantageous state of affairs by the Minister of the parish, the Reverend Andrew Beattie, a man noted for his frugality.

Andrew's wife, Flora, matched this frugality with a lavish extravagance. She knew and accepted that she had married into reduced circumstances and that money was tight, but while she had learned to be what her husband constantly referred to as 'practical' in her day-to-day dealings, the essential extravagance of her spirit could not be broken by those circumstances. Far from disapproving, Andrew adored her all the more for it. To think that this wonderful and beautiful woman had given up fashionable society in London for the life he had to offer. It made him believe in the virtue of his calling and the purity of her love.

Their two daughters, huddled in front of the fire, had inherited Flora's extravagance of spirit. Agnes Beattie, a porcelain-skinned beauty, the elder at seventeen years, pushed back her raven hair to afford herself an unbroken view of the contents of Ladies Monthly Museum. – There is the most ravishing evening gown! Do look at it, Margaret, she exclaimed wildly, thrusting the page in front of her younger sister by one year, who was idly stoking the meagre coals in the fireplace, – a bodice of blue satin, fastened in front by diamonds!

Margaret sprang up and attempted to wrestle the paper from her sister's grasp. Agnes tightened her grip, then her heart skipped a beat, from anxiety that the paper might tear, but she kept her tone admirably condescending as she laughed, – But dear sister, you are far too young to consider such things!

– Do, pray, give it me! Margaret implored her sister even as her own hold was loosening. In their frivolity, the girls failed to notice the entrance of their new tutor. The slender, spinsterly English woman pursed her lips and tutted loudly. – So this is the behaviour I must expect from the daughters of my dear friend Flora Beattie! I must think twice before absenting myself in the future!

The girls looked embarrassed, but Agnes detected the note of playfulness in the tutor's reprimand. – But madam, if I am to be introduced to society, in London too, then I must consider my attire!

The woman looked at her. – Training, education and etiquette are more important qualities for a young lady in her introduction to polite society than the detail of the finery she wears. Do you imagine that your dear mama, or your father, the good Reverend, for all his austerity, would see you embarrassed in that way at London's balls? Leave the consideration of your wardrobe in those capable hands, my girl, and turn your attention to more pressing matters!

– Yes, Miss May, Agnes said.

That girl has an untameable streak, thought Miss May, just like her dear mama, the tutor's dear old friend from many years ago – from the time, in fact, when Amanda May and Flora Kirkland were introduced to London society together.

Perky slung the manuscript back onto the coffee table. – What a load of utter nonsense, he said out loud, then, – Absolutely fucking brilliant! The bitch is on form. She'll make us another fucking fortune! He rubbed his hands together gleefully as he strode out into the garden towards the rose-bushes. Suddenly, a tumult of anxiety rose in his breast as he ran back into the conservatory and picked up the manuscript. He thumbed through it, to the back pages. It stopped at page forty-two and had, by page twenty-six, degenerated into an unintelligible series of stark sentences and ramshackle spidery notes in the margins. It was nowhere near finished.

I hope the old girl's all right, Perky thought. He felt an uncontrollable urge to be with his wife.

6 Lorraine And Yvonne's Discovery

Lorraine and Yvonne were preparing to go onto the wards. After their shifts they were going out to buy some clothes, because tonight they were hitting a jungle club where Goldie was headlining. Lorraine was slightly perturbed to find Yvonne still engrossed in her book. It was all right for her; she didn't have Sister Patel on her ward. She was about to remonstrate with her friend and tell her to get a move on when the name of the author on the cover jumped out at her. She examined the book and the picture of a glamorous young woman adorning the back. It was a very old picture, and if it hadn't been for the name she would not have recognised Rebecca Navarro.

– Fuckin hell! Lorraine's eyes widened. – See that book you're reading?

– Yeah? Yvonne looked at the glossy, embossed cover. A young woman in a bodice pouted in a dream-like trance.

– Ken her that wrote it? Her on the back?

– Rebecca Navarro? Yvonne asked, flipping it over.

– She was admitted to Dean, Ward Six, last night. She'd had a stroke!

– That's wild! What's she like?

– Dinnae ken ... well, she's fuck-all like that anyway! She seems a bit dotty tae me, but she'd just had a stroke though, eh?

– That would do it right enough, Yvonne smirked. – You gonna see if she's got any freebies?

– Aye, ah'll dae that, said Lorraine. – Aye, and she's really fat as well. That's how she had the stroke. She's a total pig now!

– Yeuch! Imagine looking like that and letting yourself go!

   – Right but, Yvonne, Lorraine looked at her watch, – we'd better be makin a move, eh no?

   – Yeah … Yvonne conceded, earmarking a page and rising to get ready.

7 Perk's Dilemma

Rebecca was crying. Just as she had been every day that week he had gone in to visit her. This gravely concerned Perky. When Rebecca cried it was because she was depressed. When Rebecca was depressed she didn't write, couldn't write. When she didn't write ... well, Rebecca always left the business side of things to Perky, who in turn painted a far glossier picture of their financial situation than was actually the case. Perky had certain expenses unknown to Rebecca. He had needs; needs, he considered, that the self-centred and egotistical old bag could never comprehend.

Their whole relationship was about him indulging her ego, subsuming all his own needs in the service of her infinite vanity, or at least that's what it would have been had he not been able to lead his private life. He deserved, he reasoned, some recompense. He was, by nature, a man of expensive tastes, as extravagant as her blasted heroines.

He looked at her clinically, drinking in the extent of the damage. It had not been what the doctors would term a severe stroke. Rebecca had not lost the power of speech (bad, Perky considered) and he was assured that her critical faculties had not been impaired (good, he thought). But it certainly appeared nasty enough to him. One side of her face looked like a piece of plastic which had been left too close to a fire. He had tried to keep a mirror away from the self-obsessed bitch, but it proved impossible. She'd insisted, until someone had furnished her with one.

– Oh Perky, I'm so horrible! Rebecca whined, gazing at her collapsed face in the mirror.

– Nonsense, my darling. It'll all get better, you'll see!

Let's face it, old girl, you were never much in the looks stakes.

Too gross, always stuffing fucking chocolates into your face, he thought to himself. The doctors had said as much. Obese was the word they had used. A woman of only forty-two years of age, nine years his junior, though you would never think it. Three stone overweight. It was a fantastic word: obese. The way the doctor had said it, clinically, medically, in its proper context. It hurt her. He noticed that. It cut her to the quick.

Despite this recognition of the change in her face, Perky was astonished that he couldn't really ascertain any real aesthetic decline in Rebecca's looks since the stroke. The truth was, he reckoned, that she had repulsed him for a long time. Perhaps, indeed, she always had: her childishness, her self-obsession, her fussing, and above all, her obesity. She was pathetic.

– Oh darling Perks, do you really think so? Rebecca moaned to herself rather than Perky, then turned to the approaching Nurse Lorraine Gillespie, – Will it get better, Nursey?

Lorraine smiled at her, – Aw, ah'm sure it will, Mrs Navarro.

– See? Listen to this lovely young lady, Perks smiled, raising a bushy eyebrow at Lorraine, and maintaining eye contact for a flirtatiously long time, before ending it with a wink.

A slow burner, this one, Perky thought. He regarded himself as a connoisseur of women. Sometimes, he considered, beauty just bit you straight away. You went *wow!*, then you acclimatised yourself to it. The best ones, though, the ones like this little Scotch nurse, they just crept up on you slowly but resolutely, showing you something else every time, with every mood, every different expression. They allowed you to form a vague woolly neutral perception of them, then they looked at you a certain way and ruthlessly mugged it.

– Yes, Rebecca pouted, – my darling little Nursey. She's so kind and gentle, aren't you, Nursey?

Lorraine felt flattered and insulted at the same time. All she could think about was finishing. Tonight was the night. Goldie!

– And I can tell that Perky likes you! Rebecca sang. – He's such a terrible flirt, aren't you, Perks?

Perky forced a smile.

– But he's such a darling, and so romantic, I don't know what I'd do without him.

His personal stock with Rebecca seemingly higher than ever, Perky instinctively placed a micro-cassette recorder on her locker, along with some blank tapes. Maybe a bit heavy-handed, he thought, but he was desperate. – Perhaps a bit of match-making with Miss May might take your mind off things, my darling ...

– Oh Perks ... I couldn't possibly write romance now. Look at me. I'm horrendous. How could I possibly think of romance?

Perky felt a sinking fear hang heavily in his chest.

– Nonsense. You're still the most beautiful woman in the world, he forced out through clenched teeth.

– Oh darling Perky ... she began, just before Lorraine stuck a thermometer in her mouth to silence her.

Perks looked coldly at what he saw as this ridiculous figure, his face still moulded in a relaxed smile. Duplicity came so easily to him. However, the nagging problem remained: without another Miss May Regency Romance manuscript, Giles at the publishers would not cough up that hundred-and-eighty-grand advance on the next book. Worse, he would sue for breach of contract and want back the ninety grand on the last one. That ninety grand; now the property of various London bookmakers, publicans, restaurateurs and prostitutes.

Rebecca was getting bigger and bigger, not just literally, but as a writer. The *Daily Mail* had described her as the 'world's greatest living romance writer', while the *Standard* referred to her as 'Britain's Princess Regent'. The next one would be the biggest yet. Perks needed that manuscript, something to follow up *Yasmin Goes To Yeovil*, *Paula Goes To Portsmouth*, *Lucy Goes To Liverpool* and *Nora Goes To Norwich*.

– I'll really have to read your books, Mrs Navarro. My friend's a big fan of yours. She's just finished reading *Yasmin Goes To Yeovil*, Lorraine told Rebecca, taking the thermometer from her mouth.

– Then you shall! Perks, be a darling, do remember to bring in some books for Nursey ... oh and, Nursey, please, please, please, please, please call me Rebecca. Of course I shall keep calling you

Nursey because I'm used to it now, although Lorraine is a most lovely name. You look just like a young French countess … in fact, you know, I think you look just like a portrait I once saw of Lady Caroline Lamb. It was a flattering portrait, as she was never as lovely as you, my darling, but she's my heroine: a wonderfully romantic figure not afraid to risk scandal for love, like all the best women throughout history. Would you risk scandal for love, Nursey darling?

God, the sow's ranting again, Perks thought.

– Dinnae ken, eh, Lorraine shrugged.

– Oh, I'm sure you would. You have that wild, ungovernable look about you. Don't you think so, Perks?

Perky felt his blood pressure rise and a layer of salt crystallise on his lips. That uniform … those buttons … removed one by one … he forced a cool smile.

– Yes, Nursey, Rebecca continued, – I see you as a consort of Lady Caroline Lamb, at one of those grand regency balls, pursued by suitors eager to waltz with you … do you waltz, Nursey?

– Naw, ah'm intae house, especially jungle n that likes. Dinnae mind trancey n garage n techno n that, bit ah like it tae kick but ken?

– Would you like to learn to waltz?

– No really bothered. Mair intae house, eh. Jungle likes. Goldie's ma man, eh.

– Oh, but you must, Nursey, you really must, Rebecca's swollen face pouted insistently.

Lorraine felt faintly embarrassed as she was aware of Perky's eyes lingering on her. She felt strangely exposed in her uniform as if she was something exotic, something to be held up for inspection. She had to get on. Sister Patel was coming on soon and there would be trouble if she didn't get a move on.

– Where about in Bonnie Scotland are you from? Perks smiled.

– Livingston, Lorraine said quickly.

– Livingston, Rebecca said, – it sounds perfectly delightful. Are you going home to visit soon?

– Aye, see ma mother n that.

Yes, there was something about that Scotch nurse, thought Perks.

She had an effect on more than his hormones; she was helping Rebecca. This girl seemed to ignite her, to bring her back to life. As Lorraine left, his wife drifted back into a litany of self-pitying whines. It was time he left as well.

8 Freddie's Indiscretion

Freddy Royle had had, by his standards, a tiring day prior to his late afternoon arrival at St Hubbin's. He had been in the television studios all morning filming an episode of *From Fred With Love*. A young boy, whom Fred had sorted out to swim with the dolphins at Morecambe's Marineland, while his grandparents were brought back to the scene of their honeymoon, was all excited in the studio and writhed around on his lap, getting Freddy so aroused and excited that they had to do several takes. — Oi loike em still, he said, — very, very still. Barry, the producer, was not at all amused. — In the name of God, Freddy, take the rest of the fucking afternoon off and go to the hospital and shag a stiff, he moaned. — Let's see if we can dampen that bloody libido of yours.

It seemed good advice. — Oi think oi moite just be doin that, me ol cocker, Freddy smiled, summoning a commissionaire to order him a cab from Shepherd's Bush down to St Hubbin's. On the ride through West London, frustrated at the grindingly slow pace of the cab in the traffic, he changed his mind and requested the driver to drop him off at a Soho bookshop he frequented.

Freddy winked at the man behind the counter of the busy establishment before sauntering through to the back. There, another man, wearing strange, horn-rimmed glasses, and drinking tea from a Gillingham F.C. mug, smiled at Freddy. — All right, Freddy? How you going, mate?

— Not baad, Bertie, moi ol mucker. Yourzelf?

— Oh, musn't grumble. Here, I got something for you ... Bertie opened a locked cupboard and rummaged around through some brown-paper packages until he saw one marked FREDDY in black felt pen.

Freddy didn't open it, but instead nodded over to a display bookcase on the wall. Bertie smiled, – Quite a few been in today, and moved over to the wall. He grabbed a handle and pulled open a door. Behind it was a small, narrow room, with metal shelving stacked with magazines and videos. Two men were browsing, as Freddy walked in and pulled the bookcase door shut behind him. Freddy knew one of them.

– Alroight, Perks, me old sport?

Perky Navarro averted his gaze from the cover of *Long-Tongued Lesbo Love-Babes No.2* and smiled at Freddy. – Freddy, old boy. How are you? He did a quick double-take to the rack, as he was convinced he saw a likeness of Nurse Lorraine Gillespie in *New Cunts 78*. He picked it up, studied it closely. No, just similar hair.

– I'm foine, me old mucker, Freddy began, then noting Perk's distraction, asked – Zeen zumthin interestin?

– I rather thought I had, but, alas, no, Perky sounded deflated.

– Oi dare zay you'll foind zumthin that takes your fancy. And what news of the Angel, ow's she farin?

– Oh, she's doing a lot better.

– Well, she's in the roight place. I'm going to drop in and see her today, cause oime headin down to St Hubbin's for a fund-raisin meetin.

– Well, I can see a huge difference, Perky smiled, perking up again. – She's even talking about starting to do some writing soon.

– Crackin show.

– Yes, that young nurse that's been looking after her … little Scotch girl … she's been good for her. A stunning little bird as well. In fact I've been scouring the wares for a likeness …

– Anything interesting in?

– There's some new stuff that Bertie tells me just came from Hamburg yesterday, but that's over there, Perks ushered Freddy to one of the racks.

Freddy picked up a magazine and thumbed through its contents. – Not baad, not baad at all. Oi got moiself a noice little vist-vuckin magazine the other week there. Ow zum of them there girlz an boyz can take one of them vists up their doo-daas oi don't know. Oi be bad enough trying to shoite if I've gone a vew days without spendin a penny!

— I think some of them must be full of those muscle-relaxant drugs, Perks told him.

This seemed to intrigue Freddy. — Muzzle-relaxint drugs … hmmm … that open them up noicely now, would it?

— Yes, that would do the trick. Read about it. You're not thinking of trying some, are you? Perky laughed.

Freddy turned a toothy grin his way and Perky found himself recoiling from the television star's pungent breath. — Oi rulz out nuttin at no toimes, Perky me boy, you knows me.

Slapping his friend on the back, the television star picked up his package and left the shop, hailing another taxi outside. He was off to see Rebecca Navarro, a woman he, like all her friends, indulged shamelessly. He had playfully, and to her delight, nicknamed her 'The Angel'. But after seeing her, Freddy would spend more time with some other friends whom most people would describe as 'absent', but who, for his purposes, were very much present and correct.

9 In The Jungle

The night before his life changed, Glen had had to plead with his friend Martin, – Come on, mate, give it a try. I got good pills, those Amsterdam Playboys. The best ever.

– Exactly, Martin sneered, – and you're gonna waste them on this fuckin jungle shit. I don't go for that shit, Glen, I just can't fucking well dance to it.

– C'mon, mate, as a favour. Give it a go.

– A favour? Why you so desperate to check out this club? Keith and Carol and Eddie, they're all going down to Sabresonic and then on to the Ministry.

– Look, mate, house music's at the forefront of everything, and jungle's at the forefront of house. It's got to have a capacity to surprise, innit, otherwise it just becomes affirmation, like country-and-western, or like rock'n'roll's become. Jungle's the music with the capacity to surprise. It's where the cutting edge is. We owe it to ourselves to check it out, Glen implored.

Martin looked at him searchingly. – There's someone you want to see at this club … someone from the hospital goes there … one of them nurses I'll bet!

Glen shrugged and smiled, – Well … yeah … but …

– All right, that's cool. You want to chase the girls, we'll chase the girls. Ain't got no objections on that score. Just don't give me all this cutting-edge bollocks.

They got to the club, and Glen felt despondent when they saw the size of the queue. Martin strode up to the front and talked to one of the bouncers. He then turned and gesticulated violently at Glen to come up. There were some moans of frustrated envy from others in the crowd as Glen and Martin strode through. At first Glen had been terrified that they would not get in. After Martin had blagged it so effectively, he worried that Lorraine might have been stuck outside.

In the club, they went straight to the chill-out zone. Martin hit the bar and bought two fizzy mineral waters. It was dark and Glen pulled a plastic bag out of his Y-fronts. It contained four pills with a Playboy bunny logo stamped on them. They swallowed one each and washed them down with water.

After about ten minutes, the pill kept coming back on Glen, as it tended to do, and he had dry, hiccupy wretches. He and Martin were unconcerned; Glen was just bad at taking pills.

Three girls sat down close to them. Martin had been quick to start chatting to them. Glen was equally quick to leave him and hit the dance-floor. These Es were good, but unless you started dancing straight away you would sit around talking in the chill-out zone all night. Glen had come to dance.

He skirted the already-busy dance-floor and quickly came across Lorraine and her friend. Glen danced a discreet distance away. He recognised Murder Dem by Ninjaman sliding into Wayne Marshall's G Spot.

Lorraine and her friend Yvonne were up there, going for it in a big way. Glen watched them dancing with each other, Lorraine blocking out all the world, focusing on Yvonne, giving her friend everything. God, for just a bit of that attention, he thought. Yvonne, though, was more disengaged, further away, taking in the whole scene. That was how it seemed to Glen. His pill was kicking in, and the music, which he had had a resistance to, was getting into him from all sides, surging through his body in waves, defining his emotions. Before it had seemed jerky and disjointed, it was pushing and pulling at him, irritating him. Now he was going with it, his body bubbling and flowing in all ways to the roaring bass-lines and the tearing dub plates. All the joy of love for everything good was in him, though he could see all the bad things in Britain; in fact this twentieth-century urban blues music defined and illustrated them more sharply than ever. Yet he wasn't scared and he wasn't down about it: he could see what needed to be done to get away from them. It was the party: he felt that you had to party, you had to party harder than ever. It was the only way. It was your duty to show that you were still alive. Political sloganeering and posturing meant nothing; you had to celebrate the joy of life in the face of all those grey forces and dead spirits who controlled everything, who fucked with your head and livelihood anyway, if you weren't one of them. You had to let them know that in spite of their best efforts to make you like them, to make you dead, you were still alive. Glen knew that this wasn't the complete answer, because it would all still be there when you stopped, but it was the best show in town right now. It was certainly the only one he wanted to be at.

He had looked back over at Lorraine and her friend. He couldn't tell at first, but he was dancing like a maniac, and when he glanced over at them, he realised. There were no poseurs here, they were all going crazy. This wasn't dance, that wasn't the word for what this was. And there they were: Lorraine and her friend Yvonne. Lorraine, the goddess. But the goddess had multiplied. There wasn't just one of them now, like when he came in, there was just Lorraine and her friend. Now it was Lorraine and Yvonne, in a dance of crazy, rapturous emotion which, while conducted at ninety miles an hour, slowed down to almost nothing under the onslaught of the throbbing strobes and jerky break-beats. Lorraine and Yvonne. Yvonne and Lorraine.

A mass scream went up from the crowd as the music left one crescendo and changed its tempo to build up to the next one. The two women, danced out, collapsed into each other's arms. At that point Glen knew that there was something wrong in their body language. Lorraine and Yvonne were kissing, but Yvonne, after a while, started to resist and was pulling away. So slowly, under the strobes. It was as if she had snapped: as if she had gone beyond the range of her emotional elasticity. She jerked free from what at first seemed a symbiotic hug with a violence the strobes couldn't disguise, and stood in cripplingly uncomfortable rigidity as Lorraine appeared to look at her with a brief, odd contempt, then ignore her.

Yvonne headed from the dance-floor, making her way towards the bar. Glen looked at her departing, then looked at Lorraine. Lorraine. Yvonne. He went after Yvonne. She was standing at the bar drinking a mineral water. On the night his life changed he tapped her on the shoulder.

– Yvonne, innit?

– Yeah … she said slowly, then, – you're Glen, aintcha? From the hospital.

– Yeah, Glen smiled. She was beautiful. It was Yvonne. Yvonne was the one. Yvonne, Yvonne, Yvonne.

– Didn't know you wos into this, she smiled. It was as if her big white teeth burrowed through his chest bone and ate a hole into his heart. She is so fucking beautiful, Glen decided. This is a woman to die for.

– Oh yeah, said Glen, – Most definitely.

– Having a good one? she asked. He was gorgeous, Yvonne thought. He was a fucking hunk. He's fucking well noticed me big time.

– I'm having the best ever, and what about you?

– It's getting better, she smiled.

This was also the night Yvonne's life changed.

10 Rebecca's Recovery

Lorraine was taking Rebecca's temprature when her illustrious patient's distinguished visitor arrived. – Angel! announced Freddy, – How goes it! Oi wos supposed to be down ere to zee you yesterday, but this vund-raisin meetin dragged on and on. Ow be you?

– Mmmm, Rebecca began, and Lorraine withdrew her thermometer, her hand trembling and unsteady. – Freddy! Darling! Rebecca outstretched her arms and gave Freddy a theatrical hug.

– That's you, Rebecca, Lorraine forced a smile. She was on a bad comedown and Yvonne had the hump with her. She'd let things get silly, out of hand. No, *she* had got out of hand. She consciously stopped the psychic self-mutilation before it gathered momentum. Now was not the time.

– Thank you, Lorraine darling … have you met darling Freddy?

– Naw … said Lorraine. She went to shake his hand. Freddy gave her a lusty shake followed by a kiss on the cheek. Lorraine winced at the cold, wet feel of the greasy saliva that Freddy's lips left on her face.

– Oi've been hearin all about you, that you've been doin a great job lookin after the Angel here, Freddy smiled.

Lorraine shrugged.

– Oh Freddy, Lorraine's been perfectly darling, haven't you, sweetheart?

– No really, it's jist ma joab, eh.

– But you do it with such style, such *savoir faire*. I absolutely insist, Freddy darling, that you bring all your considerable influence to bear on advancing Lorraine's career within this health authority.

– Oi think you're overstatin the influence of a zimple Zomerzet varmer's boy ere, Angel, but ah'll obviously be puttin the roight wurds in the roight lugs, zo to speak.

– Oh, but you must. It's due to my Nursey Lorraine that I'm going home next week. And I've lost over a stone. Oh Freddy darling, I *had* let myself go in recent years. You must promise to tell me when I'm overweight and simply not indulge me. Please, darling, do say you will!

– Anythin you say, Angel. Great newz about you gettin out though, Freddy smiled.

– Yes, and Lorraine's going to come and see me, to visit, aren't you, darling?

– Eh, well … Lorraine mumbled. This was the last thing she wanted at the moment. Her legs ached; they would ache more before the end of the shift. Her eyes were tired. She saw the beds she had to change and wanted to lie down on one so badly.

– Oh, do say you will, Rebecca pouted.

Rebecca made Lorraine feel strange. Part of her detested her patronising and moronic behaviour. Part of her had an urge to shake this stupid, bloated, naive and pampered woman, to tell her that she's been a fool, to try and get herself together, to come out off her child-like fantasyland. However, part of her pitied Rebecca, felt protective of her.

Lorraine realised that, for all her irritating ways and pitiful inadequacies, Rebecca was essentially a good, warm and honest person, – Aye, right, she told her patient.

– Wonderful! You see, Freddy, Lorraine has inspired me to write again. I'm going to base the heroine on her. I'm even going to call her Lorraine. She was going to be called Agnes, but I think I could get away with a French-sounding name. I'm thinking that Flora may have had a French lover before she met the Minister. The auld alliance, you see. God, I'm bursting with ideas again. I'll definitely dedicate this book to you, my dear dear Nursey darling Lorraine!

Lorraine cringed inwardly.

– That's great, said Freddy, impatiently wanting to get down to the path lab, – but oi must be off now. Tell me though, Angel, that woman in the next room, what's up with her?

– Oh she's very ill. I think it's only a matter of days, Rebecca sighed.

– Terrible, Freddy said, trying to stop his features shifting into a smile of gleeful anticipation. She was a hefty one. The kind of body Freddy could happily get lost in. All that meat to conquer. – It'd be loike climbin Evirizt, he said happily, thoughtfully, under his breath.

11 Untitled – Work In Progress

Page 47

It was, in the event, not until the end of March that Lorraine and Miss May set out to accomplish the long trek to London. To a young girl from the Scottish borders, who had only once been as far as Edinburgh, every new sighting on the road was viewed with eager interest. At the start of the journey, Lorraine was still in a fit of intense excitement, which was as much to do with the small fortune of sixty pounds that her father, the stoical Reverend, had surprised her with prior to her departure.

They travelled by an old coach pulled by two sturdy beasts and driven by Tam Greig, a Selkirk man who had undertaken the journey many times in the past. To those accustomed to the speed which the post-chaises were able to attain, a journey in a rather ponderous, creaking carriage drawn by only two horses often seemed so painfully slow. So while for Lorraine this was a great adventure, for her travelling companion, Miss May, it was an untold grind – the only benefit being the superior comfort.

However, they were happy to be offered excellent refreshments at most of the halts, and the beds in the posting houses were generally of an acceptable standard. Lorraine found a three-day break at York most agreeable. It was extended on the advice of Tam Greig, who had noted bad fatigue in one of the horses. So enthralled with the town was Lorraine that she begged that they stay just one more day, but the dour Scotch coachman reported the horses to be quite fresh and Miss May, as ever, had the last word. – I have a duty to get you to Lady Huntingdon's, my girl. While no time was given for your arrival, I would be less than prudent in my responsibilities were I to sanction long holidays at every interesting point we pass through! There is little gain in lingering!

With that, they set off.

The rest of the journey was uneventful until Grantham. It had been raining heavily for most of the day as they approached the Gonerby Moor, and the Lincolnshire landscape was sodden. Seemingly from nowhere, a post-chaise and four dashed by at such pace that the more docile horses drawing the carriage were thus highly vexed, and ran the vehicle off the road. The carriage tilted and Miss May banged her head. – What …

– Miss May, Lorraine held her hand, – are you all right?

– Yes, yes, yes, girl … I thought the carriage was going to tilt over … what, pray tell, has happened?

Lorraine looked out of the window to see Tam Greig shaking his fist and cursing in a guttural Scotch, the likes of which she never heard before. – Ye devils, ye! Ah'll cut oot yer feckless English herts!

– Mister Greig! Miss May barked.

– Begging your pardon, ma'am, I was fair scunnered by the recklessness of the men in yon coach. Officers they were too. Officers, but no gentlemen, I'll wager ye.

– Perhaps they were in a hurry to get to some posting, Miss May said. – We too should be in a hurry.

– I'm sorry, ma'am, but yon horse has gone lame. He'll have to be replaced in Grantham, and I'd say it'll take some time to make yon arrangements.

– Very well, Miss May sighed. – Oh, Lorraine, I am so vexed by this journey!

It took longer to get to Grantham than expected, due to the lameness of the second horse. There was no room at the Blue Inn, so they were forced to billet in a much less genteel lodging. As they disembarked, Tam the coachman cursed as he saw four officers, the occupants of the post-chaise which had caused them their grief, pass them en route to a tavern.

One of the soldiers, a dark, handsome chap with an arrogant twist to his mouth, raised an eyebrow in Lorraine's direction which caused her to look down and blush. Miss May noted the officer's gesture and nodded approvingly to herself at Lorraine's response.

The stop-off in Grantham held them up for another two days, but the final part of the journey to London was uneventful and they reached Earl Denby and Lady Huntingdon's grand town home of Radcombe House in Kensington in fine spirits.

Lorraine was overwhelmed by London; its size and scale were beyond anything she could have conceived of. Lady Huntingdon, a strikingly handsome woman, and much younger-looking than her thirty-six years (for Lorraine's mother Flora was the same age as her friend), proved to be a most amenable hostess. Lorraine also had Miss May, whom only Lady Huntingdon addressed by her Christian name of Amanda, keeping a watchful eye on her during her induction to society. Earl Denby was a dashing, handsome man, and he and his wife together seemed so full of vitality and gaiety.

The dinners at Radcombe House were grand affairs, even on the occasions where few guests were present. — Isn't this wonderful? Lorraine said to Miss May, ever present by the young Scotch beauty's side.

— This is rather modest. Wait until you see New Thorndyke Hall, my girl, she smiled. That was the family's country seat in Wiltshire, and Lorraine eagerly anticipated going there.

At a smaller Radcombe House dinner one evening, where only a few guests were present, Lorraine's attention was caught by the flirtatious eye of a handsome young man. He seemed strangely familiar, and she fancied that she might have seen him before at one of the earlier dinners. This man, an erratic young sprig of fashion, fixed his friend and host, Earl Denby, with a mocking eye and demanded in theatrical, rallying tones: — Well, Denby, you old rogue, you promise me a champion time down in Wiltshire with the hounds this weekend, but what, pray tell, do you offer me for my entertainment this evening? The young blood smiled over at Lorraine, and she instantly recalled where she had seen him before: he was one of the officers from the post-chaise which had so disrupted their progress to London, the one who had gestured at her.

— My cook, said Denby, rather nervously, — is generally thought of as an artist in her own line …

— But, interrupted the young man, smugly, as he cast another flirtatious glance over towards Lorraine, who felt herself blush, as she had done before, — I am not to be put off with a cook! I came here in the fond expectation of finding all manner of shocking orgies! he boomed. Lord Harcourt, sitting nearby, spluttered on his wine and shook his head testily.

– *Darling Marcus! You are so scandalous!* Lady Huntingdon smiled benignly.

– *My dear lady,* said Lord Harcourt, – *you are as bad as that despicable young blade himself, giving his puerile and amoral blabberings such indulgence!*

– *The lamentable influence of Lord Byron and his cohorts upon society!* Denby said, with a slightly contemptuous smile.

– *Yes, that damn poet fellow has set up such a dust!* Harcourt exclaimed.

– *But the point I seek to make,* continued the young man, – *is how can I seek to encounter old Boney at the end of the month without the sustenance of more vigorous recreation?*

– *The sort of recreation you seem to be suggesting shall not be forthcoming under my roof, Marcus!* Denby growled.

– *Marcus, do be a darling and dampen that fiery ardour for a moment while we eat, as your talk is verging on the scandalous! Entertain us with your army tales,* Lady Huntingdon sweetly implored her bullish young guest.

– *As you wish, my good lady,* the young man smiled, soothed and seduced by the soft tones and calming classical beauty of his hostess. And that was exactly what he did for the remainder of the evening: enthralling the table with tales of great wit and humour concerning his military service.

– *Who was that man?* Lorraine was moved to ask Lady Huntingdon, after the guests had taken their departure.

– *That was Marcus Cox. A perfect darling, and one of London's most eligible bachelors, but an unspeakable cad. There are many bloods in this town who are not what they seem, my angel, and you must tread warily with them. But no doubt my friends your dear mama and darling Amanda will have already told you that. Alas, many bloods will do and say almost anything to capture a maiden's virtue. When a man, even one of Marcus Cox's breeding, faces posting at the front, a certain recklessness enters his tone and bearing. For the sad truth is that many do not return, a fact of which they are only too well aware.*

– *You are so wise in the ways of the world ...* Lorraine said.

– *And it is therefore my duty to impart to you some of the wisdom I have had the good fortune to have acquired, my darling Lorraine. But now, there is work to be done. We must, with reluctance, undertake that most pressing and* arduous of tasks and finally decide what you and I are to wear to tomorrow evening's ball.

The following night, Lorraine was prepared for the ball, supervised by Lady Huntington. Lorraine could tell the operation had been a success before she studied herself in the mirror. In the eyes of her hostess she saw such a look of glowing approval that, indeed, a mirror was superfluous. She looked heavenly and striking in a red dress made from imported Indian silk. – How wonderful you look, my darling, how simply divine! Lady Huntingdon cooed.

Lorraine went over to the mirror and studied her reflection, – It cannot be I, surely not!

– Oh but it is, my darling, it most surely is. How like your darling mama you are ...

At the ball, one handsome officer after another danced with Lorraine, all keen to make her acquaintance. The waltz was the most wonderful dance, and Lorraine was intoxicated by the music and the movement.

Lady Huntington and Lord Denby took her aside after one dance with a particularly tall officer. – My darling Lorraine, we are so proud of you! How I wish your dear mama was with us to witness this, the mistress of the house said appreciatively in her ear.

Lorraine thought with fondness and love of her beloved parents back up in the Scottish border manse, and the sacrifices they had made so that this dream might be realised.

– Yes, my pretty one, your introduction to society has been more of a success than I had bargained for! I have had every young officer in my own regiment asking after you! Lord Denby noted cheerfully.

– Alas, I am always in the radiant shadow of your beautiful wife, m'Lord, Lorraine smiled at Denby. The company all knew that the pretty debutante's comment was an honest statement of the truth, rather than a sycophantic act of deference or display of gratitude to her hostess.

– Ha! You flatter me so! The eyes are on you, my little darling. Look, watch and wait, my angel, and curb any tendency towards impetuosity. The ideal one will come along and you will know, Lady Huntington smiled at her husband who touchingly squeezed her hand.

Lorraine was moved by this. She felt that she should dance with the most *handsome man in the hall. – Come and dance with me, m'Lord, she pleaded to Denby.*

– That would never do! Denby burst into a laugh of mock outrage.

– You will not get him to waltz, my child; his Lordship is a strict opponent of the importation of such music into this country.

– And I must agree with his Lordship's principles on this, Lord Harcourt, who had now come over to join them, sharply opined, – for it is but an underhand tactic of our foreign foes to import this decadent music and dance to our shores.

Lorraine was horrified that the wise lord could feel this way about such beautiful music. *– Why do you say that, m'Lord? she asked.*

Harcourt took a step backwards and Lorraine watched his chin recede into his neck. *– Why, he began with bluster, unused to being challenged in such a way by a young woman, – this unsettling proximity of gentleman to lady is a most scandalous and improper thing, and can only be a strategy by overseas enemies of the realm to weaken the resolve of the British officer, by facilitating the erosion of his moral fibre and lubricating his fall to debauchery! This filth is spreading like an unchecked virus through polite society, and I shudder to think of the ramifications for the enlisted men adopting these devilish practices!*

– Oh hush, Harcourt, Lady Huntington smiled, brushing the good lord aside as she swept majestically down the marble stairs, to the approving eye of her husband, who noted the admiring looks his handsome wife elicited.

Lorraine saw Lord Denby's expression, and was moved to address him. *– My Lord, I pray that one day I will command a presence similar to that of this divine beauty, your good wife, the Lady Huntington. What poise and grace that most radiant and ñoble woman possesses, what …*

Lorraine's words were cut short as Lady Huntington tripped on the skirts of her gown and toppled down the marble stairs. The guests watched in shocked and horrified silence, none of them being close enough to catch her, with the lady herself seemingly unable to break her fall as she tumbled on and on down the steps for what seemed like an eternity, gathering a frightening momentum, until she came to rest in a broken heap at the bottom of the staircase.

The Earl of Denby was first at her side. He lifted his wife's golden, tousled head to him, tears filling his eyes as he felt the blood run through his hands and drip onto the marble floor. Denby looked up towards the heavens, beyond and through the ornate roof of the banqueting hall. He knew that by the most random and arbitrary of cruel accidents, everything he had and held dear had gone from him. – There is no God, he said quietly, then, even more softly, he repeated, – no God.

12 Rebecca's Relapse

Rebecca thought she was having another stroke. Her heart burned as she flicked through the contents of the magazine. There were two young women inside, in various poses. One of them – as she considered one might expect from the title: *Feisty Feminist Fist-Fuckers* – appeared to have her clenched fist in the other's vagina.

Her mind raced back to last Friday, when her world had blown apart. This was worse than the stroke, it seemed even more casual, vicious and sickening. It carried a humiliation that the illness, for all its disfigurement and incapacity, had never conferred. Last Friday, following her hospital discharge, she had gone shopping. She was coming out of Harrod's with a new, morale-boosting outfit one size down from what had become her usual. Then, from the window of the taxi on the way home, she saw Perky, right there in a busy Kensington street. She had the taxi slow down and she got out to pursue him, deciding that it might be jolly good fun to follow her beloved Perks.

It started to seem less good fun as she saw him vanish into a small flat. Rebecca's heart sank, as she immediately suspected another woman. She went home under the darkest of clouds and fought the desperate urge to cram her face with food until her stomach was at bursting point. Then, the urge passed and she couldn't have eaten had she been force-fed. All she wanted to do was to know.

After this, she followed Perky many times, but he always went to the flat alone. Rebecca spent ages watching to see if anyone else was coming and going. It seemed to be unoccupied. Eventually, she went to the door and rang the bell. Nobody answered. Every subsequent time she tried it, nobody was home. She confided in Lorraine, who came over to tea at her request. It was Lorraine who suggested she look through his pockets to see if there was a key. There was, and Rebecca had it copied. Going there alone, she found a small studio flat. Inside, the place was a library of pornography: magazines, video tapes and, most ominously, a video camera on a tripod positioned over a bed that – along with the television set and the racks of books, magazines and tapes – dominated the room.

She was now sitting there alone, glancing at this one, *Feisty Feminist Fist-Fuckers*. She couldn't bring herself to look at the video tapes, especially the home-made ones. They each had the name of a different woman, written on a label on the spine. They were whores' names, she thought bitterly: Candy, Jade, Cindy, and the like. She felt the side of her face again. It didn't burn but it was wet. She dropped Perky's copy of *Feisty Feminist Fist-Fuckers* on the floor.

Something told her to do her breathing exercises. She started with forced, laboured, deep breaths, punctuated by sobs, but eventually found a rhythm. Then she coldly said out loud: – The *bastard*.

A strange, frozen calm came over her as she continued to compulsively explore the flat. Then she discovered something which proved to be the worst find of all. It was a large box-folder which contained various financial statements, cash receipts and invoices. Rebecca found herself shaking. She needed to be with someone. The only person she could think of was Lorraine. She dialled the number and her young former nurse, and now friend, answered, – Please come, Rebecca said softly to her, – please come.

Lorraine had just come off a shift and was going to bed. It had been a good one at the club last night and she was suffering, but when she heard Rebecca's voice on the other end of the line she threw on some casual clothes and jumped in a taxi to Kensington. She had never heard such pain and desperation in a human voice before.

Lorraine met Rebecca in a wine bar which was by the tube station and round the corner from the flat. She could see that something terrible had happened.

– I've been betrayed, deeply betrayed, she said in a cold, trembling voice. – I've been paying for him to ... it's all been a lie, Lorraine ... it's all been a fucking *lie*! she sobbed.

It fazed Lorraine to see Rebecca like this. It wasn't her: she was no longer the eccentric, by turns engaging and irritating woman she knew in the hospital. She seemed vulnerable and real. This woman was a troubled sister, not a dotty aunt.

– What am I going to do … she cried to Lorraine.

Lorraine looked her in the eye. – It's no what you're gaunny dae. It's what that fuckin creep, that fuckin parasite's gaunny dae. You're the one wi the money. Ye cannae rely on everybody else, Rebecca, especially some fuckin creepy man. Look around you. He's got away with it cause you've had your heid stuck up your fanny for too long in that never-never land of yours. That's how he's been able to exploit ye, tae fleece ye like that!

Rebecca was jolted by Lorraine's outburst. But she sensed that there was something behind it. Through her own pain, she was able to empathise with something coming from Lorraine.

– Lorraine, what's wrong? What is it? Rebecca couldn't believe that she was talking like this. Not Lorraine. Not Nursey …

– What's wrong is that I see people who come into the hospital who've got nothing. Then I go hame, back up the road tae Livi and they've goat nothing. And you, well, you've goat everything. And what dae ye dae wi it? Ye let some pig fuckin waste it aw away!

– I know … I know I go on about romance all the time … I know I live in that dreamworld you say. Maybe I've been writing that crap for so long I've come to believe it … I don't know. All I know is that he was always there for me, Lorraine, Perky was always there.

– Always there, watching you get fatter and more ridiculous, jist encouraging ye tae sit aboot and be a fucking fat stupid vegetable. Making a fool ay yersel for other people's amusement … ye know what we used tae say aboot ye oan the ward? We said: she's so fuckin stupid. Then ma pal Yvonne goes: she's no that daft, she's the one that's makin aw that money while we're working these back-breaking shifts for a fuckin pittance. We went, aye, right enough. It made us think differently, we thought: she's doing it, she's pretending to be daft, but she's beating the bastards. Now you tell me he's been ripping you off for years and you didn't even know about it.

Rebecca felt a rage boil up inside her, – You ... you ... just obviously hate men. I should've noticed that ... it's not romance you hate, it's men, isn't it? Isn't it!

– Ah dinnae hate men, just the kind ah always seem tae run intae!

– And what kind is that?

– Well, at school for one thing. Lorraine Gillespian, they used tae call me at Craigshill High back in Livi. They called me a lesbian just because I was a thirteen year old with tits who didnae want tae fuck every guy that leered at me or hassled me. Just because ah wouldnae get intae that fuckin shite wi them. I got eight O. Grades and I was studying for my Highers, then I was off to Uni. My mother's new husband wouldn't keep his fuckin hands off me long enough tae let me sit the exams. I had to get away, so I applied tae dae nursing here. Now I'm still getting it, still getting hassled and fucked around by wankers at the hospital. All I want is tae be left alaine. I don't know what I am, I don't even know if I am a fuckin dyke or not ... I want tae be left alaine tae work it all out.

Now Lorraine was sobbing, and it was Rebecca who was comforting her. – It's all right, darling ... it's all right. You're still so young ... it's all so confusing. You'll find someone ...

– That's just it, Lorraine sniffed, – I don't want to find someone, not yet at any rate. I want to find me first.

– Me too, Rebecca said softly, – and I need a friend to help me along.

– Aye, me n aw, Lorraine smiled. – So, what are we gaunny dae?

– Well, we're going to get pissed, then go and watch Perky's video tapes and see what the bastard has been up to, and then I'm going to do what I've always done.

– What's that? Lorraine asked.

– I'm going to write.

13 Perks Sees The Script

It was wonderful; that little Scotch nurse was round almost constantly, and the old girl was writing like a proverbial bastard out of hell. There were times when his sweet little Lorraine was present that Perky found it difficult to take leave of absence to his flat. His mind had become fevered with the prospect of getting Lorraine round there. He *had* to get her round there, he had to make his move.

One afternoon, Perky decided to take the opportunity. He had heard Lorraine laughing with Rebecca in the study and noted that she was preparing to go. – Ah, Lorraine, where are you headed?

– Back tae the hospital, eh.

– Splendid! Perks sang, – I'm off in that direction. I'll drop you there.

– That's simply wonderful, Perky, Rebecca said, – See what a darling he is, Lorraine? What would I do without him? The two women exchanged a knowing smile Perks was oblivious to.

Lorraine climbed into the passenger seat and Perky drove off. – Listen, Lorraine, I hope you don't mind, he said, pulling over and turning down a side-street where he brought the car to a halt, – but you and I need to have a talk about Rebecca.

– Aw aye?

– Well, you and her are close, so I thought that I should reward you for making such a sterling contribution to her recovery. Perks reached into the glove compartment and handed Lorraine a brown envelope.

– What's this?

– Open it and see!

Lorraine knew it was money. She saw the large notes and

estimated it was about a thousand pounds. – Great, she said, sticking the envelope in her bag, – Nice one.

The little bitch loves the folding stuff, Perks thought contentedly. He drew closer to her and let his hand fall onto her knee. – There's a lot more where that came from, I'll tell you that, my little beauty … Perks gasped.

– Aw aye, Lorraine smiled. Her hand went to his groin. She opened his flies and put her hand inside. She found his testicles and squeezed. Perky gasped. He was in heaven. She squeezed some more, then some more, and heaven started to become something else. – You ever touch me again and ah'll brek your fuckin neck, she grinned until his radiant smile vanished and her forehead crashed into his nose at full force.

Lorraine was gone, leaving Perks holding a bloody handkerchief to his nose with one hand and massaging his crushed testicles with the other. He sat for a while trying to compose himself. – Good God, he moaned, starting up the car and heading for the flat. I like them feisty, but not that damn feisty, he thought balefully, his hands trembling on the wheel.

A session watching some of the old videos cheered him up. Particularly the one with Candy, his favourite. She would do anything at all for a price, which was exactly how a good whore should be. Too many of them had predictable thresholds, a bloody disgrace to their profession, he mused. No, he'd have to get in touch with Candy again soon.

When Perky Navarro returned home in higher spirits, he noted with a satisfied glee that Rebecca's manuscript was expanding. Strangely, Rebecca was contracting. This diet-and-exercise regime they had put her on had worked wonders. Stones had been shed. She dressed differently, and even seemed different in a more fundamental sense. People were commenting. She was now more than two stone lighter than she had been at the time of the stroke. Her face looked back to normal. These changes were interesting to Perks, but the unfamiliarity was slightly unsettling and intimidating. He even found himself aroused by her presence one evening, and suggested that they forego their separate rooms to sleep together for the first time in about three years. – No, darling, I'm far, far too tired, I must finish this book, she told him.

Never mind that, he thought, the manuscript was coming along nicely. She'd been knocking out the words. This consoled him. She had taken to keeping her study locked, for some strange reason. But that evening when she said she was going out, which she seemed to be doing more and more often, she left the door not just unlocked but wide open. He picked up the document and read.

14 Untitled – Work In Progress

Page 56

It had been a sad time for all at Radcombe House since the death of Lady Huntingdon. Lorraine, now acting as the mistress of the house, was greatly concerned with the state of mind of the Earl of Denby, who had taken to drinking heavily and frequenting London's opium dens. The great lord showed such lassitude of spirit that Lorraine was glad to hear that his good friend Marcus Cox would soon be returning to England with his regiment.

On his return, however, Marcus, too, seemed a changed man. The war had taken its toll on this dashing blade, and he had come back with a fever. On meeting the officer, Lorraine was happy to find, though, that Marcus was determined that his Lordship's pain would be eased without recourse to spirit-sapping bad habits.

— Denby must be taken out of London, he said to Lorraine. — We should all go down to the ancestral home of Thorndyke Hall in Wiltshire. He must be taken out of himself and his melancholy, lest it destroy his soul.

— Yes, a spell at Thorndyke Hall would help to raise his spirits, Lorraine agreed.

Perky put the manuscript down to pour himself a large Scotch. He nodded approvingly as he thumbed through a few more pages. This was ideal. Then, the text seemed to change. Perky could not believe his eyes.

Page 72

Inside the large barn some miles from Thorndyke Hall on the road to the village, they had blindfolded the thirteenth Earl of Denby and bound his hands behind his back. His erect penis poked through a slit in the long white tunic he wore which covered his chest, stomach and thighs.

– Give me an arse, damn you! He drunkenly roared as a cheer went up from the crowd gathered in the barn.

– Patience, Denby, you blood, you! The Earl recognised the voice of his friend Harcourt. He was now hungry for sport, hungry to prove himself in this wager.

There were three wooden platforms in front of Denby. On one there was a bound, gagged and naked girl, on her knees with her buttocks sticking in the air. On the next platform, there was a boy in an identical position. On the third, a large, hardy blackface sheep was trussed up and gagged.

A series of pulleys were connected to the platforms, thus allowing for alterations in the height of the participants in the wager. Harcourt had instructed the men to make appropriate adjustments until the anal orifices of the three creatures were positioned at a similar height, lined up to meet Denby's engorged member.

Harcourt whispered in his ear, – Remember, Denby: boy, girl and sheep are no strangers to buggery.

– I well know the circumstances and history of all the little creatures concerned, Lord Harcourt. Are you losing your confidence, old friend? Denby mocked.

– Foo! Not a bit of it. You see, Denby, I firmly believe that you are nothing but an old humper, incapable, particularly after imbibing wine, of determining what it is you are in congress with, Harcourt said with great smugness.

– I shall have a wager on my friend the Earl, Marcus Cox said, to more cheers from the gathered bucks and bloods, dropping a florin in the keeper's hand.

The woman was proving the most difficult to restrain. A normally compliant servant-girl, and no stranger to the attentions of many of the present gathering, she nonetheless began to panic under the sensory deprivation caused by gag, ropes and blindfold.

– Hush, my sweet one, Harcourt whispered, straddling her and pulling her buttocks apart as Denby's cock prepared to penetrate. As he roughly greased her anus, sliding in his finger, he noted a nervous tightness he had not experienced in this young wench since he had personally broken her in. Surely, *despite their experience, both the sheep and the boy would also display such nerves and the contest would be even.*

Harland was relieved to see Denby's organ slide in with little resistance. He was glad that he'd picked this one, serviced anally from eight years of age, as her sphincter muscle yielded easily.

— Mmmm, Denby smiled, continuing his push, then thrusting savagely for a while.

After a few more strokes he withdrew without spilling his seed, his penis still erect.

Harcourt stood over the boy and held his buttocks open, applying the grease with more care and tenderness than he had shown to the girl. This boy was his favourite and he harboured a concern that Denby might put him out of commission for a while with the ferocity of his fucking. Steered by his manservants, Denby's blood- and shit-stained member found its target. — Damn you ... he gasped, as the boy — who, like the girl, had been subjected to anal attentions from an early age by his master — groaned under his mask.

— The next one! Denby roared, withdrawing to a cheer.

With a look of slight distaste, Harcourt straddled the sheep and a man apiece held each of its back legs. He examined the smoothly shaved area around the animal's anal passage. He then had one of the men grease the orifice of the animal.

Despite the strength of the manservants who held the animal, it would not yield readily to Denby. He struggled inside as the creature twisted and bucked, the men endeavouring to hold it still. Denby pushed harder, his face reddening as his cries filled the air. — YIELD, DAMN YOU! ... I AM THE EARL OF DENBY! I COMMAND YOU TO YIELD!

The animal continued its struggle and Denby could not control his elation.

— I AM DENBY ... he shouted, his sperm pumping into the creature.

Cheers went up as Denby withdrew to gasps, and composed himself.

— Well, Denby? said Marcus Cox.

Denby let his heavy breathing calm down. — I have never more enjoyed such a wager, Sir, and never had the pleasure of such a wonderful tup as that last adorable creature. No blindly docile beast of the fields bred for slaughter could have responded to my promptings in that way ... nay, it was more than a common coupling — the spiritual communion I enjoyed with that delicious and most rapturous creature transcended all bounds … there was a meeting of minds, of souls … this delicious communion was all too human.

The bucks stifled their laughter as Denby continued, – That last one, that beautiful fuck, it was either the pretty wench or the obedient house-boy … it matters not. I know that the creature is destined to be mine. I state now that I will pay the master of that third one the sum of one hundred pounds for the services of that ride!

– A handsome offer, Lord Denby, and one which I am bound to accept.

Denby immediately recognised Harcourt's voice. – The boy! I knew it! That lovely young boy! One hundred pounds well spent! Denby said to great laughter. Sheep, girl and boy, in that order! That was it, I'll wager!

There was a short silence followed by a volley of hysterical laughter. As the blind was pulled off him, Denby let out a sporting roar. – My God! The sheep! I don't believe it! That beautiful stoical beast!

– Gentlemen! Harcourt raised his voice with his glass, – Gentlemen! As one who has little time for the parlour controversies of idle theorists, an interesting social point has surely been proved here! Let our friends in the legal profession take note! Buggery is buggery!

The farmhands sang in a lusty chorus:

> *Some men they loikes wimmin*
> *some men they loikes boys*
> *but moi sheep's warm and beautiful*
> *an makes a barrin noise.*

Perks let the manuscript fall through his fingers onto the floor of the study. He picked up the phone and got straight onto Rebecca's publishers. – Giles, I think you should come over here. Straight away.

Giles recognised the panic in Perky's voice. – What's wrong? Is it Rebecca? Is she all right?

– No, Perks sneered, – she's not fucking well all right. She's very fucking far from all right.

– I'll be straight over, Giles said.

15 Perks Is Upset

Giles wasted no time in arriving at Perky and Rebecca's Kensington home. He read the manuscript with horror. It got worse and worse. Rebecca returned later that afternoon and came upon them in the study.

– Giles! Darling! How are you? Oh, I see you've been looking at the manuscript. What do you think?

Giles, in spite of his anger and anxiety, had been preparing to soft-soap Rebecca. He detested writers; they were invariably tedious, self-righteous, fucked-up bores. The ones who had artistic pretensions were by far the most unbearable. That's what had happened to the silly cow, he considered, far too much time to think in that hospital, and she'd gone and got fucking art! Confronted by her illness with the prospect of mortality, she wanted to make her mark and she wanted to do it at the expense of his profit margins! However, nothing could be gained by irritating her. She had to be seduced, to be wooed into seeing the error of her ways. Giles was just about to launch into an 'interesting new direction, darling, but … ' speech, when Perky, seething with anger, got in first.

– Becca, darling, Perks said through gritted teeth, – I don't know what you're trying to give us here …

– Don't you like it, Perky? Don't you find it more racy, more … raw?

– It's hardly a Miss May Romance, darling, Giles lisped.

– Now, Giles, it's full of realism. One can't, how should I put it, live with one's head stuck up one's fanny forever, can one?

It's the medication, Perks thought. The old girl's finally lost her marbles.

– Darling Rebecca, Giles implored, – Do try to see reason. He started pacing up and down, moving his hands expansively. – Who reads your books? Mumsie-Wumsie, of course, she who doth hold the entire fabric of our great society together. She who does all the essential maintenance on the chappie who goes out to work, she who rears the kiddies. You know her, you see her all the time on the washing-powder adverts. Yes, she works ever so hard; and like the slaves in the field she does it with a smile on her face and, yes, a song in her heart! It's a dull, thankless life of drudgery, so she needs a little escape hatch. Oh, yes, afternoon telly helps, of course, but what is the real sweet little pill that makes it all bearable? It's getting out Rebecca Navarro's Miss May novels and escaping into that beautiful world of romance and gaiety you so passionately re-create. All the mumsies and the young mumsies-to-be need that.

– Precisely, Perky nodded sternly, – you go introducing buggery and revolution into things and those valium-headed bovine tarts will be throwing down their books in horror – and then where will we be?

– Do tell me, darling? Rebecca teased.

– On the fucking street selling *The Big Issue*, that's where! Perky roared.

16 A Bugger In
The Scrum

Nick Armitage-Welsby picked up a loose ball on the edge of the scrum and accelerated, weaving deep into opposition territory, deftly swivelling past two desperate tackles. The small crowd at Richmond experienced a tingling of anticipation, as Armitage-Welsby had the pace and power to go all the way to the line. However, with the opposition rearguard in disarray, Armitage-Welsby weakly passed to a colleague then collapsed onto the mud.

He was dead on arrival at St Hubbin's Hospital, the victim of a massive cardio-vascular accident.

The body lay on a trolley in the hospital morgue and was eagerly inspected by Freddy Royle. – Oooh ar, that's been a good un! Ung loike an ars boi the looks of things ... He prepared to take a closer look.

– Eh, Freddy, Glen said warily, – we got this new pathologist geezer, this fellow called Clements, and he ... eh, hasn't really sussed out the way we do things here. He's on duty later on, and he'll want to see our friend, so sort of go easy on him.

– Yeah, aal be noice n gentle wif you, won't oi me ol vlower? Freddy smiled and winked at the corpse. He turned to Glen, – now are you goin to be a lad and look out zum noice ztring vor Vreddy?

Glen huffed and puffed but rummaged in a drawer and produced a ball of string. Let Freddy do what he wanted, Glen thought. He was going out with Yvonne tonight. The cinema, then out clubbing. He would buy her something nice with Freddy's cash. Perfume. Expensive perfume, he thought. To see her face when he gave it to her. That would do him.

Freddy took two splints and tied them around the corpse's flaccid penis. He then stuck a rectangular biscuit tin between the dead man's legs, balancing the splinted cock on top.

– Just wait vor this little beauty to go n zet, with that there rigour martiz, then we'll have ourzelves zum praber vun! Freddy smiled.

Glen made his excuses and went into the ante-room.

17 Lorraine
And Love

Lorraine had been spending a lot of time at Rebecca's. She had helped her with the manuscript. They had been to the British Museum, to Cardboard City, through the Underground stations where mothers begged, holding up malnourished children. – I saw them do that in Mexico City about ten years ago, Rebecca sighed, – and I always thought: that could never happen here, never in England. You want to look the other way all the time. You want to believe everything, that it's all a con, a fake; you want to believe everything but the truth.

– Which is that they've no money to feed their kids and the Government don't give a fuck, Lorraine sneered, – they'd rather make sure that the rich have got miles more than enough.

Lorraine was so hard sometimes, Rebecca thought. It wasn't good. If you allowed those who would brutalise you to make you hard, then surely you've lost to them. They had achieved their goal. Romance was more than her creative imagination. Surely there had to be room for romance, for true romance? Romance for everyone, and not just from the pages of a book.

These thoughts pounded through Rebecca's head as Lorraine went back to the nurses' home. She too had concerns. She hadn't really talked properly to Yvonne for ages. She had been avoiding her since that night at the club. She was now going out with that Glen guy, and she seemed so happy. When she got back to the home, Lorraine heard some house music coming from Yvonne's room. It was that Slam tape she'd given her ages ago.

Bracing herself, she knocked on the door. – It's open, Yvonne said.

She was alone when Lorraine entered. – Hiya, Lorraine said.

– Hi, Yvonne replied.

– Listen, Yvonne, Lorraine began, then started talking quickly, – I came to apologise about how I was in the club that time. It's really weird, but I was so E'd up and emotional and you just looked so fucking cool and gorgeous and you're my best pal and you're the only person who never gives me a hard time …

– Yeah, that's all good and well, but I ain't, you know, like that …

– The thing is, Lorraine laughed, – I don't know if I am either. I was just going through a downer on men … oh, I don't know … maybe I am, I don't know where the fuck I'm coming from! When I kissed you, I was treating you like guys treat me … it was out of order. It was weird, but I wanted to see what they felt. I wanted to feel how they felt. I wanted to fancy you, but I didn't. I thought that if I was a dyke, then it would be easier, at least I'd know something about myself. But I couldn't get aroused by you.

– I don't know whether to be pleased or insulted, Yvonne smiled.

– Thing is, I don't seem to really fancy guys either. Every time with one of them has been a disappointment. Nobody does it for me like I do it for myself … Lorraine put her hand to her mouth, – what a fuckin weird cow, eh.

– Just ain't found the right one yet, Lorraine. It don't matter who it is, a bloke or a bird, you just gotta find the right one.

– Voice of experience, eh?

– I think so, Yvonne smiled. – why don't you come out with us to the club tonight?

– Naw, I'm gaunny keep off the Es for a bit, it's fucking my head up. I think I love everyone, then I think I'm incapable of loving anyone. The comedowns are getting pretty bad.

– Yeah, I think you're wise, you've put in a fair old bit over the last couple of years. You've well paid your dues, gel, ya know? Yvonne laughed then she stood up and embraced Lorraine in a hug which meant more to each woman than either could ever have told each other.

As she left, Lorraine reflected on Yvonne's love for Glen. No, she wouldn't be going to the club with them. When two people were in love you had to leave them to it. Especially when you weren't in love and wished that you were. That could embarrass. That could hurt.

18 Untitled — Work In Progress

The decline of the Earl of Denby continued apace. Servants complained that Flossie, the sheep, made a mess of the quarters, yet he insisted that she would be waited on by a team of hand-maidens, who would keep the animal in luxury and contentment, particularly ensuring that the beast's fleece was well-groomed and spotless.

— Flossie, my darling angel, Denby said, rubbing his erect penis against his beloved blackface's fleece, — you have rescued me from a life of emptiness and despondency since the untimely demise of my wonderful wife … ah, Flossie, please do not mind me talking of that divine lady. I do wish that the two of you could have met! That would have been wonderful. Alas, it can never be, it is just the two of us now, my darling. How you arouse and tantalise me! I am bewitched … The Earl felt himself sliding into the sheep. — … what bliss …

19 The Pathologist's Report

The Trust Manager, Alan Sweet, had that sinking feeling he'd anticipated for some time. Someone had to be the bearer of bad news. Sweet had a bad feeling about the bumptious Geoffrey Clements, the new pathologist, right from the start. Clements came into his office, without making an appointment, sat down, and thrust a typed report in front of him. After letting Sweet glance through it, he started to speak in deep, stern tones. – ... and I have to conclude that the body of Mr Armitage-Welsby has been interfered with in the way I described, since it came into our possession, here at St Hubbin's.

– Listen, Mr Clements ... , Sweet said, looking at the report, – ... eh, Geoffrey ... we have to be quite sure about this.

– I am quite sure. Hence the report, Clements gruffly observed.

– But surely there are other factors to consider ...

– Such as?

– I mean to say, Sweet began, adding a matey wink which he immediately knew was a bad move before Clements' bearded face could register a disapproving scowl, – Nick Armitage-Welsby attended an English public school and played rugby at all levels. These two factors should be enough to ensure that he was no stranger to these kind of, eh, attentions ...

Clements looked astonished.

– I mean, Sweet continued – could the stretching and contusions around the sphincter and the traces of semen not perhaps be the result of some dressing-room pranks and frolics, perhaps at half-time, shortly before the poor unfortunate fellow was brought to us?

– Not in my professional opinion, Clements retorted frostily. – And incidentally, I would like you to know that I attended an

English public school and I play rugby with great enthusiasm, though at nowhere near the same level as Nick Armitage-Welsby used to. I have certainly never encountered those practices you talk about and I take great offence at the bland recital of such an offensive stereotype.

– I apologise for any offence caused, Geoffrey. However, as Trust Manager, you appreciate that I have a responsibility to the Trustees who are accountable for any alleged malpractice ...

– What about your responsibility to the patients and their relatives?

– Why, that goes without saying, surely. I regard the two as synonymous. But the point is that I can't go around accusing members of staff of necrophiliac practices. If the press got hold of it, they would have a field day! Public confidence in the hospital and its management would be severely undermined. The Trust relies to a great extent for some of its innovative practices, like the state-of-the-art screening equipment in the new preventative medicine unit, on the goodwill, expressed through charitable donations, of its many wealthy benefactors. Why, if I started pushing needless panic buttons ...

– As manager, you and your team also have a duty to the public to investigate this, Clements snapped.

Sweet decided that Clements stood for almost everything he detested, perhaps even more than the working classes he himself sprang from. That arrogant public-school assumption of in-bred superior morality. Bastards like that could afford it; no money worries there. Sweet, though, had staked everything on purchasing that large property on the Thames at Richmond, no more than a shell when he bought it. Now the bills had to be repaid, and things were coming along nicely, thanks to Freddy's patronage. Now all that was being threatened, his very livelihood, by an arrogant little fuss-pot with a silver spoon in his mouth!

Taking a deep breath, Sweet tried to resume his air of detached professionalism. – Of course, a full investigation will take place ...

– See that it does, Clements barked, – and see also that I'm kept informed.

 – Of course … Geoffrey … Sweet simpered through gritted teeth.

 – Goodbye, *Mister* Sweet, Clements snapped.

Sweet grasped a pen in his fist and scraped the word CUNT across the paper of a lined notepad with such venom that it tore through six pages and left its impression on another dozen. He then picked up the phone and dialled a number. – Freddy Royle?

20 Untitled – Work In Progress

Lorraine had been following the Earl of Denby, all the way across the city to the opium den he frequented in Limehouse. Dressed in old clothes and with a scarf over her face to avoid being recognised by the Earl, she looked for all the world like a humble servant-girl. The disguise proved to be effective; in some ways too effective. Lorraine was subjected to continual harassment from the assorted reprobates and ne'er-do-wells who were returning home through the dark city streets after a night of revelry.

She maintained her demeanour and walked on, but one persistent pair, dressed in military colours, had been making comments, and now they jumped in front of her to block her path.

— This pretty maid will be fair game for some sport, I'll wager, one of the men said wryly.

— And I think I know the sport you have in mind, the other smiled lewdly.

Lorraine froze to the spot. These drunken soldiers had mistaken her for a common maid. She was about to speak but was then aware of another presence behind her.

— I caution you not to bother this lady, a voice was heard.

Lorraine turned to see a handsome man emerging from the shadows.

— Who do you think you are? One of the bloods shouted, — be about your business!

The man stood impassively. Lorraine recognised the familiar contemptuous scowl on his lips, though his hat kept his eyes in shadow. When he deigned to address the young soldiers, he did so with authority. — I've been observing your revels, Sirs, and I have to inform you that your drunken verse displays a taste for the bawdy that would shame the most undisciplined conscripts from the coal towns of Lancashire!

The other soldier, recognising the bearing of a fellow officer, seemed more wary. — And who might you be, Sir?

— Colonel Marcus Cox, of the House of Cranborough, and of the 3rd Division of the Sussex Rangers. And you: who would be the rogue who sullies the colours of his fine regiment by insulting a lady of status in society and a ward of the Earl of Denby?

— You know, Sir? Lorraine asked in surprise. Her disguise had been enough to fool the grieving Denby, he who could not wait to return from his London duties to his stupid sheep, but had not deceived Marcus Cox, restored as he was to full health and alertness.

— Begging your pardon, my dear Miss Lorraine, the gallant young Colonel said, turning back to the bucks, — well, what have you to say for yourselves?

— Why, madam, one thousand apologies ... we took you for a maid ...

— Evidently, said Marcus, — and in my capacity as enforcer of discipline within my own regiment how, pray tell, would my good friend Colonel 'Sandy' Alexander react to learning of his junior officers setting such an unseemly example of debauchery?

— Sir ... let me explain my circumstances ... we are soon to be dispatched to the front to see off Boney's mob. We ... did not realise that the lady was ... of society. My people are not wealthy, Sir, this commission means so much to them ... I beseech you ... the young soldier who had seemed the more arrogant pleaded openly, his face pained with anguish.

Lorraine thought of her own circumstances, and the sacrifices made by her parents to introduce her to society. — It was my fault for dressing like this, Marcus, I only did it so that I could follow our beloved Denby undetected ... she cried.

Marcus Cox turned briefly to Lorraine, then glanced back at the two men. He let his bottom lip curl downwards and rested one hand on his hip as he looked them up and down. — I am not a man who lacks compassion by nature, Cox explained to the two young officers, — nor am I one who is immune to the temptations of sport, particularly before the stresses of battle, which I understand only too well. However, when an officer of a British regiment insults a lady of breeding, and one of my acquaintance, I can only demand satisfaction. All other considerations pale, he said ominously, his voice lowered almost to a whisper. Then he boomed, — Will you give me satisfaction?

— Dear Sir, said the more silent of the soldiers, who was now in much

distress, literally shaking, as if he was facing Napoleon's rifles, – we cannot consent to duel with a senior officer! Let alone a man of your standing! It would be barbaric! To engage in combat with someone whom we should be standing with side by side for England, why, it is nothing short of perverse! Please, my noble Sir, I accept that we have erred badly and that some recompense is due to you for our dastardly behaviour towards the good lady, but please, I implore you, do not seek your satisfaction from us in this way!

– And that is the feeling of you both? Cox asked.

– Yes, Sir, it is, the other soldier answered.

– I will have satisfaction, damn you! Cox roared into the night, – Will you give me satisfaction?

– Sir … I beg you … how can we? The two young men were cowed and timid under the thunderous ferocity of the senior officer's tones.

Marcus felt his raw, tingling lips spattered with his froth, and a powerful throbbing in his chest. – I see before me a man of no consequence, unused to society and unfit to wear those colours, and an arrogant milksop who will sell his soul to save his quivering, goose-bumped flesh!

– Please, Sir … I beseech you, in the name of England herself! How can we give you satisfaction in the manner you suggest?

– Very well, said Cox, after a contemplative silence. – As you refuse to comply with my request to settle this matter in a time-honoured way, it leaves me to fall back upon the traditions of my own regiment to guide me. These traditions of punishment for junior officers who transgress, in this or any manner, are the punishments which I myself now feel duty-bound to administer. Drop your trousers, the both of you! Obey! Marcus turned to Lorraine, – Please get into the carriage, Lorraine, this is not for the eyes of a lady.

Lorraine complied, but could not stop herself from pulling back the blind and observing the men strip from the waist and bend over a railing. She could watch no more, but she did hear the screams of one man and then the other, followed by Marcus shouting: – I will have satisfaction!

He joined her shortly afterwards in the carriage, a little breathless. – I am sorry, Lorraine, that you had to be exposed, in this manner, to the harsher side of military discipline. It hurt me gravely to be forced to administer such a punishment, but the lot of a senior army officer is not always a pleasant one.

– But your way of disciplining these officers, Marcus, was that usual?

Marcus raised an eyebow at Lorraine. – There are many methods one can call upon, but in this particular situation, these were the ones I would expect to find most effective. When one is entrusted with the responsibility of administering punishment upon one's brother officers it is important to remember that one still cannot relinquish one's equally compelling role in ensuring that the sense of esprit de corps, the sense of togetherness and, yes, the sense of love for the regiment and for brother officers be maintained. This is absolutely essential for the purposes of morale.

Lorraine looked doubtful, but was moved by Marcus's eloquence to concede, – Alas, Sir, as a mere woman I am far from wise in military ways …

– That is as it should be, Marcus nodded, – And now, what news of our friend, the Earl of Denby?

– Oh, my Lord is still in such a sorry way, Marcus! It tears my heart! The gluttonous taking of wine and opium, the bizarre congress with that sheep … it vexes me so! He is going to Wiltshire in a few days, and he will be with that beast the entire time!

– We must accompany him. We must endeavour to do something that will bring him to his senses. It was a trauma that enfeebled his mind, so perhaps it requires some trauma to shake him out off it. We must think.

– Marcus, Lorraine began, after an impressively small pause for such thought, – I think I have something in mind …

21 Lord Of The Rings

The corpse had been pulled out of the burning warehouse early that morning. Glen winced as he looked at it; desensitised as he had become to dead bodies, some of them in abominable states, he had never come across one like this. The flesh was burned from the top half of the body, the face unrecognisable. Ominously, as Glen heard the heavy breathing of Freddy Royle behind him, he saw that the buttocks were almost untouched by the consuming flames.

– Zo this un woz a regular arze bandit then, woz e? Freddy drawled.

– Well, yeah, I mean it was a fire in a gay disco. The geezer's boyfriend came in to identify the body, Glen nodded at the charred mess. – He could only recognise the ring, that's how he was able to make the identification.

Freddy thrust his index finger into the corpse's arsehole. – Yeah, it's about the only thing that ain't been damaged … I dunno how he could tell the difference, though, most of them look the same to me. Must've been true love, eh?

Glen shook his head and pointed at the gold band which was on one of the body's charred fingers. – *That* ring, Freddy, he said.

– Oh! Oi see wot you mean, me ol moite! Freddy laughed.

Glen was almost gagging on the sickly scent of the charred flesh. It seemed to get everywhere. He stuck more of the blocking cream under his nostrils.

After he had his way with the corpse, Freddy poured lighter fuel into the arsehole and set it on fire.

– What are you doing? Glen screamed.

– Just makin it a little bit more divigult vor that there patholigizt fella to vind evidinz, Freddy smiled as Glen started gagging again.

22 Untitled – Work In Progress

– *The tenderest and most succulent lamb I have tasted in many years, Denby said, then froze. The word 'lamb' seemed to echo in his skull. Flossie. He glanced up at Harcourt who was filling his goblet with wine.*

– *Indeed, Harcourt smiled, – meat, I hear, which has been marinated internally with the juices of the finest English aristocrat.*

Denby looked across at Marcus Cox. It was not the smirk he expected on the face of his friend, but the odd look of compassion and pity that convinced him some terrible deed had been perpetrated. Harcourt, though, demonstrated no such compassion. His shoulders began to shake and a giggling sound vibrated from his bulky frame.

– *You … Denby rose and shouted, – Damn your eyes … if anything has happened to my Flossie I swear by God … he broke off and stormed into the kitchens.*

He saw the terrified face of the cook, Mrs Hurst, just as he came across the head of his beloved sheep, Flossie, decapitated and staring at him from the kitchen table with what he thought was a look of sadness and recrimination.

He buckled as if from the impact of a blow, then quickly straightened and advanced towards the shivering old woman.

– *Damn you, you evil witch! I'll consign your scrawny body to the grave and your twisted soul to hell!*

– *This was not my work, Sir! the woman screamed.*

– *Who sanctioned this sick, criminal butchery? Denby roared.*

– *It were the young mistress, Sir, Miss Lorraine, it were her that told I to do this …*

– *LIAR! Denby screamed, reaching for a meat cleaver on the table.*

Lorraine stood in the doorway. – My Lord, if you are to wreak vengance, vent your spleen on me. For it is true, it was I who sanctioned this!

Denby looked at his ward. As his eyes met hers he could fathom no duplicity, only an unerring devotion in the beautiful young woman, who had, indeed, since the departure of his wife, unstintingly taken on the mantle of mistress of the hall. It had the effect of squeezing the anger from him like the juice from an orange. – But Lorraine, my sweet, tender blossom of wild Scotch heather ... how could you do such an unspeakably vile thing!

Lorraine turned away, and let the tears run from her eyes. Then she turned back to Denby. – I beg you, my Lord, believe me that I surely had to! The relationship between my beloved Earl and this unfortunate beast of the fields was making him the laughing-stock of society ...

– But ...

– ... there was even talk of the corrosive power of syphilis on the faculties of his Lordship. You were, noble Sir, being steadfastly undermined by this scurrilous chatter, the idle banter of fools and reprobates, granted, yet still serving the foulest and most despicable of purposes ...

– I did not realise ... I had no idea ...

– No, Sir, you did not, so bewitched by a spell of evil were you, so torn by heartbreak that the devil got into you while your defences were devastated by the loss of your darling wife. But that sheep is no replacement ... only a woman can love a man, Sir, this I contend.

Denby let a smile play across his lips as he studied this enchanting young creature fondly. – And what, my little darling, would you know of love?

– Alas, Sir, I too harbour my passions, passions which burn all the more sorely for being so guarded ...

– A pretty, innocent young thing like you? Denby said. Yet so devious, he thought.

– Even in a world so warped by the madness of men as our own, my good Lord, I cannot bring myself to regard trickery, subterfuge, manipulation and seduction as the legitimate behaviour of a young woman, let alone one preparing to take up her place in society, but these concerns of morality are always tempered by passions ... grand passions which justify anything!

– You've fallen for Marcus Cox! Lorraine, I will have you know that the dashing blood commands my utmost respect as a soldier and a friend and, moreover, in his vagabond ways I see echoes of a younger self. This is why I

could never consent to such a liaison with a ward of mine. Cox is a wild stallion whose entire raison d'être *is to win the hearts, and thus the virtue, of innocent maidens, then discard them ruthlessly in pursuit of the next prey!*

– *No, Sir, you may rest assured on the matter of Marcus Cox. Charming and dashing though he may be, Marcus is not the one who has captured my heart … you are, my Lord. There. I have said it.*

Denby looked at Lorraine. He was then aware of the presence of someone else in the room. He turned, anticipating Marcus Cox. However, it was a female figure. He gazed at his departed wife's great friend, the match-maker Miss May. – *Miss May. You have, I take it, played a part in these proceedings?*

– *Not as much as I generally do, for affairs of the heart can only be resolved by the parties concerned. It is for you to now make that resolution, my Lord. What do you say?*

Lord Denby looked into the dark pools that were the eyes of the fair Lorraine. – *I say …* he staggered forward and held her in his arms, – *… I love you … my darling … my sweet, sweet darling Lorraine!* He kissed the beautiful young woman and he was aware of cheers in the room as Harcourt and Cox had gathered round. Nonetheless, the Lord held his lips on the lovely lady's.

– *Now,* Cox commented loudly to Harcourt, – *we shall surely get a day out with those blasted hounds!*

23 Perk's End

He was on his third bottle of red wine in the Kensington bar, but two inches past the bottleneck he could drink no more and he decided that he was as drunk as could be without passing out. He wearily raised his hand to the barman and staggered out into the street.

It was still light but Perky Navarro was too dazed with drink to react to the oncoming car. He felt nothing until it hit him and he went over its bonnet, realised nothing at all until he briefly came to in the hospital.

Through his heavy, stunned state Perky could see the assorted strange faces around his bed, the faces of the medical team. One face was familiar, though, one leering face which twisted grotesquely into focus from behind the bland expressions of concerned detachment from the medical people.

Perks could feel himself slipping away, but he could see that face getting closer to him and the last words Perky Navarro heard were: — You're in good haaaands ere, Perky, moi ol zun. We'll take praber gare of thee ...

Unfortunately, Perky Navarro passed away. That evening, Yvonne Croft was on her break so she went down to the path lab to see Glen. She heard noises coming from the behind a door in the lab. — Who's in there? she asked Glen.

— It's just Freddy, Glen smiled, — he's an old friend of the deceased. He's a bit emotional; he's just paying his last respects in his own way.

— Oh, said Yvonne, — that's nice.

— Yeah, said Glen. — Fancy a coffee?

She smiled and he ushered her out, along to the canteen.

24 Pathologically Yours

There were two men who played a particularly prominent role in the St Hubbin's Hospital Trust. It was profitable to them both in different ways. Both men had known that they were not going to give up what they had, what they valued.

Alan Sweet, who was one of these men, had requested the clear-the-air meeting with the increasingly truculent pathologist Geoffrey Clements, to discuss his continuing allegations of malpractice in the department.

The pathologist had just started to speak when he felt the chloroform gag over his mouth. He struggled, but Freddy Royle, the second of the men most concerned about the ramifications of the pathologist's findings, came from good farming stock, and he had an exceptionally tight grip.

Alan Sweet was soon over by his side, helping to restrain the pathologist until he fell into unconsciousness.

When Geoffrey Clements was able to gain partial consciousness, he could only strain fitfully against his bonds. Even though a girl with bleached-blonde hair called Candy was riding him, and the huge dildo strapped to her stomach was well into his anus, and in spite of the other girl, Jade, rubbing her crotch into his bearded face, Clements felt blissfully relaxed.

– Ooh ar, looks like a good un! Freddy Royle shouted as the camera in Perky's old apartment started recording the scene. – Them muzzel-relaxint drugs look loike the bizzniz, don't they, Geoffrey, me old sport?

All Clements could do was moan quietly into Jade's bush in his blissed-out state.

    — A lot of people could see this video, Geoffrey. Of course, you and I know that isn't going to happen, Sweet smiled.

    — In fact, oi think that itz bizzniz as usual, Freddy laughed, — Ooh aar, looks like a good un!

25 Lorraine Goes To Livingston

Rebecca was having the time of her life at The Forum. The drug was taking her to new heights with the music. She took it easy, sitting in the chill-out room, enjoying the waves of MDMA and sound inside her. She looked at Lorraine, dancing away to the crazy apocalyptic sounds of the car horns and sirens blaring, crazy urban nightmare FX over a seductive, irresistible break-beat. Rebecca had accompanied Lorraine home to Livingston for a break. Lorraine was dancing with a group of men and women she knew. It was the first ever jungle night at The Forum, with a couple of top London jocks up doing the business. Lorraine looked happy. Rebecca thought of the title for her book: *Lorraine Goes To Livingston*. It would probably never be published. It didn't matter.

And in the midst of the Livingston jungle, something happened to Lorraine. She found herself necking with somebody, snogging the lips on a face that had been close to hers all night. It felt good. It felt right. She was glad she had come back up to Livingston. Come home.

Fortune's Always Hiding

A Corporate
Drug Romance

For Kenny Macmillan

Prologue

Stoldorf was a very beautiful village, picture-postcard Bavarian. It was located some eighty miles north-east of the city of Munich, nestling on the edge of the Bayrischer Wald, the lush Bavarian forest. The present village was actually the second Stoldorf; the medieval ruins of the first lay just over a mile down the road, where, long ago, the swelling Danube had burst its banks and swept part of the original settlement away. To avoid the risk of future flooding the village had been moved back from the great river, up onto the base of the slopes of the mountainous forest which rose in towering layers to the Czech border.

Gunther Emmerich, who had family connections in the area, had chosen to make this idyllic and unspoiled hamlet his home. The local pharmacy had become available, and six years ago Emmerich had decided to take it over, giving up corporate life and its attendant stresses.

It had been a good move. Gunther Emmerich was a contented man who felt that he had everything. Additionally, there was the wry satisfaction of knowing that this was how he was perceived by others: an old man with a young wife, a beautiful baby, health and wealth. As the local pharmacist in Stoldorf, Emmerich also had a status, and his family connections enabled him to be assimilated into the village community more easily than someone without the advantage of such a background. Emmerich was far too self-effacing by nature to be smug about his lot and therefore tended not to incite jealousy. This had been a flaw in his corporate life; lesser talents had obtained greater career advancement purely on their ability to beat their own drums. Here in Stoldorf, however, this liability was a decided asset. The locals respected this quiet, courteous and diligent man, admired his pretty young wife and their baby. So while Gunther Emmerich had reason to be contented, there was always a vaguely fatalistic unease about him; it was as if he knew that what he had could, and perhaps would, be someday taken from him. What Gunther Emmerich understood was the fragility of life.

Brigitte Emmerich was, if anything, even more at one with the world than her husband. From an adolescence littered with drug and personality problems, she considered that the best move she had ever made had been to marry the old pharmacist. She would think of her days in Munich's Neuperlach District, consuming and dealing amphetamines. The irony that she had married a pharmacist! It was not, she knew, a relationship based on love, but there was a strong affection which had grown over the four years they had been together and this had cemented further with the birth of their son.

This postcard appearance of the village of Stoldorf, though entirely persuasive, was inherently superficial; like most places it had more than one facet. Stoldorf was located in a region which had, until recently, been one of the most inaccessible in Europe, tucked alongside the old east-west divide of the Iron Curtain. In the darkness of the night, the forest which loomed over the village gave off an aura of foreboding which lent substance to the age-old myths of the Superbeasts lurking in its recesses. Gunther Emmerich was a religious man, but also a man of science. He didn't believe that a Superbeast stalked through the forest, observing the villagers just out of the line of their vision – though sometimes he felt as if *he* was being watched, spied on, singled out. Gunther knew far more about the evil that people, rather than monsters, were capable of. Bavaria had been the key region in the development and rise of Nazism. Many older people in Stoldorf had their secrets, and they never asked too many questions about the past. That local characteristic appealed to Gunther Emmerich. He knew all about secrets.

One cold, late December morning, Brigitte had taken their young child, Dieter, into Munich to do some Christmas shopping. As a Christian, Gunther Emmerich was opposed to the commercialisation of Christmas, but enjoyed the occasion and the exchange of gifts. As the child had been born just before last Christmas, this would be their first real family Christmas together. There had been problems last year. Following the birth of the baby, Brigitte had become depressed. Gunther was supportive, and urged prayer. This was a bulwark in their lives: they had met at a Christian mission in Munich, where they had both worked as volunteers. Brigitte had subsequently made a full recovery and was relishing this festive period.

A few minutes changed everything.

She left the child outside a gift shop in Munich's crowded Fussgängerzone for just a few minutes, to nip inside and get Gunther a tie-pin that had taken her fancy. When she emerged, the child and his buggy were gone: in their place just a sickening vacuum. A jagged, frozen sensation exploded in the base of her spine and travelled up each vertebra, disintegrating them one by one. Shaking off fear's paralysis, she looked around frantically – nothing, just throngs of Christmas shoppers. Buggies there were, but not *her* buggy, not *her* baby. As if the corrosive trail of fear had eaten through the very structure that held her upright, all Brigitte Emmerich could do was let out a loud moan as she buckled and collapsed against the window of the shop.

– Was ist los? Bist du krank? An elderly woman asked her.

Brigitte just kept screaming, all the faces of the shoppers turning towards her.

The police had little to go on. A young couple had been seen pushing a child in a buggy away from the shop around the time Brigitte's child had vanished. Nobody really remembered what they looked like. Nobody took any notice: another young couple with a baby. Yet there was an impression from the witnesses that there was *something* about that young couple. Something that was difficult to be specific about. Something perhaps in the way that they moved.

Eight days later the distraught Emmerichs received an anonymous package from Berlin. It contained, wrapped in polythene, two small blue, puffy, chubby arms. Both knew straight away what it was and what it meant: only Gunther knew why.

The police doctors said that there was no way the child could have survived such an amputation, performed with a crude implement, like a saw. There were marks above the elbow joints to show that the arms had been secured in a vice. If the shock hadn't killed Dieter Emmerich, the child would have bled to death in minutes.

Gunther Emmerich knew that his own past had caught up with him with a vengeance. He went into his garage and blew his face off with a shotgun his wife didn't even know he kept. Brigitte Emmerich was found by neighbours drugged and in a pool of blood where she had slashed her wrists. She was taken to a mental hospital on the outskirts of Munich where she has spent the last six years catatonic.

Aggravation

If the truth be known I can fucking well do without this bleedin aggravation, on account of the little job we got planned for tonight. Well, that was the way it panned out. You don't come down here mob-handed like that. Not on our fucking manor, you bleedin well don't.

– Came down here to clear the air, didn't we, this cocky Ilford cunt says.

I turned to Bal, then back to this mouthy Ilford slag, – Yeah, well let's fucking well clear it then. Outside.

Now I could tell that that took the wind out of the cunt's sails because the geezer with the mouth and his mate that was all fucking sly, well they were looking a bit fucking sad at that point, I should fucking well say.

Les from the Ilford, he ain't so bad, he was saying, – Look lads, we don't need all this aggravation. Come on, Dave, he says to me.

But nah, they don't come down here mouthing. That ain't on. I ignore the cunt; I nod to Bal and we make for the door.

– You, Bal points to this Hypo geezer and his mate, the cunt with the mouth, – out you fucking well come, you cunts!

They follow us, but I don't reckon that their bottle's up to it. A few Ilford slags make to go out behind them but Riggsie says, – Sit fucking down and drink your fucking beer. They'll sort it all out.

So me n Bal are right over to the two Ilford ponces and there ain't nowhere for them cunts to go, they are like lambs to the bleedin slaughter. But then I see that one cunt's tooled; he pulls a blade, and him and Bal are having this stand-off. This peps up the other geezer cause I thought that he was just gonna stand there and take a slapping, but he's steaming in, the cunt. He gets in a couple quite tasty style n

all but what he don't realise is that I'm a heavyweight and he's a
lightweight so I don't mind taking a few to get in close – which I do –
then it's over in no time. I hit him in the jaw and boot him a couple of
times and he goes down onto the tarmac of the pub car-park. – It's
the fucking Rembrandt Kid we got here! Always on the fucking
canvas! I shout at the slag who's all cowed on the deck, not so fucking
cocky now. My brogue goes down hard on his throat and he makes a
shrieking, choking noise. I kick him a couple of times. Very
disappointing this is n all; ain't no fight left in this cunt so I steam over
and give Bal a hand.

Thing is, at first Bal ain't nowhere to be seen, then he comes back,
eyes all fucking glazed, hand dripping with blood. It looks quite bad.
The cunt's cut him and run, the fucking conniving little toe-rag.

– Slag fucking got my hand! Tooled the cunt was! A fucking toe-
to-toe we was on! That slag's fucking history! Fucking history! Bal
screams, then a light comes into his eye when he sees the geezer that
I've given the slapping to, just lying there, groaning on the fucking
deck. – CAHHNNTS! FUCKING ILFORD CAHHNTS! He
starts booting fuck out off this Ilford slag who's gone into a ball to try
to protect his fucking face. – Hold on, Bal, I'll open this cunt up for
you, I says, and starts booting at the base of the cunt's spine and that
makes him buckle, giving Bal cleaner shots at the fucker's nut. – I'LL
TEACH YOU CAHHNTS TO PULL A FUCKING BLADE
IN A TOE-TO-TOE YOU CAHHNNTS!

We left the Ilford wanker lying there. He'd have got worse if he
hadn't been one of our geezers, I mean not Mile End, but like Firm.
Well, they call themselves Firm but they ain't the real Firm. We
proved that fucking point. Foot-soldiers, them cunts. Ideas above
their fucking station.

Anyway, we leaves the cunt in the car-park and goes into the
Grapes to finish our drinks. Bal took off his T-shirt and wrapped his
hand in it. Standing there like fucking Tarzan, he was. It was bad n
all, the hand like, needed stitching pretty sharpish at the A&E at the
London Hospital down the road. It would have to wait though; this
was about show, about flash.

Cause it felt great walking into that bar: grinning like a pair of bleeding Cheshire Cats we was. Our boys cheered when we got in; some Ilford cunts skulked out the fucking door there and then. Les from their mob came over.

– Well, you got the result, fair and square, lads, he said. Not a bad geezer, Les: decent sort of bloke if you know what I mean.

Bal ain't a happy man though. No wonder with his bleedin mit cut up. – Weren't fair n square at all, you cunt. Some slag slipped that Hypo geezer a tool!

Les just shrugs like he dunno nothing about it. Maybe he don't. Not a bad geezer, Les. – Dunno nothing about that Bal. Where are they, Greenie and Hypo?

– The mouthy slag, Greenie, is it? Last seen in small fucking pieces outside in the car-park. That Hypo cunt, he was heading for the fucking Tube. Probably caught the East London line across the fucking river. He'll be running with the fucking Millwall next season!

– Come on, Bal, we're all West Ham. No fucking doubts about that, Les said. Les was okay, but there was something about the slag that was giving me the hump. I drew my head back and stuck one on his nose. I heard the crack and saw him stagger back, trying to stem the flow of blood with his hand.

– Fuck me, Thorny ... we're on the same fucking side ... we shouldn't be fighting each other ... he says, all fucking gasping as the blood splashes out onto the deck. It's fairly coming out n all. That was a nice one. That blood though. He should hold his fucking head back, the daft cunt. Somebody should give the fucker a hankie.

– And don't you Ilford cunts ever forget it, Bal shouted, giving me a nod. He looked over at Shorthand and Riggsie. – Come on, lads, get 'em in for Les and the boys over there. We're all fucking Firm after all!

– Oi! I shouts over at the Ilford, – One of you cunt's get old Les a hanky, or a towel from the shithouse or something! Want him to fucking well bleed to death?

They jump n all, the fuckers.

I looked over to Chris, the landlord, who was washing some glasses. Looked like he had the hump. – Sorry, Chris, I shouted, – just putting a slag right on one or two little things. No aggravation like. He nodded over. An alright geezer, Chris.

The Ilford cunts stay for a couple but their hearts aren't really in it and they're queuing up to make their excuses and leave. Bal had to stay until the last one had gone: put on a brave face on account of the hand. Don't want that Hypo slag boasting about how he'd given Barry Leitch a bad cut.

Once they'd gone Riggsie says to me, – Bit out of order there, Thorny, nutting Les like that. He's an okay geezer. We're all on the same fucking side.

Yeah, and he's out off his nut on ecstasy, the fucking ponce. I ain't getting into it with him.

– Bollocks it was, Bal said. – Thorny was in the right. You beat me to it there, Dave. Yeah, we need these slags, but not as much as they fucking think.

– Something about the cunt's attitude I didn't like, I tell them. – He didn't show enough respect, you know?

Riggsie's shaking his head, all humped up and everything, so he don't stay for too long, which is good, cause after taking Bal down to the A&E to get him stitched up, me, him and Shorthand are straight back to his place to plan tonight's job, which was the real order of business before those Ilford wankers came down here disrupting things.

So back at his we're all pretty fucking well pleased with ourselves; well, Bal's a bit broody on account of his hand I suppose. I look at myself in the full-length mirror he's got: well fucking hard I am. I've been fairly hammering the old weights in the gym. I got quite a few things to sort out.

I look at my mates; they can be cunts at times, but they're the best mates you could have.

Bal, he's a head shorter than me, but he's a heavyweight n all. Shorthand's a bit of a wimp; he's the joker in the pack, ain't he. He gets on your bleedin tits at times but he's all right. Riggsie ain't with us so much these days. It was always the four of us, now it's just the three, innit. He ain't with us, but he's still always with us, if you know what I mean.

– Riggsie, Bal scoffs, – Mister fucking love n peace these days ain't he?

We had a good bleeding laugh at the cunt.

London, 1961

Bruce Sturgess was, as was his habit, in the boardroom fifteen minutes before the meeting was due to start. He went over his slides, checking the sharpness and clarity of the image the projector threw onto the screen from all seating points in the musty, wood-panelled room. Content, Sturgess strolled over to the window and looked at the new office block which was being constructed opposite. They seemed to spend forever on the foundations, but once they were complete, the structure rose into the sky rapidly, and it would change the city skyline for a least a couple of living memories. Sturgess envied the architects, the planners. They have their monuments, he considered.

His thoughts were distracted by the arrival of the others. Mike Horton came in first, followed by the ebullient Barney Drysdale, with whom he had enjoyed a robust evening of drink and conspiracy last night in the bar of The White Horse public house, just off Trafalgar Square. In the small, crowded bar, populated largely by staff from the nearby South African Embassy, he and Barney had spent a great deal of time discussing this meeting. Barney tipped him a wink and then started making gregarious remarks to the other executives who were coming in and filling the chairs around the large, polished oak table.

As usual, Sir Alfred Woodcock was the last to arrive, languidly taking his seat at the top of the table. Bruce Sturgess thought what he always thought when Sir Alfred sat down: I WANT TO BE WHERE YOU ARE NOW.

The buzz of the chatter immediately ceased, though Barney's booming voice went on a little longer and was apparent in its isolation. – Oh … sorry, Sir Alfred, he said in crisp apology.

Sir Alfred's smile was impatient but carried a redeeming dose of indulgent paternalism which Barney alone seemed able to elicit. – Good morning, gentlemen ... we are here today to talk largely about Tenazadrine, our proposed new product lead ... or rather, I should say, Bruce will be telling us exactly why this should be our new product lead. Bruce, Sir Alfred nodded.

Sturgess stood up, feeling a surge of power. With an assertive swagger brought on in response to an icy scowl from Mike Horton, he clicked on the projector. Bloody Horton pushing the promotion of a useless fucking mouth-ulcer cure. Well, Tenazadrine would blow all that away. Bruce Sturgess believed in this product, but much more than that, Bruce Sturgess believed in Bruce Sturgess. – Thank you, Sir Alfred. Gentlemen, I am going to tell you why, if we do not lead off on this product, this company would be missing an opportunity which probably only comes along perhaps two or three times in a lifetime in the pharmaceutical industry.

That was exactly what Bruce Sturgess did in his presentation of Tenazadrine. Horton could feel the cool reticence in the room thaw. He was aware of the empathetic nods and then the mood of growing excitement. He could feel his own mouth drying out and was soon wishing for a swig of his vaunted mouth-ulcer cure: a product, which, he realised, would be a long, long time in the making.

Suburbia

This fucking ski-mask's too bleedin hot, innit: that's the problem with them. Don't bear thinking about. This one was a piece of fucking piss though. We had the place well sussed out, knew the whole family's M.O. backwards. That's one thing I gotta give Shorthand: he does his surveillance well. Mind you, them suburban types don't exactly make it hard for ya. They are creatures of habit and no mistake. And long may it bleedin well continue, cause it's good for business; and, as Maggie herself once said, what's good for business is good for Britain; or something like that.

The only spot of nastiness about the whole thing was that it was the bleedin Doris that answered the door. Well, I was in the striker role so I just punched her square in the gob and she fell backwards into the house, crashing down heavily and just sort of lying there twitching on the floor like she was having a bleeding fit. She didn't even make a sound, like cry out or nothing. I stepped in and shut the door. The way she was just lying there: fucking pathetic; it made me all sort of angry at her, you know? Bal bends down and holds a blade at her throat. As it comes into focus and she realises what it is, her eyes are popping out of her bleedin head. Then she's holding her skirt down against her thighs. That gets my fucking goat, that does; as if we want any of her, the cheeky slag, as if we're sick or something.

Bal talks to her softly in his put-on coon voice, sort of West Indian like, – Keep it shut an you live. Fuck wit us an your white ass is yesturday's noos, woomun.

Total pro is our Bal, ya gotta give him that. He even has his eyes and mouth blacked under that ski-mask. This Doris just stares at him; her pupils huge, like some cunt's dropped an ecstasy on her.

Then this geezer, the husband, comes through. – Jackie … for god sake …

– SHUT YIR FUCKIN MOOTH SLAG! I shout at him in my Jock accent. – IF YE WAAHNT YIR WUMMIN HERE IN WAAHN PIECE YI'LL KEEP IT FUCKIN SHUT! RIGHT? He nods all timid like and says, – Please, take anything, just don't …

I move over and bounce his head hard off the wall. Three times I do it: once for business, once for fun – cause I hate slags like that – and once for luck. Then I stick my knee into his bollocks. He slumps down the fucking wall with a groan, pathetic little cunt. – Ah telt ye tae shut the fuck up! Ah sais tae shut up n dae whit we ask n that wey nae cunt gits hurt, right? He nods all fucking cowed, cringing into the bleedin wall, pathetic wanker. – Now if ah git any bother fae you, son, your missus here's no even gaunny be good fir donatin organs. Right?

He nodded at me, fucking shitting himself.

It's funny, but when I was a nipper, people always used to say to my old man – who's Scotch – people like this smarmy scumbag, that they never understood the Jock accent. Funny thing is, when I do these little jobs, they always seem to get the message loud n clear and no mistake.

– Now dat's di attitude we loike ta see, Shorthand says, sounding like a bleedin Mick. – Now. Right sor, I'll be tankin you to be gettin all di mooney and jewellery you got in di house. Now. You stick it in dis hold-all, right? If you're noice n quiet, sure, we won't even be havin to be wakenin up dem poor little children up di stairs now will we? Now.

The accents is a great stroke: tactics to throw the filth off the track. I do a good Jock one on account of my old gel and my old man. Shorthand's Irish is alright, a bit over the top sometimes, but Bal's West Indian dread is fucking brilliant.

The shit-out cunt of a husband runs around with Shorthand, while Bal keeps a tight grip on the missus with the knife at her throat; too bleedin tight if you ask me, the dirty slag. I make us all a nice cup of tea, which ain't that fucking easy with them gloves on n everything.

– Goat any biscuits, hen? I ask her, but the poor bleedin cow can't even speak. She's pointing to a cupboard above the worktops. I check it out. – Fuck me, a pack ah Kit Kats. That's pure dead brilliant, so it is, by the way.

God, this bleedin ski-mask is hot.

– Sit doon oan the couch, hen, I tell her. She don't move. – Sit hur doon oan her erse, Bobby, I say to Bal. Her gets her onto the couch, with his arm around her like he was her bleedin fellah or something.

I put the tea down in front of her. – Dinnae even think of flingin yon tea in anybody's face, hen, I tell her, – or see they weans up the stair? Thair fuckin wormfood!

– I wasn't … she stammered. Poor bleedin Doris. Sitting at home watching the telly and this happens. Don't bear thinking about really.

Bal ain't best pleased. – Drink youah fuckan tea, woman. My friend Hursty here, he make you nice tea. Drink Hursty's tea. You think we you fuckan slave? White bitch!

– Hey, hey, c'moan you. The lassie disnae wahnt nae tea, the lassie disnae huv tae have ony tea, I told Bal, or Bobby as I called him.

When we went on jobs like this, it was always Hursty, Bobby and Martin we called ourselves. This was after Bobby Moore, Geoff Hurst and Martin Peters: the Hammers who won the World Cup for us in 1966. Barry was Bobby, the general; I was Hursty, the up-front striker. Shorthand – well, he saw himself as Martin Peters, the schemer: ten years ahead of his time and all that bollocks.

Of course, there wasn't much bleedin cash around: we only got about two hundred. There's never a fucking farthing in these bleedin places. We only really do it cause it's easy and it gives us a bit of buzz. It also keeps your hand in with planning and all that. You can't allow yourself to get all rusty. That's why we're the country's number one firm: it's the planning, innit. Any silly cunt can steam in; it's the planning and organisation that sorts out the real professionals from the bleedin mob. Anyhow, Shorthand, he gets the card numbers from the husband geezer then tours around a few cashpoints and comes back with six hundred quid. These fucking machines and their bastard limits. It's best to wait until midnight, then at 11.56 or whatever, you draw out two hundred, then another two hundred at

12.01. It's only 11.25 now, which is too long to hang about. You always have to leave a bit of extra time in case of struggle. This one though, it was too fucking easy.

We got em trussed up and Bal slashed the phone wires. Shorthand put his hand on the geezer's shoulder. – Now. Don't you people be goin and talkin to di officers of di law now, you hear me? Sure, you've two lovely children upstairs there who go by the names of Andy and Jessica now, don't they just?

They nod at him in shock.

– You wouldn't want us to be comin back here for dem, now would you? Now.

They stared at him in fear, the crapping cunts. I said: – We know yon school yir weans go tae, the scout troop, the fuckin guide pack; we know everything. But youse forget us and we forget youse, right? Yis goat oaf lucky!

– So no plaice in-volv-mant, Bal says softly, touching the gel's face with the flat end of his knife.

The side of the skirt's face had swollen right up an all. That made me feel funny. I don't hold with hitting a Doris: not like my old man. He don't hit my mum now though, not since I told the cunt he better hadn't. That's one thing I'd never do is to hit a Doris. Tonight, well, that don't count cause that's business, that's all there is to it. You're in the striker's role and you can't let the side down. First cunt who opens that fucking door gets it, Doris or no fucking Doris, as hard as you can fucking well give it. And I can give it fucking hard all right. It's like the whole job depends on it and you can't let the side down. Gotta be professional, innit. Like I said it's business, and what's good for business is good for Britain and I like to do my bit for the Union Jack. You gotta just put all them personal likes and dislikes aside, they don't come into it. But punching a Doris ain't something I go for: not in a personal way like. I ain't saying it's really wrong cause I know some Dorises that deserve a fucking good slapping; all I'm saying is that their ain't no real satisfaction in it.

– Sure, it's a pleasure doin business with such foine folks, Shorthand says, and we just piss off leaving the family in peace, while we're buzzing on the old adrenalin. One thing I am glad of is that we didn't have to wake any of them kiddies. I got a little un of my own and the thought of some cunt doing something like that there … well, no cunt would fucking well dare. The thought makes me wary though, sort of puts me in mind to check up on the little un. Maybe go round there tomorrow morning like.

Wolverhampton, 1963

Spike laughed and raised the glass of Bank's bitter, halting it an inch from his lips. – Cheers, Bob, he grinned, his deep-set eyes furrowing into one narrow slit which looked like a mouth, – moy all your problems be little uns!

Bob winked, and took a sip from the pint. He smiled at his workmates around the table. He felt good about them all, even Spike. Spike wasn't so bad. If he didn't want to get on, that was up to him. Spike would be happy to be stuck in The Scotlands for the rest of his life; no ambition but to use up the big wages on more drink and more hopeless horses. He'd felt the gulf grow between them since he'd flitted, and it was to do with more than his physical displacement out to the Ford Houses Estate. He remembered what Spike had said: Y'all don't want tall boi movink out there, spending all that good brass on a bloody house when the council'll rent ya'll woon chayp. Ya'll got to enjoy loife!

That was Spike's view of enjoyment, tipping Bank's down his neck. Molyneux's North Bank on a Saturday, after the bookies. That was his life, but he was standing still. Bob was working-class and proud of it, but he was a skilled man. He wanted the best for his family.

His family. The first one on the way. The thought warmed him with the rum he had with his pint.

– Another one, Bob? Spike urged.

– Don know about that. Oive got the hospital tonight. Could happen any toime, they said.

– Roobeesh! Ferst woons ur orlweys loite, everywoon knows that! Spike roared as Tony and Clem gave a drum-roll of encouragement on the table with their empty glasses.

But Bob got up and left. He knew that they'd be talking about him and what they'd be saying: that he had gone soft, that he was spoiling their excuse to get drunk, but he didn't care. He just wanted to see Mary.

It was raining outside: a dull slow drizzle. Although it was still the afternoon, the winter darkness was starting to fall and Bob pulled his collar tight against a whipping wind. A Midland Red bus came into view, then it was upon him, then it was zooming past his outstretched hand. It was half empty and he was at the bus stop and it hadn't stopped. The stupid injustice of it bemused and angered him. – Fucking bastard Midland Red! he shouted at the vehicle's waddling, teasing rear as it receded away from him. He trudged on.

He sensed that something was wrong when he got to the hospital. It was just a flash, that fleeting sensation that something was amiss. Every expectant father must feel this, he thought to himself. Then he felt it again.

Something had gone wrong. But what could? This was the twentieth century. Nothing went wrong these days. This was Britain.

Bob's breath was almost knocked from him when he saw his wife in the bed, howling through her obvious sedation. She looked terrible. – Bob … she wailed.

– Mary … what happened … you had it … is it okay … where's the baby!

– You have a little girl, a healthy little girl, a nurse said without enthusiasm or conviction.

– They won't let me see it, Bob, they won't let me hold my baby, Mary whined.

– What's happening ere! Bob shouted.

Another nurse had appeared behind him. She had a long, tortured face. She looked like someone who had seen something that was both terrifying and incomprehensible. She wore her professional demeanour like a tramp wears a new tuxedo. – There are one or two irregularities … she said slowly.

A Slag's Habit

She ain't changed the fucking lock yet; she knows what she'd get if she tried that one. I'd kept my set of the keys for this shithole after I moved out. I told her that I needed a place of my own. It was best all round. But yeh, I still kept a key for this gaff though, so I could come round and see the little un; stands to reason that I'd want to do that. She hears my key in the lock and looks at me all funny as I step in. The little fellah's here though, he comes out from behind her.

She smokes in front of him n all. Forty a day she fucking well smokes. Slag's habit. I hate to see skirt smoking. Different in a geezer like, but common in skirt, especially young skirt. I mean, I ain't talking about my old gel like. I mean she gets little enough bleedin pleasure out of life as it is, I wouldn't deny her her snout. In young skirt though it's too fucking tarty. Then there's the health aspect to be considered. That's what I said to her the last time I was up. I warned the slut about smoking in front of the nipper. You gotta consider the bleedin health aspect, I told her. Don't bear thinking about.

– He needs new shoes, Dave, she says.

– Yeah? Well I'll get him a pair then, won't I, I tell her. I ain't giving her no more bleedin dosh. It'll only go on the cheapest pair with the balance on snout for that slag. I ain't that fucking soft.

The little un's looking at me.

– Ow's my boy then, eh?

– All right, he says.

– All right? I goes, – Wot's all this about all right? Wot about a kiss for your old pop then, eh? He comes over and gives me a nice wet slammer on the side of my gob. – That's my boy, I tell him, ruffling his hair. I'll have to stop this kissing lark though, he's getting far too bleedin big for that. Could make him soft, that palaver could; even worse, turn him into one of them queer blouses you see hanging around. Ain't natural that. I turn to her, – Oi, that queer-arsed nonce ain't still hanging around the school, is he?

– Nah, ain't heard no more about it.

– Well if you do let me know straight away. Ain't no sick-beast coming near my boy, ain't that right, son? Remember what I told you, if anybody mucks about with you at that school?

– Kick em in the bollocks! he says. I laugh, and give him a bit of shadow boxing. Heavy hands for a little kiddie; a chip off the old block that one, if The Slag brings him up good n proper that is.

The Slag. She does look pretty tasty today though, made up n all. – You seein anybody, gel? I ask her.

– Not at the moment, she goes, all sort of snooty like.

– Get your fucking knickers orf then.

– Dave! Don't talk like that. Not in front of Gary, she says, pointing at the little fellah.

– Yeah, right. Listen, Gal, you take this dosh n get yerself some sweets. There's the car keys, this one opens the door. Wait for us in the motor, right? I'll just be a few minutes. Got some things to say to your mum; grown-up's things like.

The little geezer toddles off with the dosh, then she starts giving me a hard time.

– I don't wanna, she says.

– I don't bleedin well care what you bleedin well want, do I, I tell her. No fucking respect, that was always The Slag's problem, a sort of personality defect. She puts on that fucking face, but she knows the score and she's getting her kit off and going through to the bedroom. I get her on the bed and start kissing her, my tongue in that horrible ashtray mouth. I get her legs open and get up between her easy enough, the dirty slag's like a sodding dripping sponge down there, and I start giving her one. I just want to blow my fucking load and get on out of there, down to the bleeding car. The thing is, whenever I get into her, I can't bleedin well come … and it's fucking well happening again, I should've known better. She's going fucking mad; her that didn't fucking want any of it n all, she's going bleeding well mad and I can't fucking well come.

I FUCKING HATE THE CUNT THE FUCKING DIRTY COW AND I CAN'T BLEEDING WELL COME.

I want to rip her fucking smelly cunt apart, to really fucking hurt that dirty bitch, but the harder I go at it, the easier she takes it all, loving every minute of it she is, the fucking filthy warped evil fucking slag … it ain't supposed to be this … I keep seeing him, Lyonsy from the Millwall, I keep seeing him in my head. I'm trying to fuck off Lyonsy instead of her. That rumble we had down the Rotherhithe Tunnel when I got in first and hit that big cunt three fucking times and he just stood there and took it all, gave me that fucking look as if I was just a little fucking toy.

Then he hit me.

– DAAAAAVEEE! DAAAAVEE! she's fucking well screaming her head off innit, – STAY, ALWAYS STAY, WE CAN MAKE IT WORK, OH DAVE … OH DAAAAVEEE! She's bucking like a fucking stallion, I can feel the power of her under me and the size of her to me n all and I'm feeling dead inside as she come to rest and I pull out still as fucking hard as a brick and I got to get well away from this bleedin slag, cause if I don't I ain't gonna be responsible for what I might do.

I'm getting dressed and she's got a big smile on her face and she's going on about how nobody'll ever change me and when she said that before it used to make me feel special, no doubt about that, but now it makes me feel like a big fucking stupid lemon that the whole world's laughing up its fucking sleeve at.

– Yeah, I tell her, getting the fuck out of it and going down to the car, but I ain't in the mood for the bleedin kid. Not now: now that that fucking slag's spoiled everything. I dump him off at my sister's: he's happier there, playing with her little uns. I ain't really much one for the kiddies if the truth be known.

I go back to my flat and pull out a copy of *Playboy*, the one with that Opal Ronson slag in it. I've taken out the staples so I stick it on the fridge using the magnets. It ain't like I buy dirt mags usually, just if one of the stars is in getting their kit off. It's good to see the fucking stars in the buff, sort of like seeing someone you know. Takes away the fucking mystique, makes them seem more sort of available like.

I've got a fresh melon in the fridge and I've already dug in three holes the width and depth of my erection; two at one end and one at the other, for Opal's cunt, arsehole and mouth. I put a bit lipstick on the mouth one. Then I squirt some Pond's hand cream in the others and we're fucking well off … where do you fucking want it, girl, your gob or your arse or your cunt … I'm concentrating on the image of Opal bending over, her back arched and I can't work out what she's saying to me, whether or not she wants it up her cunt or her arsehole and something about those dark eyes says to me that maybe Opal ain't the sort orf gel to take it up the tradesman's on a first date, I'm thinking of her in that *Seductive Affairs* … naah … but then in that *Paranoid*, definitely; then I think, fuck it, the bitch maybe needs to be taught a fucking lesson and in it fucking well goes … phoah, this is going to fucking well spilt you in two, my gel … phoah … KWWAAWWW!

My head's fucking dizzy as my muck just pumps and pumps into the melon. A few imaginary seconds in Opal's crapbox does it for me. God bless ya, my gel.

I take a little doze on my couch and when I wake I try to watch the box but I can't bleedin settle. I do some work with the dumb-bells and examine my pecs. The definition's coming on, but it's still a bit poofhouse, like the strutting queerbeasts at the club. It's beef I want, for punching power. After a bit I go down the Blind Beggar. There ain't no cunt in, so I try the Grave Maurice. They're all there: Bal, Riggsie, Shorthand, Roj, John n all. I get a pint of brown and bitter up and go over. It's a nice crack n all and I'm just starting to relax and get into it when I hears this noise at the bar.

– HEEEYYYYGGGHHHH!

I turn around and see him. That pathetic old bastard, my bleedin old man. Look at him: lurching around out of his fucking tree, bothering people. Fucking pathetic, that's what he is, that's what he always was. Now the pest had fucking clocked us and he's coming over here. Bal, Riggsie n Shorthand, well these cunts are loving every minute of my fucking embarrassment, ain't they.

– Awright, ma boey! Buy yir auld fella a drink then, eh? Eh! He says. He's fucking sozzled, the cunt.

– I'm trying to have a bleeding conversation here, I tell him.

He raises his eyebrows n looks at me like I'm some kind of arsehole. Then he puts his hands on his hips. – Oh, a conversation, is it …

– 'Salroight Mr T., I'm just getting them in, ain't I, Bal says and hits the bar. He comes back with a pint and a large Scotch for the old cunt.

– That's a man, he points at Bal. – Young Barry thair … Barry Leitch … that's a *real* fuckin man! he smiles, raising his glass to Bal, who does the same back. Then he clocks me staring at him. – Hi, whit's wrang wi your face!

I'm fucking well seething at the old cunt.

– Whit's wraaaannng …

That fucking ugly beery Scotch face, that stupid, breathless Jock voice; it never stops, not for one bleedin minute. I really want to shut that stupid voice up.

– Nuffink! I snap. Then the old cunt's got an arm around me and he's turned to Bal n Riggsie. I'm going to swing for the old cunt, fucking sure as Christ …

– This is ma boey here. And he's a fuckin arsehole! A FUCKIN EEEEERRRRRSSSSE! Bit he's still ma boey, he says. Then: – Hi son, gaunny sub us but? Ah'm expectin a big insurance cheque, son. They telt us it wid've been here by now, so thair wis me up the dug track last night, thinkin ah'd be flush n ah wid be sorted oot this mornin … ye know what ah mean, David … eh, son?

I pulled out a couple of tenners. Anything, anything to get rid of the fucking old ponce.

– Yir a good boey, son. A good PRAWSTINT boey!

He looked around, then rolled up his sleeve. – Ma blood, he said to Riggsie, – Prawstint blood.

– I'm sure it's one hundred per cent proof, Mr T., Riggsie says, n Bal n Shorthand n Roj n Johnny n that, they all have a bleedin laugh n I do n all, but I don't like Riggsie's mouth. Cunt or no cunt, this is still my old man we're talking about here. A bit of fucking respect is called for.

– That's it, son. One hunner per cent prawstint! The old clown says. Then thankfully he looks around and sees another old pisshead staggering into the bar. – Ah'm gaunny huv tae love yis and leave yis, boys. Ower thair at the bar, a very good friend of mine's ah'll have ye know … well, take care ma boeys. Nae fitba bother! Ah'm relyin oan youse boys tae screw the nut. Yis huv goat tae huv the big match temperament … interfuckincityfirm … shite! The Billy Boeys … we could've showed youse a thing or two … that wis *real* hard men … the Bricktin Billy Boeys, the original Bricktin Billy Boeys ah'm talkin aboot here! Remember, boeys, yuv goat tae git in first n take nae prisoners. Yuv goat tae huv the big match temperament!

– That's the game, Mr T., Bal says.

The old cunt stands up and lurches over to this other sad old fucker at the bar.

– BIG MATCH TEMPERAMENT! he turns back and shouts over.

I'm fucking well wound up. There's only one place to go when you're feeling like this. I turn to Bal. – I fancy a little walk over the river. A bus to London Bridge and a pleasant stroll down Tooley Street, along Jamaica Road and back home by Tube from Rotherhithe. Just the six of us.

Bal smiled, – I'm up for that. Let's piss all over the bastards.

Riggsie shrugs, so does Shorthand and the rest. They'll come along, but their bottle ain't really up for it.

Mine is. I down the pint, relaxing my gullet and taking it in one swallow and feeling that gassy burp as it fills my gut. It's time to move.

Toronto, 1967

Bob looked at the youngster in his wife's arms. For a second he thought about another country, another wife and another child … no. He stopped himself as he stroked the baby's warm red cheek. That was another time, another place. That was Wolverhampton Bob Worthington. This Bob Worthington had made a new life for himself in Toronto.

He stayed at the hospital for a few hours, then, exhausted but elated after sitting up all night, took the long drive home out to the suburbs. All the houses were different in his street, not like the mass-built redbrick slums he'd come from, yet a strange air of uniformity still pervaded his district. He parked the car in the narrow driveway outside the garage.

Bob looked at the basketball hoop which was suspended the regular ten feet above the garage door, and imagined his son growing – even saw him as a young man, leaping up like a salmon to send the ball home. This child would have the opportunities which circumstance had denied him. He would make sure of that. Tomorrow he had to go back to work; that was what you had to do when you worked for yourself. Just now he was shattered. As he went to bed, Bob prayed for a deep sleep with his dreams defined by the marvellous events of the day. He hoped the demons wouldn't come.

That was what he hoped more than anything.

Decent Skirt

There's us fucking sitting out in the car-park, in the back of the van. No cunt wants our fucking gear; it's all been a waste of bleeding time. Well, I'm thinking that if things don't liven up around here soon, I'm gonna take a good E and just get right into the flaming action. Bal's with some geezers in the other motor, he ain't up for going in. Well, he can do as he pleases, I ain't hanging about, am I; flaming skirt galore in there.

– That was a great fucking ruck the other week, in that pub like, Shorthand says.

– Yeah, after I pulled them geezers off you, I told him. If I hadn't the slag would have been finished. – Final fucking chapter, weren't it.

– Yeah, I thought that I was well fucked there for a bit. See once I got hold of them glasses though, phoarr … I was taking all them cunts out: left, right and bleeding centre.

– That fat bastard behind the bar, Johnny says, – he was pretty fucking tasty.

– Yeah, I goes, – he was until I copped him with that metal bar-stool. That was fucking ace. I remember that all right: fucking brilliant the way the cunt's eyebrow just split right open.

I clock Shorthand ferreting in the plastic bag for beer. – Oi, Shorthand! Give us a fucking can, you cunt, I shout over at him. He passes a lager. McEwan's.

– Fucking Jock piss, he says, then: – Sorry, mate, I forgot.

– Don't worry about it.

– I mean, it ain't as if you're really flaming Scotch n all. It's like my old man, he's a Mick, and my old gel, she's Polish, innit. Don't make me a flamin Pole now, does it?

I just fucking shrug, – We're all sodding mongrels, mate.

– Yeah, Shorthand goes, – but we're all white men though, innit. Purity of race n all of that.

– Yeah, I suppose you got a point there, mate, I say.

– I mean, I ain't saying that Hitler neccessarily had it right, mind you. It ain't his fault he wasn't an Englishman.

– Yeah, Hitler was a fucking wanker, I tell him, – Two World Wars and one World Cup, mate. All won by the claret n blue.

Shorthand starts singing. Ain't no holding him when he gets started on some of the old West Ham classics. – No re-li-ga-shin for the claret n blue, just ju-bi-la-shin, for the claret n blue …

Riggsie climbs into the van. Bal's behind him with that cunt Rodger. – Come inside, you cunts! Riggsie says, – It's fucking kicking in there! The sounds, I'm tellin ya, make the hairs stand up on the back of your bleedin neck!

– Tell ya wot makes the fucking hairs stand up on the back of my neck, I say.

– The bagpipes, Shorthand goes.

– Nah. There's cunt's dealin in there, and they ain't bleedin Firm, I tell Riggsie.

Bal says, – Yeah, that's fucking well right, Thorny. Some fucker's on a broken face in there.

That shuts Riggsie up good n proper. He's a fucking soft touch, the stupid cunt. Them smarmy gits, the skinny fuckers with the big bags full of pills, they just crawl up his arse. It's no bleedin wonder we can't shift our paracetamols and bicarbs.

– Nah, it ain't that, Riggsie's going, – What's happened is that every fucker seems to have got sorted out before they came along tonight. He hands Bal a pill, – Here, take one of them.

– Fuck off, Bal snorts. He still ain't up for it. Fuck it, I swallow an E and head indoors with Riggsie. Shorthand's necked one n all and he's right behind us.

Inside I'm checking out this group of skirt standing by the wall. One of them I can't stop looking at. I'm feeling a bit ropey, like I need to do a big fucking shit and then I realise that it's because I'm coming right up off my fucking threepenny bits on this fucking gear and them bleedin sounds.

— Wot you fucking well staring at? She just came over and said it right out to me. I don't really stare at skirt as such. I mean, as far as I see things it's down to manners. Shorthand, well, he just intimidates a Doris. Stares straight at them; they probably think that they're gonna get fucking raped or something. I've pulled him up about it. Don't you fucking well stare down skirt, I tell him. You wanna stare some cunt down, you go down the Old Kent Road and try it with some Millwall geezers. You gotta treat birds with respect, I said to him. How'd you like some Bushwacker or Headhunter starin at your sis like that?

But here I am, staring at this gel. And it ain't just cause she's so pretty, cause she is, she's fucking beautiful. It's just that I've had this ecstasy and I'm staring at this gel who ain't got any arms.

— Wasn't you on the telly? It's all I can think to say.

— Nah, I wasn't on no telly and I wasn't in no bleedin freak show either.

— I never …

— Well, just piss off, she snaps at me, turning away. Her mate puts an arm around her neck. I just stands there like a right bleedin turnip. I mean, nobody likes a slag with a mouth; let's just take that one as given, but what can you say to a gel who ain't got no bleedin arms?

— Oi, Dave, you ain't gonna let some freaky skirt talk to ya like that, are ya? Shorthand smiles at me with his rotten teeth exposed.

Teeth which could so easily be smashed.

— You shut your bleedin mouth, you wanker, or I'll shut it for ya. No doubt about it, I am well pissed off with that cunt; pretty gel who ain't got no bleedin arms, a crying shame in anybody's book, that's what that is. Her mate comes across to me, another looker, all pupils, E'd out of her nut.

— Sorry about her. Bad acid like.

— What about her arms then, eh? I shouldn't really have said that, but sometimes things just sort of slip out. Best to say what's on your mind though, I suppose.

— Tenazadrine, innit.

Shorthand has to stick his bleedin oar in at that. – That's the smallest boozer in the world, innit: The Tenazadrine Arms.

– Shut it, you mouthy slag! I snap at the wanker and he knows what the stare I'm giving him means and he's pissing off. Mate or no mate, that slag's on a collision course with a good slapping. I turns to the Doris. – Tell your mate I didn't mean to upset her none.

She smiles at me, – Come over and tell her yourself.

That sort of floors me, cause I get all sort of shy in front of a gel I really like. We're not talking slags here, cause they're ten a penny, but with a gel I like it's really sort of all different. The Ecstasy helps though. I go across.

– Oi, eh sorry about starin at you n all, like.

– I'm used to it, she says.

– I don't usually stare at people ...

– Only ones without arms.

– It ain't cause of the arms ... it's because I was getting a great rush off the E and I felt so good ... and you ... you just look so fucking beautiful, I just let it all come out, – I'm Dave, by the way.

– Samantha. Don't ever call me Sam. Never. My name's Samantha, she says, almost smiling.

Almost is more than enough for me. – Samantha, I repeat, – well, don't you ever call me David. It's Dave.

Then she smiles at that and something happens to me inside. This Doris is like a fucking white dove crammed full of more MDMA than I've ever had in my fucking life.

London, 1979

She sat in the Oxford Street branch of the fast-food chain with her chocolate milkshake, sucking the sugary liquid through the straw. She had elected to take the Tube into town after signing on down in Hammersmith. She couldn't face being in the flat she was squatting in; a group of young Scots guys had recently moved in and spent most of the day sitting around drinking bottles of cider and arguing with pointless dogmatism about the bands they were into. The West End had seemed a better bet on this hot day, but her head was a soupy void, an opium party into which the odd unwelcome thought occasionally gatecrashed. She thought of another gig, another band, another face, another fuck; another mechanical, loveless fuck. She tightened the muscles of her vagina and let a shiver convulse her body. Feeling the onset of self-loathing, she forced herself to subvert this bad line of thought by contemplating the mundane scene of shoppers bustling into the ridiculously crowded eating-house.

It was at this point that she felt his eyes on her.

She didn't know how long he had been staring at her. It was the smile she noticed first, but she was determined not to acknowledge it. Another fucking creep. The ones that wanted to talk about her disability, they were always the worst. There was the old fucker who told her he was a Church of England minister. She didn't want any more of that shit just at the moment.

When he came over and sat down beside her, she felt a familiar shock of recognition. He was another punk. His hair was pink, and he wore a leather jacket, unimaginatively held together with safety pins. There was something sterile about his look: too pristine, too contrived. A total plastic. – Mind if I join you? he asked. His accent was foreign, possibly German. She noticed this, noticed the dress.

With his jacket draped across his shoulders it took a little longer
before it dawned on her that he was more like her than she had at first
perceived.

– I'm Andreas. I would shake hands, he laughed, but somehow I
don't think that is appropriate. He shook off the jacket to expose
flippers which, like her own, grew out of his shoulders. – Perhaps, he
smiled, – we will kiss instead?

Samantha felt her jaw tighten aggressively, but she realised that this
response had to compete with another; a nauseous, nervy, queasy
rush of embarrassed attraction. – I don't wanna fucking kiss you, she
snapped, in a clichéd punk mode. It sounded as fake as Andreas's gear
looked.

– That makes me sad, Andreas said, and he did look sad. – I sense
that you are a very angry person, yes?

– You what? she said, genuinely upset, yet intrigued, at this
continuing intrusion.

– As I thought. This is good. Anger is good. But when it goes on
for too long it can become bad, yes? The badness inside. I know all
about it. But what is the saying: do not get angry, get even. Do you
know that?

– Yeah.

Samantha had met other Tenazadrine kids before. It had always
been an embarrassment. A topic of conversation, their deformity,
was staring them in the face. How could you ignore it, how could
you not ignore it? It hung over every casual conversation like a black
cloud. There was more: part of her hated them. They reminded her
of how she looked, how she would be perceived by the rest of the
world. Someone with a deficiency: a deficiency of arms. And once
people pinned the label of deficiency on you, they tended to make it
a universal one, applying it to all areas; intellect, luck, hope. Andreas,
though, he inspired none of that sense of awkwardness or loathing.
There was no sense of deficiency here, despite his physical form. All
he radiated was a staggering impression of surplus: she could feel the
confidence ooze from him. While she had learned to cover up her
fears with sneers, she saw in him someone who would take on the
world exactly on his own terms.

– Are you going to The Vortex tonight?

– Might be, she found herself saying. She didn't like The Vortex, hated that crowd. She didn't even know who was on.

– 999 are playing. They are a pretty poor band, but one is much the same as the other if you are full of the speed and the beer, yes?

– Yeah, that's right.

– My name is Andreas.

– Yeah, she replied curtly, then, giving ground to his raised eyebrows which made him look slightly bizarre, – Sam. Not Samantha, right? Sam.

– Samantha is better. Sam is a man's name, not a lovely girl's. Do not let them shorten you, Samantha. Do not let them do that any more.

She felt a small bolt of fury rising up. Who did he think he was? She was about to react, when he said: – Samantha … you are very lovely. We must meet at The Ship pub in Wardour Street at eight o'clock. Yes?

– Yeah, well, maybe, Samantha said, knowing that she'd be there. She looked into his eyes. What she saw in them felt strong and warm. Then she thought that they looked ludicrously blue against his pink hair.

– Did you break into London Zoo or something? What you doing with that fucking flamingo stuck on your head?

Andreas looked at her quizzically. Samantha thought she saw a cruel anger briefly suggest itself in his face, before it settled back into a calmness so complete she felt that she must have imagined it. – I see … a flamingo. Samantha has made a joke, yes?

– Aintcha got a sense of humour or what?

– You are very young, Samantha, very young, Andreas observed.

– What you talking about? I'm the same age as you. We must have been born within weeks of each other.

– I too am very young. The issue, though, is substance.

She was about to give in again to a surge of anger, but Andreas was rising in his chair. – Now I go. But first, I have that kiss, yes?

Samantha didn't move as he bent down and kissed her on the

mouth. It was a tender kiss. He lingered briefly and she felt herself
tentatively responding. Then he moved away. – Eight is good, yes?

– Yeah, she said, then he was gone. She was left by herself, of
which she was painfully conscious. She knew what they were all
thinking: Two Tenazadrines, kissing.

Well, Samantha thought, at least he can't be after my compensation money.

She left shortly after this, walking aimlessly down Charing Cross
Road, then cutting through to Soho Square, lying in the sun with the
office workers. Then she moved through Soho's streets and walked
up and down Carnaby Street twice until exasperation set in and she
took the Tube back to the Shepherd's Bush squat she shared with a
group of other young punks whose personnel changed intermit-
tently.

In the kitchen, a painfully thin, red-haired young Scots punk with
bad spots, called Mark, was eating bacon, eggs and beans straight
from the frying pan. – Awright, Samantha? he smiled, – goat any
speed oan ye?

– No, she said curtly.

– Matty n Spud are away intae toon. Ah couldnae move this
mornin. Fuckin wrecked last night. This is jist me gittin breakfast
now. Ye hungry? he nodded at the food congealed in the grease.

– No … no thanks, Mark, Samantha forced a smile. She could feel
the spots starting to form on *her* face, just being in the vicinity of
Mark's frying pan. The Scots guys in the squat were only sixteen, but
they were a pest: filthy, loud and naive about the music. They were
friendly enough; in fact the problem was that they were too friendly:
they panted after you like a litter of enthusiastic puppies. She went to
the room she shared with two other girls, Julie and Linda, and
switched on the black-and-white set and clockwatched constantly
until it was time to go out again.

She arrived at The Ship ten minutes late. He was sitting there, in
the corner. She went over to the bar and bought herself a pint of
cider. Then she sat down beside him. It seemed a long walk to the
seat, and she felt that every eye in the pub was on her. It was a surprise
that, after she returned his smile and looked around nervously,

nobody seemed to have noticed them. They drank steadily and dabbed at some speed she'd had but told Scots Mark she hadn't.

That night at the club, the band thrashed through a set as Andreas and Samantha pogoed unselfconsciously. Samantha felt a freedom and a lack of inhibition unlike anything she'd experienced before. It went beyond drugs and alcohol: it was Andreas and his liberating, infectious confidence and enthusiasm.

She knew that she was going home with him. She didn't want the gig to end, and she did, all at once.

On their way down the road, Samatha felt her paradise being lost as they were confronted by a trio of drunk and whistling skinheads.

– It's a fucking freak show! one shouted.

– Leave em be, another said, – it's a bleedin shame. You wouldn't like it.

– She's got a nice pair of tits though! Giz a feel then, darlin! The first young skin moved towards Samantha.

– Fuck off! she shouted. Then Andreas was standing in front of her, blocking his path.

The young skinhead's face was briefly tentative and quizzical and, for a crucial few moments, it seemed that he was frighteningly aware of the power of events to move outside of both his expectations and his will. – Get out my fucking road, you freak! he hissed at Andreas.

– Get away, Samantha said, – I don't need anyone to fight my battles!

Andreas, though, did not move. He looked his would-be-tormentor steadily in the eye. He moved his jaws around slowly, languidly. It appeared as if he was almost enjoying this distraction; he seemed in complete control. He appeared in no hurry to speak, but when he did, it was in a slow, uniform monotone. – If you do not leave us alone I will bite your fucking face off. Understand this: you will have no face left.

He held his gaze. The shaven-headed youth's eyes started watering, then twitching. He began to shout, but even as he was doing that, he seemed only partially aware that he was simultaneously moving away.

– C'mon, Tony, fuck that Kraut freak, let's get out of here before some filth come by, his friend said.

They screamed further abuse as they departed, but in the manic, desperately defiant way of the humiliated and defeated.

Samantha was impressed. She was fighting against being impressed, but she was more and more impressed by this German. – You got some bottle.

Andreas nodded to one side. A finger from the stump that was his hand tapped his head. – I am not a fighter. I do not have the reach, he smiled, – and that is why you must use the head. This is where I win and lose my battles. Sometimes it works, other times ... it's not so good, you see. He shook his head with a *c'est la vie* smile.

– Yeah, but you really psyched those bastards out, Samantha said. She realised that the skinheads were not the only ones psyched out.

She realised that she was in love with Andreas.

Mouthy Slags

We talked for ages, just bleedin talked. I ain't never rabbited so much in my life, not to skirt at any rate. Thing is, I didn't even feel embarrassed. It wasn't like talking to skirt; not skirt in the normal sense of the word, as I would usually mean skirt. I talked about me, Bal, and the yard; my mum and the old tosser; The Slag and the little fellah; but most of all about the Firm, about the rucks we had been in and the ones we was planning and how I was going to sort out that Lyonsy geezer from the Milwall. Sort the cunt out for good.

I couldn't stop looking at her face though. I was even talking like some queer-beast. — Mind if I touch your face, I asked her.

— No, she says.

So I couldn't stop touching her face. I didn't really want to do nothing else, well maybe like hug her for a bit. Not like shagging or nothing like that, just like, being together with her. I was thinking like some fucking great poof-house. It wasn't, I mean, it was like … love or something, weren't it.

When the music died I had to ask her to come into town with me. The thing about her was that she was interested in all of this, she was interested in *me*. Even when I talked about all the aggro n all of that, she seemed really fucking interested.

I borrowed a motor from one of the security geezers I knew and we drove into Bournemouth and spent the day together. I never felt this before. I felt like someone else. Someone different.

Then we was in this caff, still having a proper old chinwag, we was, and when we came out these three geezers were just all sort of standing there, staring and sniggering at Samantha. At my Samantha.

— Wot you fucking staring at? I says. One of the geezers, his bottle just crashes.

– Nothing.

– C'mon Dave, Samantha says, – they weren't doing anything.

– Oi, what's your problem then, eh? this other slag, the mouthy type, says. Well, blow me if I'm having any of that.

At times like this I always go back to them old Bruce Lee films. All that Kung Fu is a load of old bollocks, but there was always this one thing that Bruce Lee said, one bit of advice that he gave which has always stood me in good stead. He said: you don't bleedin well punch some cunt, you punch *through* them. This geezer with the mouth, all I could see was that orange brick wall behind his face. That was what I was going for, what I wanted to demolish.

The next thing I realise is that I'm standing looking at this other geezer sayin: – Who's next then, eh?

They just stood frozen, looking at this arsehole on the deck, who seemed in quite a bad way. A few nosey parkers were sticking their oars in, so I thought it was best we headed back to the Smoke, as Samantha stayed over in Islington, quite near me, which I was chuffed about. That little incident, though: proper spoiled our day, it did.

– Why did you do that? she asked me in the car as we got onto the dual carriageway.

She didn't seem too angry, though, more sort of curious like. She's so fucking beautiful it don't bear thinking about. I could hardly keep my eyes on the fucking road. I sort of felt like I was wasting time whenever I wasn't looking at her face.

– They was having a fucking go, not showing you proper respect.

– That's important to you, is it, that people don't bother me, that they don't hurt me?

– It's more important to me than anything in the world, I told her.
– I ain't never felt this way before.

She looks at me, all sort of thoughtfully like, but she don't say nothing. I've been saying too fucking much. It's the chemicals, I know it is, but it's only what's inside me and I don't give a toss.

We drove back to her place. I felt a bit funny when we were there cause there was a picture of her and this geezer. It was when they were younger. The thing was, he was like her, with no bleedin arms.

– He your boyfriend then? I asked her. I couldn't help it.

She laughed at me. – Just because he's got no arms, he has to be my boyfriend?

– Nah, I didn't mean it like that …

– He's a German guy I know, she said.

A bleedin Kraut. Two World Wars and one World Cup, you cunt. – So is he then? Your boyfriend?

– No, he's not. He's just a good friend, that's all.

I felt a glow in my chest and I even started to like the bleedin Kraut. I mean, poor geezer, no arms n all, can't be much bleedin fun now, can it?

So we talked for a bit more and Samantha told me a few things. Things about her past. Things which made my fucking blood boil.

New York City, 1982

For someone who was where he wanted to be, in a well-appointed office in a midtown Manhattan building, Bruce Sturgess was being persecuted by a line of awkward, persistent thought. He looked out of the north-facing window at the splendid view which took in Central Park. The magnificent Chrysler and Empire State buildings towered above, looking contemptuously down on his great height like disapproving nightclub bouncers. There was always somebody looking down on you, he thought with a rueful smile, no matter how high you climb. They were extraordinary, those buildings, particularly the art-deco Chrysler. He thought of Frank Sinatra and Gene Kelly turning the city into a massive set of props in *A Night On The Town*. Freedom, that was what New York epitomised for him. It was clichéd and predictable, he thought, but never less than the truth. The view, however, failed to obliterate the wincing images of deformities that burned relentlessly in his mind. This was the worst he had been. It led to him dialling Barney Drysdale's number in London. There was something about Barney's voice, its untroubled, gruff positiveness, which always calmed Bruce when he was troubled in this way.

Barney Drysdale, busy packing in his Holland Park flat, was less than amused to hear the sound of the phone ringing. – What now? he moaned, irritated. Barney was preparing to set off to the cottage in Wales for a long weekend; preparing for the family's big, semi-permanent move out there next month.

– Hello …

– Old boy! Bruce said, almost tauntingly.

– Bruce! Barney laughed, his temper improving at the sound of his friend's voice, – You old devil! How are they treating you in Yankeeland?

Sturgess offered some bland platitudes. Yes, it was good to hear Barney's voice. He only felt a little frost in his voice when his old friend mentioned Philippa and the boys. He was not getting on with her. The lads had settled well, in their place over in Long Island, but she hated America. Her fixes of shopping expeditions to Blooming-dale's and Macy's failed to soothe her burgeoning discontent. Sturgess, though, loved New York. He loved the anonymity he had, as someone who had not yet made all the contacts he soon would. He loved the clubs. He thought of the boy he'd fucked in the toilets the night before in that wonderfully filthy club in the East Village ...

– You caught me at a rather bad time, old man, Barney explained – I'm cottaging this weekend.

So, dear boy, mused Sturgess, rubbing his crotch as he looked out of his office window at Manhattan's towering skyline, am I.

– How wonderful, he said.

How wonderful, he thought. But his mind was troubled. Deformities and obsessions with young boys: he would have to watch himself. He could so easily throw away what he'd worked for. It was good to talk to Barney. Thank God for Barney.

Injustice

I'm seeing more and more of Samantha. Thing is, we ain't done anything. I wish I knew where I bleedin well stood with her. As if it bothers me that she ain't got no arms. We just talk when we're together, but the thing is I don't really like the way the conversation heads. She keeps going on about her arms and about the geezers that sold the stuff that made her like that. I don't wanna hear all that: I just like to look at her.

Thing is, I can't do anything other than go along with it, cause the truth is, I ain't really all that bothered about anything else but being with her.

– You look at me, and you want to sleep with me. You want to fuck me, she says. She just sort of says these things out of the blue.

– Well, so what if I do? Ain't no law against it, is there? No law against fancying someone, I tell her. Then I get a slight panic attack, cause this is round at mine's and I'm sure she was in the fridge. I hope she didn't see the fucking melon and the cream. Thank fuck I took the Opal poster down.

– You don't know what it's like for me. A freak, an incomplete woman. They took something from me. I ain't whole, and I want to make them pay. Not a few bob in the bank; I want justice. I want Bruce Sturgess, the bastard who marketed that drug, who butchered us.

– You want me to help you sort out this Sturgess geezer? Fine, I'll do it.

– You don't understand! I don't want you to slap him around. This ain't some fucking wanker that goes to football or that drinks in the pub round the corner. I don't want this bastard frightened! I want his arms. I want his limbs hacked off. I want him to know how it feels!

– You can't do that ... you'll get put away ...

– What's wrong, Firm man? You lost your bottle? she taunted me, her face changing, looking different, not like her.

– Nah, I ain't ...

– I'll have that fucking bastard, with or without your help. I want the fucker to know how it feels to be made into a freak. He changed the way I am. I just want to change him. You understand? I don't want their fucking money. I want to take what they took from me and let them see how useful their fucking money is. I want them to know how it feels when somebody you don't know causes damage, how it feels when they change you ... when they deny you your place in the world. Bastards like him do it all the time: they take jobs, homes, lives, by the decisions they make and they never see the destruction they cause, are never held to account. I want him to see it, but I also want him to feel it. I want him to know how it feels to be a freak.

– You aint no freak! You're beautiful! I love ya!

Her face opened up like I'd never seen it before, like she felt the same as I did. – Ever been foot-wanked before? she asked me.

Pembrokeshire, 1982

Barney Drysdale always felt that surge of contentment as he teased and bullied the old Land-Rover up the steep path towards the cottage. Alighting from the vehicle, he looked at the old stone dwelling, then took a breath of the fresh air and gazed across the landscape around his home. Nothing but hills, streams, a couple of small farm houses and sheep. That would do him.

Tomorrow he would have company, Beth and Gillian would arrive from London. It was part of their family ritual that Barney always went on ahead to the cottage, to 'light the fire' as he put it. He enjoyed surveying the place in solitude, looking at what he had achieved in its restoration. In reality, the workmen had achieved it, turning a derelict pile of stone into a dream home. Barney had come out, made out he was mucking in, huffing and puffing and trying to be one of the lads, never quite winning over the suspicious workmen – even when he arrived with beers, or insisted they knocked off early for a session at the village pub. He thought that they were just a little shy, those local types, and embarrassed. He couldn't see that they were embarrassed for him. In the pub, they'd make excuses and go, one by one. Then they would phone the bar to check whether Barney had left and return to carry on the session without him.

There was a damp chill throughout the cottage and Barney set about getting the coal fire set up. In the short time he had been procrastinating, touring his holiday home, night had fallen. Barney went to bring in some coal from the outside shed, which was almost in pitch darkness, out of range of illumination from the house lights. He felt good making his way in the dark, enjoyed the cold of the night air against his skin.

As his tentative steps crunched the path, Barney thought he heard a noise, like a cough. A spasm of fear exploded in his chest, but it was over instantly and he laughed at his jumpiness. He returned with the coal and the logs.

To his dismay, Barney noticed for the first time that he was out of firelighters. The village shop would now be shut.

– Fiddlesticks, he said.

He piled up some twists of newspaper, the wood kindling, then small pieces of coal. It was a slow job and it took patience, but he was pleased to have started up a satisfactory blaze.

He sat in front of it for a while then, restless, he drove down to the village and had a couple of solitary drinks in the pub, combing through the *Telegraph*. He was disappointed not to recognise anyone: neither local workmen nor professional incomers. After a while, that gentle melancholy that only isolation can engender settled upon him and he returned home.

Back at the cottage, Barney placed himself in the chair in front of the fire: relaxing with some television, sipping at a glass of port and munching at some Stilton he had brought with him. The boiler from the blaze had warmed the house quickly and Barney felt drowsy and retired to bed.

Downstairs, someone else was inside the cottage.

The figure moved with great grace and stealth in the darkness. Swinging from the shoulder of the silhouette, where the arm should have been, was a large can. The contents of this can were used to soak the carpet and the curtains in paraffin.

Outside, someone else had a paintbrush in their mouth. With incredible speed and dexterity, head flicking backwards and forwards, the dark figure drew slogans against the wall of the cottage:

CYMRU I'R CYMRU
LLOEGR I'R MOCH

Sacred Cows

We take the truck up to Romford where this silly git's got this old Aston Martin lying outside his door. – Give us fifty quid, mate, and it's yours, he says, the mad slag, – I can't be bothered fucking around with it. I've had a lot done to it; it don't need much to get it going. I'm just a bit fed up with it.

I open up the bonnet and have a poke around. It don't look too bad. Bal has a look and tips us the nod.

– Naah … this is fucked, mate. We can take it off your hands for a tenner scrap.

– Leave it out. I paid a ton for that motor. I've spent that again on it, the git says.

– Yeah, but this is gonna cost ya two hundred minimum to get this little lot sorted out. Gears seem fucked up to me, for one thing. You'd be throwin good money after bad, mate, take my word for it.

– What about forty? he says.

– We're businessmen, mate. We gotta make a living here, Bal shrugs.

The mug screws up his face and takes the tenner. I'll have this little beauty back on the road in no time. We hook it up and tow it back down to the yard.

Something about our fucking lock-up really fucking depresses me. Especially being here on a hot summer's day like this one. I think what it is is that it never seems to get the heat from the sun, it's always in the fucking shadow, cause of these tall buildings around it. Inside here there's no fucking natural light, just those fucking old lamps. One day, I swear, I'm gonna cut a fucking hole in that roof, put in a skylight of some sort. The smell of paraffin from the heater, and oil from the parts lying around, proper goes for me sometimes that does.

The other thing is that I always come out fucking manky. All those parts dumped around on the floor and on that big fucking table. Then there's that huge fucking swinging door which don't even have a bolt for it any more. We have to padlock the bastard. I get proper narked most mornings, trying to get the fucking thing opened.

Bal loves it in here though. He's got all his fucking tools, even this big fucking chainsaw he used last winter when he started that sideline of cutting down trees in Epping Forest, selling them as bundles of firewood through the *Advertiser*.

Yeah, it's far too hot to be in the yard today.

– One born every minute, eh, mate? Bal laughs, slapping the hood of the car.

– Yeah, fucking stupid cunt. Gor blimey, it's bleedin hot today. Listen, mate, my throat's tryin ta tell me something. Fancy a drink?

– Yeah, all right. I'll see ya down the Grave Maurice. I want to have a little fuck about with this first, he says, patting the bonnet of the car again, touching it like it was a bird's arse or tits or something. Well, he's welcome to it: motor mad, that cunt. I'm more into the idea of Samantha's tits and arse. Whoah. This fucking heat's giving me the horn in a big way. I sometimes wonder whether or not it's scientific, or whether it's just cause all the skirt walk around half bleedin naked at this time of the year. Anyway, I can't wait to get my hands on her, but in the meantime a nice, cool, pint of lager'll do me. I leave him to it.

Community fucking policing. I'm in the pub five fucking minutes and had two bleedin gulps, then that cunt Nesbitt from the Old Bill – just walks straight into the bar of the Maurice, like he owns the fucking shop.

– All right, Thorny?

– D.C. Nesbitt. What a pleasant surprise.

– It's never a pleasure to call on the criminal classes.

– Know wotcha mean, John. I avoid them like the plague. Must be tricky doing that, though, in your line of work. Don't really give

you much scope, does it? A career switch might be in order there.
Ever fancy trying your hand at the motor trade?

The cunt stands there taking the hump, trying to stare me down
like I should apologise. Billy and the new gel behind the bar are
having a proper old giggle. I just raise my glass at the filth cunt, –
Cheers!

– Where's your mate, Leitchy?

– Barry Leitch ... ain't seen Bal in a while, I tell him. – I mean, at
work n all, hard not to in a two-man business, but we ain't hanging
around together much socially. Tend to move in different circles
these days, if you get my drift.

– So what circles does he move in then?

– You'd have to ask him that. We're far too busy graftin these days
to waste time on idle chit-chat about our social life.

– You're at Millwall next week, he says.

– I beg your pardon?

– Don't fuck me about, Thorny. Millwall v. West Ham.
Endsleigh Insurance League Division One. Next week.

– Sorry, guv, I don't take much of an interest in the fixture list
these days. Since Bonzo filled the manager's chair I've lost interest.
Great servant on the park, but he don't cut it as a manager, you
know. Sad when that happens, but it's life, innit.

– I'm glad to hear it, cause if I see your miserable arse across the
other side of the river in any way, shape or form on Saturday, I'll have
you down for inciting a riot. Even if you're down in the shopping
centre in Croydon loaded with bags of toys for the starving orphans
of the neighbourhood, you're fucking well nicked. Stay away from
South London.

– Glad to, Mr N. Never liked it, ain't nothing across there.

Filth I've never been partial to. Not just cause of the job they do,
but as people, like. It takes a certain type, if you know what I mean. It
was always the sneaky, cowardly little kids you used to give a good
slapping to at school what went on to become filth. Like they was
trying to put on a uniform and get their own back against the world.
The main problem with filth, though, is that they poke their noses in,
don't they. That cunt Nesbitt, once he gets his teeth in, he never lets

go. You get them noncing queers that hang around the playground touching up little kiddies. That's the sick people that the filth ought to be watching out for: not giving bleeding aggravation to someone who's trying to earn a shagging living.

I bell Bal back at the yard once the filthy cunt Nesbitt had fucked off. — Got to call off Millwall. Nesbitt's wide for it. He's been around here, in the Maurice, making threats.

— He comes that bleedin lark: that means he ain't got the manpower to handle it. Overtime cutbacks, innit. The *Advertiser*'s full of it. If he had the bodies he'd keep *shtum* and try and catch us in action. You know as well as I do that the filth love a big rumble; lets them say to the politicians that this public order thing's getting out of hand, so give us more money for more filth.

— Yeah, and if we call off, the Millwall cunt's 'll think the East London have lost it.

— One thing though, Bal says, — we got Newcastle in a couple of weeks.

— Yeah. Get the Firm together for that one. Better than Millwall; bit of fucking travel, innit. Might make the nationals. They're all sick of aggravation in London. Be lucky if it makes the bleedin *Standard*, a ruck with Millwall.

Newcastle suited me better. Lyonsy was still inside. I'd been at the weights, increasing my punching power, just preparing for that cunt. I don't want Millwall without big Lyonsy. I could see that the thought of Newcastle excited Bal, cause he was round the pub in a bleedin flash, and had me right through to the back room. Stared out any cunt who tried to come in, he did.

— You know, he told me, — I'm worried about Riggsie n all them. All that Ecstasy, Thorny, all that love n peace shit.

— Yeah, I know, I say, thinking of Samantha. I'm seeing her tonight. Over at hers, at Islington. The things she can do with her feet. The way she got my cock between both sets of her toes and just tugged so softly at it that I just spurted out like a bleedin fountain before I fucking well knew what was happening.

— It gets to me, Bal's saying, — proper winds me up it does, Dave.

— Yeah, I know, I tell him.

Samantha. Gor blimey. Can't be long now before we do the business good and proper. But that cunt Bal: he can read me like a fucking book.

– Listen, mate, Bal goes, all serious like, – you'd never let no skirt fuck things up would ya? Like you n me, the business, the Firm n all that?

– Course not, I tell him. – It ain't like that with me and Samantha. She's all right about the violence. I think it turns her on.

I do n all.

– Yeah? he smiles, but I'm saying no more to him, not about Samantha. I've said enough as things stand. He lets it go. – It's just that I worry about the main men these days. I mean, Riggsie and Shorthand for instance. They ain't really up to it any more. It's fucking decadence, innit. It's like ancient Rome with these cunts, one big fucking sex trip. No wonder the Ilford fancied their chances. Who's next? That smart arsed-mob from Basildon? The East Ham? The Gray's crew?

– Do me a favour! I snorted, – Anyway, it don't matter who fancies their chances. We'll have the bastards!

He smiles and we clink our glasses together. Bal n me, we're closer than fucking blood brothers. Fucking spiritual partners and the like. Always have been.

Now there's Samantha to think about though … it makes me think about that ABC song which is one of my favourites, when they go on about the past being your bleedin' sacred cow, and how we all gotta fucking change.

That's Bal's problem, he tries to make the past too much of a sacred cow. I think it was old Maggie that said something about how we all got to innovate to meet new challenges. You don't do that – you end up like all them sad cunts up north crying into their beer over some bleedin factory or mine that's shut down.

You can't make the past your bleedin sacred cow.

The present is me and her: Samantha n all. I can't sit here listening to Bal, I got to get ready to meet her. This could be the night.

When I get home there's a message on the machine; it's the Slag's voice. I don't even listen to what she's got to say for herself. It makes me feel horrible because I was thinking of Samantha and it was good and then she tries to spoil it by coming into my fucking life when it's got nothing to do with her.

It's Samantha I want.

I get ready and round to hers in double quick time. I'm back in a great mood just thinking about her because this fucking slagheap pulls out in front of me and instead of peeping him and tearing after him and giving him a mouthful, I just smile and raise my hand. Too nice a day to get all hot and bothered about a load of bleeding bollocks, innit.

She's got that look on her face. She ain't wasting any time.

– Take all your clothes off and lie on the bed, she said to me.

Well, right, I did just that. I got out of those jeans, shirt and shoes. I took off my socks and my pants. As I climbed onto the bed I could feel the old knob starting to firm up.

– I've always liked pricks, she said, wriggling out off her top like a snake. That's what she moved like, a snake. – I find all limbs beautiful. You've got five and I've only got two. That means you have to give me one, doesn't it?

– Yeah, right … I said, my head starting to spin and my bleeding voice going all hoarse.

She pulled off her leggings using her other foot, one leg at a time. They were like hands, them bleedin feet. The more I saw of her in action, the less I believed.

I look at her naked for the first time. I'd thought about it n all, pulled myself off on the thought of it for fucking days. Funny, I always felt sort of, like guilty afterwards. Not on account of her having no arms, but like cause it was somebody you really care about which is fucking weird but I can't help the sort of geezer I am or what I feel inside. She's there in front of me. Her legs are so long and shapely, just like a gel's should be, and she's got that lovely flat stomach, a beautiful arse, great tits and that face. That fucking face, like a fucking angel's. Then I looked at where her arms should be and I felt … sad.

Sad, and fucking angry.

– I love to fuck, she says. – I didn't have to learn how. I was a natural. The first guy I had, I was twelve and he was twenty-eight. In the home. I blew his mind. It's all in the hips, and nobody can use their hips like somebody like me. Nobody can use their mouth like me. A lot of men really like it, you know. Oh, I know, there's the old pervy thing about fucking a freak …

– Nah, you ain't no freak. Don't go talking about yourself in that way …

She just smiles at me. – What it's all about, though, is having access. No arms to fight off the boys. They like to think that there's nothing I can do about it, no awkward arms to push them away, to stop them doing what they want to do. You like that, don't you? You've got it all there, access to my breasts, my cunt, my arse. Anything you like. If only I had no legs either, eh? Just a fuck toy. You could rig up a harness, put me in it and have me any way you wanted, any time. You think I'm just defenceless, just here for you, for your steamy cock to penetrate, any time.

This ain't fucking right, her talking like that. It just ain't fucking right. I'm getting paranoid here. She must've found that melon in the fridge that time … she must've.

– If this is about the melon …

– Wot you talking about? she asks.

It ain't that, thank fuck. I say back to her, – Wot *you* talking like that for? Eh? I love ya. I fucking love ya!

– You mean you want to fuck me.

– Nah, I love ya, don't I.

– You're a bit of a disappointment to me, Mile End boy. Didn't anybody ever tell you that there ain't no love in this world? It's all money and power. That's what I understood: power. I grew up learning about it. The power we ran up against when we tried to get our compensation, our justice from them: the industrialists, the Government, the judiciary, from the whole fucking clique of them that run things. The way they fucking closed ranks and stuck together. It would've done you proud, Dave. Ain't that what you and your Firm's all about, in your own toytown way? The power to hurt. The power to have. The power to be somebody, to be so feared that nobody'll ever fuck you around? Ever? But it's misguided, though, Dave, cause there will always be somebody to fuck you around.

– Maybe that's wot I felt then, but I ain't like that now. I know what I feel inside, I say to her. I cup my hand over my balls. My erection's going and I feel fucking weird sitting here starkers with a naked bird and not doing nothing.

– Well that's too bad, my sweet little Firm boy. Because if that's the case, you're no good to me. I don't need some fool who's lost it. You men: you talk tough, but you always run away. Right from the start. My own fucking father ran away.

– I ain't fucking lost it! I'll do anything for ya!

– Good. In that case I'm going to suck you off until you're as hard as you once were and then let you choose what you want to do with me. Your imagination is, as they say, the only frontier.

That was what she said, and I couldn't do nothing. I loved her and I wanted to look after her. I needed her to love me, not to talk like some fucking weird slut. I don't go for gels talking like that. She must be reading some pretty grotty things or mixing with funny people to pick up that kind of talk.

So I couldn't do nothing, and you know what? I think she fucking well knew it would be that way: I'm fucking well sure she knew.

She put a gown over her shoulders. It made her look so beautiful, cause the way it hung it made me think for a minute that she had arms. But if she had arms she wouldn't even be sitting here with the likes of me. – When are you going to do Sturgess? she asked.

– I can't do that. I bleedin can't.

– If you really love me you'll do it! *Anything* you fucking said! She screamed at me. She started crying. Fuck me, I can't stand to see her crying.

– It ain't right. I dunno the geezer. It's murder, innit.

She looked at me, then sat down on the bed beside me. – Let me tell you a little story, she said. She sobbed it all out.

When she was born, her old man scarpered. Couldn't handle having a kiddie wot didn't have no arms. Her old gel, well, she only went and bleedin well topped herself, didn't she. So Samantha grew up in care. The Government and them in the courts took the side of them that made the drug, they didn't even want to give her none of that compensation, for her or any of them kiddies born with no arms. That was the thing. It was only when the papers got a hold of it and started a campaign that they bleedin well coughed up. That fucking Sturgess, he was the cunt that caused it all, he got a bleedin knighthood, that fucking old slag. He was the main man, but they all protected him. He did that to my gel, my Samantha, and they gave him a sodding knighthood for his services to industry. There's got to be a bit of justice going on here, innit. Don't bear thinking about.

So I just said to her that I would I do it.

After that me n Samantha went to bed and made love. It was really beautiful, not like with The Slag. I got there proper n all, which made me feel so fucking good. And when I done it with her, I could only see her face, her beautiful face, and not that fucking Millwall queer-beast's.

Orgreave, 1984

The term 'terrorist' sounded faintly ridiculous to Samantha Worthington's ears. International terrorist sounded crazier still. Samantha
Worthington, who grew up in a home outside Wolverhampton, and
had been abroad once, to Germany. There was also another trip to
Wales. Two trips, where the prospect of capture had always been
present. Two occasions where she felt more alive, more redeemed
than ever, and more motivated for her next one. – It does not work
like that, Andreas told her. – We go to sleep for a long time. Then we
wake and strike. And then, it is time to sleep again.

Part of Samantha had done more than see the possibility of
capture; in one corner of her mind she'd embraced it as her destiny.
Her story would be told, and although there would be revulsion at
her actions, there would be sympathy as well. It would polarise
things, and that was what was needed. She knew that she'd either be
portrayed as a cold-blooded psychopath, 'Red Sam, International
Terrorist', or as a silly, innocent young girl, duped by more sinister
figures. Wicked Witch or Gullible Angel: a misleading but inevitable
choice. Which one would she play up to? The fantasy crossed her
mind time and time again as she rehearsed both the roles in her head.

Samantha knew that the truth about her was infinitely more
complex. She looked at the force that was pushing her: revenge; and
the one that was pulling her: love; and reasoned that she could do
nothing else. She was a prisoner, but a willing one. There was a
lightness about Andreas that indicated that he could forget all this,
once the wrongs had been righted. It was just an indication and,
again, Samatha knew deep down that it was improbable. Hadn't he
started talking about moving from single-issue causes to the whole

business of state oppression? Yes, it was a mere indication, but as long as it existed, she would be with him.

Andreas, for his part, understood that all it took was discipline. That and discretion. The difference between them and the people who were ostentatiously radical or revolutionary was in their low profiles. They were ordinary citizens, not politicos, to the outside world. Samantha let this guard drop only once.

Some friends of hers in London were on a Miners' Support Committee and they talked her into going to Orgreave. The sight of beleaguered representatives of the working class in full battle with the oppressive forces of the state proved too much. She had snaked her way to the front line where the pickets pushed against the police cordons which protected the scabs. She was compelled to act.

The young Met white-shirt drafted up from London on the promise of a healthy pay-packet bloated by overtime in service to his Government masters could not believe that the girl with no arms had just dispatched a violent kick to his testicles. As his eyes watered and he struggled to draw breath, he watched her disappear into the mob.

A hidden camera, positioned in a white van, had also witnessed Samantha's actions and departure.

London, 1990

Bruce Sturgess sat in a chair in his spacious garden on the banks of the Thames at Richmond. It was a hot, fresh summer's day as Sturgess looked languidly out onto the rolling waters of the river. A horn from a passing boat sounded and some people waved from the deck as it cruised by him. As he wasn't wearing his spectacles, Sturgess didn't recognise the boat, far less the people on it, but he lazily waved back at the collection of smiles and sunglasses, feeling at one with his small part of the world. Then, for some reason that he didn't want to explore, he pulled a scrap of paper from his pocket. It read, in spidery handwriting:

MY MYSTERY MAN, PLEASE PHONE ME. JONATHAN.

There was a number with a large X beside it. That pathetic little urchin. Did he really think that he, Bruce Sturgess, *Sir* Bruce Sturgess, would compromise himself with a mercenary little rent-boy from the meat-rack? There were plenty more of those filthy ten-a-penny queen whores down there, their faces set in artificial innocence, just the way he liked it. No, thought Sturgess, there were many choice cuts to select from on the rack. What he really needed, though, was someone who could be relied upon to be discreet. He crushed the slip of paper in his hand, allowing himself to be overwhelmed by a delicious surge of violence. After this wave subsided, it was replaced by a fleeting sense of panic as he flattened out the paper and slipped it back into his pocket. Bruce Sturgess couldn't bring himself to throw it away. Instead he settled back to watch the boats slide idly down the Thames.

Sturgess began reflecting back on his life, something which he tended to do quite a lot since his retiral. This generally never gave him anything less than satisfaction. The afterglow from the knighthood had still not worn off. It was good to be called Sir Bruce – not just for the best restaurant tables, hotel suites, directorships and all the other trappings – it just sounded good to him, aesthetically pleasing to his ear. – Sir Bruce, he repeated softly to himself. He did this often. However, if anyone deserved it, they all said, it was him. He'd steadily climbed the corporate ladder, moving from a professional scientific research and development background into management, then into the boardroom at United Pharmacology, the drugs, food and alcoholic beverages conglomerate. Tenazadrine had undoubtedly been something of a blemish. Heads had rolled after it, but it was just another corporate disaster for Bruce Sturgess to worm out of. Somebody less senior and less shrewd would always be there to take the rap, and there were many in that position *vis-à-vis* Bruce Sturgess. His cool manoeuvrings on this issue had only increased his stock as a smooth operator.

The tragedy had been one he assessed purely in terms of pounds: the monies lost to the company. Sturgess refused to look at the newspaper 'human-interest' reports and the television pictures of the Tenazadrine children. Limbs and deformities seldom entered his thinking. There was a period when it was not so: during his stint in New York, where the tempting anonymity of life in that city had become too much, he had been forced to come to terms with a side of his sexuality he'd repressed since his schooldays. It was then he realised what it was like to be different, and a terrifying empathy had stricken him for a while. Thankfully it hadn't lasted.

He remembered the very first time his Tenazadrine legacy forcibly impacted on his life. He had set up a game of cricket with his two young sons on Richmond Common. The stumps were positioned and Sturgess was ready to bat when something crossed his line of vision. In the distance he saw a small child without any legs. The boy was propelling himself along on some kind of trolley, like a skateboard, using his arms. It was perverse, obscene. Briefly Sturgess felt like Dr Frankenstein in the Baron's lowest moments.

He didn't make the drug, he told himself over and over, he only bought it from the Krauts and sold it. Yes, there were the murmurings – more than murmurings, there was the report he suppressed indicating that the tests were not as stringent as they could have been and that the toxicity of the drug was greater than at first believed. As a former chemist, he really ought to have taken a greater interest in that side of things. But this was Tenazadrine, the wonder pill for pain-relief. Nothing had gone wrong in the past, with similar products. Besides, there were competitors for the franchise to market the drug in the UK. They would not hang about and Sturgess felt that he could not afford to either. He signed the deal with the German, the strange fellow, in the lounge at Heathrow. The Kraut had got cold feet, started bleating on about more tests needing to be done, and passed him over a copy of this report.

Too much, though, was invested in the drug not to put it on the market. Too much time, too much money, and too much in terms of the credibility of certain corporate careers, his being one of them. The report was never passed on, it was incinerated on the open fire at Sturgess's West London home.

All this flashed back when Sturgess saw this child, and for the first time he felt a crippling flood of guilt. – You chaps carry on, he squeaked to his bemused sons as he staggered back to the car, trying to compose himself, breathing hard until the apparition had gone from his sight. Then he got on with the game of cricket. You coped, he reasoned. It was the English way: that ability to compartmentalise pain and guilt into a separate and secure part of your psyche, like burying sealed vats of radio-active waste inside granite.

He remembered old Barney Drysdale; Barney who had been with him all the way.

– I feel bloody haunted, Barney, he had told his colleague.

– Pull yourself together, old son. We make one dodgy product and we get all this bad publicity. We just have to tough it out; the gentlemen of the press will soon find another fad to concern themselves with. All the life-saving work we've done through advances in drug technology and nobody gives a monkey's. We all have to stand together at a time like this. All those prying journalists and bleeding hearts think you never have to pay a price for progress. Well, they are wrong!

It had been a good talk; done wonders for Bruce Sturgess's state of mind. Barney was a reassuring fellow. He taught him to be selective about what one deliberates on, to concentrate on one's virtues, to leave the guilt to our foreign friends. Yes, it was the English way. He missed Barney greatly. His friend had perished in a fire in his Pembrokeshire cottage several years ago. They blamed some Welsh Nationalist extremists. Scum, thought Sturgess. Some might say just retribution, but Bruce Sturgess didn't believe in that. It was just bloody bad luck.

Who was the Kraut again? he sleepily thought as he dozed in the heat. Emmerich. Gunther Emmerich. Sir Bruce drifted off with the sun in his face. I never forget a name, he thought smugly.

Fitted Up

We got just over a hundred of the Firm together to trash Newcastle. Things were getting a bit fucking tight. With this Taylor Report and these all-seated stadiums on the way, this might be one of the last seasons for a full-scale terracing ruck. They were already starting work on grounds up and down the bleedin country. Killing the fucking game, those cunts.

For this one we knew that the filth would be out in force so there was no prospect of a major toe-to-toe. Bal and I gave strict instructions on Friday night down the Grave Maurice: no cunt was to be tooled up as such. The filth were arresting people for anything these days. The whole operation was to be a show of strength, a bit of PR: show them fucking fat Geordie gits that the Cockney lads ain't lost it. We'll fling them a few sharpened pound coins, sing a few songs and generally treat their slum like the fucking toilet it is. But we won't do nothing in the ground itself: nothing that's gonna fill the cells with the Firm. Bal n me was giving all the orders; nobody from the Ilford was batting a fucking eyelid, nor none of them other fuckers.

Anyway, thirty-two of us were to get up on the train from King's Cross, hitting a boozer we'd picked out in Geordieland for opening time at eleven. Another thirty-odds would be coming up on the nine o'clock to get into this other pub, a few hundred yards away. The third were coming up on a supporters' bus, done up as scarfers for the journey, and they would get into Newcastle about one. The idea was that they would split up into two factions and head for both the pubs. They would be the bait to entice out the Geordie gits who wanted some, then we'd steam in and do them. We'd sent two Scouts up on Friday lunchtime, and they were keeping us posted on the mobiles.

Well, as the old man would say: the best laid schemes of mice n men and all that shit, cause it didn't flaming well work quite as we planned it, did it. Newcastle's one of my favourite trips, cause of edge. It's so bleedin far, for one thing, so different. Let's face it, those cunts are more like Jocks than real Englishmen: sort of all dirty and uncivilised. There's something about the place that gives you the fucking creeps. It's all bleedin hill, with them ugly bridges hanging over that dirty river. The geezers are typically thick northern sods who couldn't organise a piss-up in a brewery, but they can fair dish out the old stick, and take it, when it comes to a punch up. Generally takes quite a bit to put one of them cunts down. Anyway, that don't bother me none cause usually I've got quite a bit, and I'm usually drinking fucking vibes like these, but today I just ain't feeling up for it. I wanted to be back with her; miles away, back in the bleedin Smoke. Some fucking club, or maybe even a full-scale rave or something like that, E'd up. Just me and her.

Anyway, we gets up to the station. There were a couple of pigs at King's Cross. They got on the train, but they got off at Durham. I thought they'd be radioing Newcastle and I was prepared for a reception of the local Old Bill. When we got off at the station, though, it was almost deserted.

– No fucking filth! Where's all the fucking coppers then? Bal shouted.

– What's happening ere then? Riggsie asked.

But I could hear something. A rustling sound in the distance, then shouting. Then they came, steaming across the concourse, some of them tooled up with baseball bats.

– IT'S A FUCKING SET-UP! I shouted, – THESE FUCKING GEORDIE BASTARDS AND THE OLD BILL! WE BEEN FUCKING FITTED UP!

– NO CUNT BACK OFF! GET THESE CAHHHNNTS! Bal steamed in, and we followed suit. I got hit fucking hard across the back but I kept swinging, driving on into the centre of them. It felt good. I forgot everything. There was no tension now, just the connection. I was on a run. This was what it was all about. I had forgotten how good it felt. Then I slipped on the concourse and went down. I could feel the boots going in, but I didn't even curl, just kept

writhing, lashing and kicking out. I managed to get up, cause Riggsie
had made space by picking up a mobile barrier and charging them
with it. I caught this skinny geezer with Coke-bottle T.Rex and just
kept punching the cunt as hard as I could. He dropped this note-pad
and I realised that he was just some poor little trainspotting cunt
who'd got caught up in all this bother.

The Old Bill eventually showed and this was the cue for
everybody to scarper off in different directions. Out in the street, this
geezer with a swollen eye approached me. – Fuckin Cockney
bastard, he said in a Geordie accent, but the cunt was laughing. I
started to n all.

– Aye, that was a fuckin good one n ahl, he said.

– Yeah, it was pretty tasty, wasn't it, I agreed.

– Ah man, ah'm too fuckin E'd up to get into ahl this just now, he
smiled.

– Yeah, right, I nodded.

He gave me the thumbs up, and said, – Ah'll see ye later, man.

– You can count on it, Geordie, I laughed, and we went our
different ways. I headed back down towards the pub we was in. Two
other Geordies approached me and I couldn't be bothered fighting,
my adrenalin had dipped.

– You fuckin West Ham? one asked.

– Git tae fuck, ah'm fae Scotland, I growled in my Jock accent.

– Aw right, man, sorry bout that, he said.

I left them and hit the boozer. Riggsie and some other geezers
were there so we made our way down to the ground and took up
seats in the stand surrounded by fucking Geordies. I thought that I'd
start swinging to see what happened, but Riggsie spotted some
undercover filth, who'd clocked us. We stayed for the first half, but
we was bored shitless so we left and went back to the pub. I gave a
couple of geezers on the pool table a good slapping and we broke
some glasses and kicked over a couple of tables before heading off.

When we got out into the streets at the end of the game, we saw
the main body of the Firm getting a police escort down to the station,
a baying Geordie mob behind them. The filth were well in control,
they had the horses and the cars out in force now. We couldn't do no

more, but I was glad that I was getting on the train and back down to Samantha.

Bal was well high on the choo-choo home. – These cunts fucking well know who we are! he shouted.

There wasn't no cunt, Ilford, Grays, East Ham or that, who was saying otherwise. I took an E off Riggsie and came up somewhere around Doncaster.

Sheffield Steel

I see the fucking cunt. Sturgess. That's the cunt that must die; for what he did to my Samantha. I'll fucking well have you, you cunt.

The cunt stops his motor on Piccadilly Circus and in jumps this young geezer and they swing round the roundabout and head down the Dilly, taking a right to detour at Hyde Park. I'm in pursuit. The car stops by the Serpentine. I can't see a lot in the dark, but I know what that queer-beast is doing, don't I.

After about half an hour, the car starts off. They head back up to Piccadilly Circus and this young fucking sleaze-bag gets out. I can spot a sodding arse-bandit a mile away. I drive round for a bit and then this rent boy's back in the same fucking location and Sturgess is well gone. I pull up alongside the young queer-beast.

— Oi, want a lift? I ask.

— Yeah, all right, he says, in a northern accent, but not a real northern accent, not a lad's northern accent like.

— What about a blow-job then, sweetheart? I ask as he climbs in. Dirty, that's what he makes me feel like. It don't bear thinking about too much.

— He looks carefully at me with those sodding girl's eyes. — Twenty quid, Hyde Park, and I get driven back here after, he says.

— Done, I say, starting up the car.

— To this very spot, he minces.

— Yeah, all right, you're on, I tell him. I put the car stereo back on. ABC: *The Lexicon of Love*, my favourite album of all time. The greatest album ever fuckin made, innit.

We drove into the park and I pulled up at the same spot this fucking sick thing had stopped at with Sturgess.

— You've done this before, he smiled. — Funny, I didn't think you looked like a punter … you being so young. I'm going to enjoy this, he lisped.

– So am I, mate, so am I. So where about's is it you come from then, eh?

– Sheffield, he says.

I finger a scar on my chin. I got that at Sheffield two years ago. Bramall Lane: bicycle chain. I'm a poet and I don't bleedin well know it. These geezers were pretty classy at United. Never rated the Wednesday mob though: fucking wankers.

– You an Owl or a Blade then?

– What? he lisped.

– Football, innit. You support Wednesday or United?

– I don't really care about football, he said.

– This band, ABC, they was from Sheffield. The geezer in the gold suit. That's him on the stereo: 'Show Me'.

I get the little scumbag working on my dick. I sit there smiling, looking at the back of his head, his close-shaven queer head. Nothing happens.

He stops in a bit and looks up. – Don't worry, he says, – just one of these things.

– Oh, I ain't worried, mate, I smile, handing him a twenty, for effort n all.

That ABC geezer is still giving it big licks with that 'Show Me'. What are you gonna fucking show me, you cunt?

– You know, he says, – for a while I thought you were a cop.

– Ha ha ha … nah, mate, not me. The law's bad news, but's that all they are, innit. Me, well, I'm more what you might call a fucking catastrophe.

He looks at me for a bit, all puzzled like. He tries to smile, but the fear's paralysed his queer face before I grab his scrawny neck and smash that sick boat-race against the dashboard. It bursts open and blood splatters all over the bleedin motor. I bash him again, and again, and again.

– YOU FUCKING QUEER-BEAST! I'M GONNA KNOCK YOUR FUCKING TEETH OUT! I'M GONNA MAKE YOUR MOUTH ALL NICE AND SOFT, JUST LIKE

A NICE GIRL'S PRIVATES, THEN I'M GONNA GET A
PROPER FUCKING SUCK!

I saw his face, the Millwall geezer. Lyonsy. Lyonsy the Lion, they
call him. He'll be out again soon. Everytime I brought the queer-
beast's head down he screamed, and everytime I brought it up he
pleaded: – Please ... I don't want to die ... I don't want to die ...

I was hard now. I pushed his head down on me and pumped and
pumped, and he started gagging and puking, his blood and sick
spilling over my bollocks and thighs ...

– COME ON, YOU CUNT, FUCKING SHOW ME!

... much more blood than the Slag's when I'm giving her one and
she's on the rag ... but I'm coming now and all I can see is Samantha
as I'm filling that queer face with spunk ... this is for you, gel, this is
for you, I'm thinking, but I realise that what I'm doing is shooting
into the head of this bleeding monster, this thing ...

– OOOOHHHH YOU FUCKING SICK LITTLE
PANSY!

Then I pull his head up and watch the blood and spunk and sick
trickle out of his burst face.

I should kill him. For what he's bleedin well made me do, I should
fucking well kill him.

– I'm gonna teach you a song, I tell him, switching off the car
stereo. – All right? You don't fucking well sing, you soppy little
Yorkshire pudding, I'll rip your fucking balls right off and stuff them
down your throat, all right?

He nods, fucking wretched little pansy.

– I'm foreveah blowing bubbles ... SING YOU CUNT!

He mumbles something through his burst mouth.

– Pretty bubbles in the ayyyahhh ... they fly so high, nearly reach
the sky, then like my dreams they fade and doiii ... SING! ... fortune's always hiding, I've looked ev-ary-where, I'm forevah
blowing bubbles, pretty bubbles in theee ...

UNITED!

I fucking well screamed as I slammed my fist into that poof face.
Then I opened the door and shoved him out into the park. – Gerrout

orf it, you fucking horrible sick little monster! I shout as he lays there, fucking well out off it.

I drove off, then reversed alongside him. I felt like running him over, didn't I. It ain't him I'm after though. – Oi, queer face, tell your fucking old sick cunt of a boyfriend that he's fucking next!

Samantha ain't got no arms, ain't got no mum or dad, was brought up in a fucking home, all because of some fucking rich old queer-beast. Well, I planned to sort all that right fucking out, didn't I.

I get back to the flat and there's a bleedin message on the fucking answerphone. It's my mum, who never phones me. She sounds really shit up: – Come and see me straight away, son. Something awfay's happened. Phone me as soon as you get in.

My old mum; never done nobody a bad turn, never in her life, and what's she got to show for it? Nothing, that's what. A queer-beast on the other hand, one that made all them kiddies freaks, the likes of them have got the bleedin lot. Then I'm thinking what could be wrong with my mum and I think about the old cunt, the drunken old fucker. If he's hurt my mum, if he's laid a finger on my old mother …

London, 1991

It had been three years. Three years and he was coming to see her at last. There had been the phone calls, but now she was actually going to *see* Andreas. The last time had been their one weekend in five years. One weekend since Berlin, when they'd butchered the Emmerich child together. Something snapped in her then, his taunting driving her into a frenzy of violence. She would have done anything for him. She did. The blood of the child, the bitter communion wine of their warped relationship.

The joke was that she had fantasised about keeping the baby. Them living in Berlin, a Tenazadrine couple, with a baby. She could have been one of the mothers in the Tiergarten in the lazy summer months. But he wanted the baby as a sacrifice, to prove her devotion to what they were trying to do.

When she killed the baby, part of her died with it. When she surveyed its small, broken, armless corpse, she realised that her life was also effectively over. She wondered if it had ever really started. She tried to remember times she had felt truly happy; they just seemed like embarrassingly small harbours of respite in a life that was a sea of torment. No, there was no chance of happiness, only opportunity for further revenge. Andreas kept saying that you had to get beyond the self, beyond the ego. Agents of change could not be happy.

Samantha had been in shock, almost catatonic herself for the best part of two years. When she came out of this trance, she found she didn't love Andreas any more. Moreover, she couldn't feel her capacity for love. She was going to see Andreas for the first time in three years, and the only person she could think about was Bruce Sturgess.

Now they'd found Sturgess. He was hers. Andreas, she chillingly acknowledged, she now had no feeling for. All she wanted was Sturgess. He was the last.

The other one, the one in the cottage in Wales, had been easy. He was unguarded. They had seen him in the lounge bar in the village. She had often thought that when she crawled through that window, she'd feel fear. But no, nothing. After that time in Germany, nothing.

Andreas came to the door. She noted dispassionately that his hair had thinned, but his face retained that youthful freshness. He wore steel-rimmed glasses.

– Samantha, he kissed her cheek. She froze.

– Hello, she said.

– Why so sad? he smiled.

She looked at him for a while. – I'm not sad, she said, – just tired. Then, without bitterness, she told him, – You know, you've taken away more of my life than the Tenazadrine crowd did. But I don't hate you for it. It had to be that way. It's the way I reacted to it all, it's my nature. Some people can let go of pain, but not me. I want Sturgess. After him, I'll achieve some kind of peace.

– There can be no peace as long as an economic system founded on exploitation ...

– No, she raised a hand to silence him. – I can't take on that responsibility, Andreas. There is no emotional connection. I can't blame a system. People I can blame; I can't abstract myself to the level of taking out my anger on a system.

– Which is precisely why you will remain a slave to that system.

– I don't want to argue with you. I know why you're here. Keep away from Sturgess. He's mine.

– I'm afraid I cannot risk ...

– I want first shot at the bastard.

– As you wish, Andreas said, rolling his eyes. – But I came tonight to talk about love. Tomorrow we plan, but tonight is for love, no?

– There is no love, Andreas, fuck off.

– So sad, he smiled, – Never mind! Tonight will be for drinking beer instead. Perhaps go to a club, yes? I have not had much time to catch up with all the acid house and techno stuff ... I have taken the

Ecstasy of course, but just in the house with Marlene, to be all loved on … or loved up, is it …

She froze, then, at the mention of the other name, at what it might mean. He confirmed it with a picture of a woman and two small children, a baby and an infant. The image was one of idyllic contentment. Samantha stared at the photograph, at the look of love and pride on Andreas's face. She wondered what sort of expression her own father must have had when he saw her for the first time.

– No peace until the end of the system, eh, she laughed coldly. It was a harsh distant laugh, and it seemed to unnerve Andreas. She smiled contentedly. It was the first time she'd seen him uneasy in this way and she felt pleased that she had been the cause of it. – All those little limbs … she continued, intoxicated by her sense of power over him.

His claw snatched the picture from her. He scowled, – I am here, am I not? Am I enjoying the peace and contentment? No. Sturgess is here, and I am here, Samantha. Part of me is always here, always where he is. You see, I too cannot let go of the pain.

You Want Some?

When I get round to my old girl's place the first person I notice is The Slag. – What's she doin here? I ask.

– Don't you talk like that, David! That's the mother of your wee boy, bichrist, my old gel says.

– What's happened? Where's Gal?

– He got taken into the hospital, The Slag says, cigarette in her hand, blowing out that fucking sick smoke through her nose. – Meningitis. He's going to be all right though, Dave, the doctor said so, didn't he, Mum?

That fucking slag, calling *my* old mum Mum, like she was part of things here.

– Aye, we goat a wee fright, but he's all right.

– Yeah, we was ever so worried, The Slag says.

I look at the fucking cow-faced slag, – Where abouts is he?

– Ward Eight of the London …

– If anything happens to him, it's down to you! I snap, then I run over to her handbag on the table and pull out her fags. – You and this! This fucking snout in his fucking lungs all day every day! I crush the cigarette packet. – If I ever catch you smoking round my boy again, I'll do to you what I did to that flaming packet of snout! You shouldn't be here! You ain't got no business here! You ain't nothing to do with me no more, you understand!

I'm right out the fucking door and my old mum's shouting on me to come back, but I'm off. I go round to the hospital, my heart racing. That fucking slag had to make him ill with her snout at this precise moment in time when I got things to do. When I get there, the little un's asleep. He looks like an angel. They tell me he's gonna be all right. I have to leave. I got a date.

I'm proper wound up when I get round to that fucking place. I've been watching them; I've seen them coming and going, but now I've got to go in for the first time.

It gives me the fucking creeps. I get a quick proposition from a beast already, who rolls his eyes and says something about a party in the toilets. I tell him where to fucking well get off. There's only one I want, and he's at the bar. Easily clocked: he's the oldest cunt here. I'm over and sitting down beside him.

— A large brandy, he says to the barman.

— That's a very distinguished accent you got there, I tell him.

He turns and looks at me with that queer-beast face: the mouth loose and rubbery, those dead, girlish eyes. It makes me feel proper sick n all, him looking me up and down, like I'm a piece of fucking meat.

— Let's not talk about me. Let's talk about you. Drink?

— Eh, yeah. Whisky please.

— So, I suppose I should ask if you come here often or something equally bland, he smiles.

Filthy fucking old cunt.

— First time, I say. — To tell ya the truth, I felt I wanted to for a while … I mean, I'm sorry talking to you like this, but I thought that as, well, as an older bloke, you might be a bit discreet. I've got a wife and a kid and I don't want them to know I've been here … to a place like this … I mean …

He raises his sick, manicured hand as if to shut me up. — I think we have what our economist friends might term a mutual coincidence of wants.

— You what?

— I think we both want a bit of good sport, but in secret, with discretion assured.

— Yeah … discretion. That's what I want. Good sport, yeah. That'll do me fine.

— Let's get out of this fucking pit, he snaps, — this place gives me the creeps.

I feel like saying to him, well, you shouldn't be such a sick old queer-beast then, should ya, but I button it, and we leave. Samantha'll be waiting, back at the yard, where I gave her the keys.

For a bit I thought that this thing, old sick trousers here, wasn't into going back over to the motor yard at the East End, but it seemed to turn the diseased beast on, the thought of fucking well slumming it. Well, we'll see how much it turns him on in a minute.

We take my motor, and while we drive in silence I'm looking at that wrinkled, tortoise head in the mirror; he reminds me of that Touche Turtle cunt from the cartoons; and I'm thinking about how Samantha's using me and I'm acting like a big fucking soft blouse but it don't matter cause when you feel about someone like I feel about her you'll do anything, anyfuckingthing for them and that's all there bleedin well is to it and I'm going to fucking send this thing to the next fucking world, to a hell for the sick and diseased minds …

The Yard

I've got ABC on the car stereo and I'm just getting into 'All Of My Heart' which makes me feel so sad when applied to my own sort of personal circumstances. I feel like crying like a girl and I can tell I'm giving off a poof-house vibe because the queer-beast is asking me:

– Is everything all right?

We're at the yard. I stop the motor.

– Yeah … I mean … you been around a bit, mate. It's just that I feel confused. Just cause you n I are like going to do it, like, it don't mean that we don't love our own now, does it …

The sick fruit puts a hand on my arm. – Don't worry. You're just nervous. C'mon, he says, getting out the car, – we've gone too far to turn back now.

He's right n all. I get out and head for the lock-up. I undo the padlock and swing open the doors. I shut them behind us, then I lead him through the back towards the garage.

Samantha clicks the lights on, and I wrap my hand around this Touche Turtle cunt's scrawny throat and smack the sick monster in the face with my nut. Glasgow kiss, the old man calls it. I push him to the ground and boot him in the bollocks.

Samantha's over and she's like doing a dance on the spot and her little flippers are going like the ones on a pinball machine and she's like a kid and she's going: – You got him, Dave! You got the bastard! He's ours! She boots the gasping beast in the stomach. – Sturgess! You are accused of drug crimes! How do you fucking well plead! she screams, bending down over him.

– Who are you … I have money … I can get you all the money you need … the wheezing beast moans.

She looks at him as if he's a fucking lunatic. – MUNNEEE-
... she's screeching, – I DON'T NEED YOUR FUCKING
MUNNEEE ... what do I want with fucking money! I want you!
You're more important to me than all the fucking money in the
world! I'll bet you never thought you'd live to hear anybody say that
about you, eh?

I've been locking us in with the padlock and chain, then going
round the back and small-bolting the office door. Samantha's still
taunting the queer-beast, who's begging for mercy like a big girl.

She nods to me and I pick up the queer-beast and drag him over to
the table. His sick gob is dribbling blood and snot and he's crying like
a sad cunt, can't even take his fucking punishment like a man. Not
that I ever expected anything different from a trouser ponce.

I pull him across the big table, face down. I see a strange expression
come into his eyes as this sick creature actually thinks I'm gonna
fucking give him one up the arse ... as if that was what we wanted
him for. I bind his wrists to the table legs using electrical flex, and
Samantha's up on the table sitting on his legs, holding them down
while I do them next.

I start up the chainsaw and this Sturgess cunt is screaming, but I
hear other noises, and there's a banging at the door. It's the fucking
Old Bill and it sounds like there's loads of them out there.

Samantha's shouting: – Keep them out, keep them fucking out,
and she's trying to manipulate the chainsaw into position with her
feet at the front of Sturgess, who's just fucking well beside himself,
struggling against the bonds. That padlock and chain won't hold the
door for long. I can't think of what to do, then I see the huge
aluminium bolt-hole: fucking massive, but with no bolt. I slide my
arm through it, the elbow past the join of the door and wall. I can
hear some silly filth cunt's voice at a loudspeaker but I can't make out
what he's saying, all I hear is the song 'Poison Arrow' blasting inside
my head. Because it's her that broke my fucking heart, cause she
knew how it would turn out right from the start.

And Samantha's getting him, I can hear the searing of the saw, and
the pain on my arm's fucking unbearable; this arm'll never be able to

deck Lyonsy of the Millwall after this, as if it matters, and I look over to shout to Samantha: – Do the cunt, Sam! Go on, my gel! Do him!

The sound of the saw changes as it rips into the flesh of the queer-beast, just below the shoulder, and blood spurts and splashes across the garage floor. I'm thinking about the mess it's gonna leave for poor old Bal, who won't be best pleased, and that's a funny thing to think about because the saw's torn through Sturgess's flesh and it's grinding into the bone. Samantha, there on her arse, saw in her feet, ripping the screaming captive beast's limb from him … God, she looks like she does when I'm giving her one and I hear another splintering and it's me this time, it's my fucking arm, and the pain is just so much I'm gonna black out but I'm catching Samantha's look at me as I fall and she's shouting something which I can't hear but I know what it is, I can see it on her lips. She's covered in his blood which is fucking well spurting everywhere but she's smiling like a little girl playing in mud and she's mouthing: I love you … and I'm doing it back and I'm blacking out and I don't care because this is the greatest feeling in the world … fortune's always hiding … but I found it cause I love her and I've done it … I've looked everywhere … the Old Bill can do what they fucking well like, it's all over now, but I don't fucking well care … I'm forever blowing bubbles …

pretty

      bubbles

               in

                         the …

The
Undefeated

*An Acid
House Romance*

For Colin Campbell and Dougie Webster

We're the undefeated
TV in the shade
girls at all our parties
we have really got it made

Iggy Pop

Prologue

Ah am fuckin well fed up because there's nothing happening and ah've probably done a paracetamol but fuck it you need to have positive vibes and wee Amber, she's rubbing away at the back ay ma neck saying it'll happen when this operatic slab of syth seems to be 3 D and ah realise that I'm coming up in a big way as that invisible hand grabs a hud ay me and sticks me onto the roof because the music is in me around me and everywhere, it's just leaking from my body, this is the game this is the game and ah look around and we're all going phoah and our eyes are just big black pools of love and energy and my guts are doing a big turn as the quease zooms through my body and we're up to the floor one by one and ah think I'm going tae need tae shit but ah hold on and it passes and I'm riding this rocket to Russia …

— No bad gear, eh, ah say tae Amber, as we dance ourselves slowly into it.

— Aye, sound.

— Awright, eh, says Ally.

Then it's ma main man on the decks, and he's on the form tonight, just pulling away at our collective psychic sex organs as they lay splayed out before us and ah get a big rosy smile off this goddess in a Lycra top, who, with her tanned skin and veneer of sweat, looks as enticing as a bottle of Becks from the cold shelf on a hot, muggy day, and my heart just goes bong bong bong Lloyd Buist reporting for duty, and the dance NRG the dance U4E ahhhh gets a hud ay me and I'm doing a sexy wee shuffle with Ally and Amber and Hazel and this big bone-heided cunt falls into me and gives me a hug and apologies and I'm slapping his hard wall of a stomach and thanking my lucky stars we're E'd and at this club and not pished at The Edge or somewhere brain-dead no that ah would touch that fuckin rubbish ... whoa rockets ... whoa it's still coming and I'm thinking *now* is the time to fall in love now now now but not with the world with that one special *her*, just do it, just do it now, just change your whole fuckin life in the space of a heartbeat, do it *now* ... but nah ... this is just entertainment ...

Later it's time to chill at Hazel's gaff. Ally hits us all with some Slam which is all very nice except that he wants to spraff wildly and I'm in a dancy mood, naw, I'm in a shagging mood really. These Amsterdam Playboys do something tae ye behind your nuts. Woaf!

There are a lot of lassies back here. Ah love lassies because they just look so fuckin brilliant, especially when you're E'd. It seems a wee bit obvious tae think that though, cause maist guys feel the same wey. Ah was reading somewhere about lassies being seen as either saints or whores. That's too simple ... that sound's like shite to me. Maybe it was about laddies thinking of lassies in that way. Ah ask Ally about this.

— Naw, that's shite, man, much too simplistic, he says. Ally's got an amazing smile and his eyes seem to eat every word that comes from your mouth. — Ah've got ma ain classification, Lloyd. Lassies are either, one: Party Chicks; two: Straight-Pegs; three: Skankers; four: Party Chicks ...

— You sais Party Chicks already but, ah told him.

— Let ays see ... Party Chicks, Straight-Pegs, Skankers or Hounds, that's the four types ay bird, he smiles, casting his eyes round the room. — Maistly Party Chicks in here, thank fuck.

— So what dae ye class as a Party Chick?

— Fuck knows ... it's obviously aw doon tae attitude, this whole classification ... right ... listen Lloyd, you necked that other pill yet?

Ah hadnae. Some crusties are burning incense in the corner and ah get a nice whiff which fills my nostrils and ah nod over at them. — Naw ...

— Ye gaunny dae it soon?

— Naw ... ah'm still up here, man. Ah might save it fir the fitba the morn, eh.

– Ah dinnae ken but eh, Lloyd … Ally pouts, looking like a toddler who's had his sweeties taken away.

– Fuck it, special occasion, eh, ah say to him, as either he or ah or some other cunt says every weekend as every weekend is, indeed, a special occasion. We neck our pills and the adrenalin rush of just having taken more chems has set Ally off again.

– Party Chicks can be subdivided, man, intae like two groups: Hiya Lassies and Sexy Feminists. Straight-Pegs are women who dinnae touch drugs, eh no man, and they shag only dull twats like themselves who are intae aw that home-and-garden shite. These are mainstream straight-pegs, man, dead easy tae spot. There are alternative straight-pegs, the kind ay po-faced feminists who read the *Guardian* or the *Independent* and that and are intae career-development paths and aw that sort ay shite. You have to watch them, if they arenae dykes, man, you can sometimes mistake them for Sexy Feminists. No always, but sometimes.

This is magic. Ally's off. – The Boyle Laddie is off on a mazy! ah shout, and a few other people come over as Ally continues his rant.

– Hiya Lassies are the best but, man, but mair ay that in a bit. Skankers drink a lot ay alcohol and shag draftpak guys. They dress crassly, and seldom, if ever, touch Class As, although mair Skankers are daein them now. They're type of women whae go tae discos and dance around their handbags. Hounds are the lowest ay the low, man; they'll shag anything and are often alcoholics. Hiya Lassies are called so because they always say hi-ya-uh … when they meet you.

– You say that aw the time, Amber, Hazel says.

– So? Amber says, wondering what's going down.

– You have to watch though, Ally says to me, – because Skankers say this as well sometimes. It's the *wey* they say it that's important.

– Are you callin me a fuckin Skanker son? Amber asks Ally.

– Naw, man … you say hiya in a cool wey, he smiles at her and she melts. Fuck me if we arenae aw coming up again. – You're a Hiya Lassie, and they are easygoing, young, salt-of-the-earth Party Chicks. The best acquire that certain edge and become Sexy Feminists; the worst get stuck with a closet twat and become Straight-Pegs. Tell ye something else, Lloyd, he sais, turnin tae me, in eighty per cent ay cases the man always gets straight and boring before the woman.

– That's fuckin knob-cheese, Ally.

– Naw, Ally's right, somebody chips in. It's Nukes.

– See? It's just that you've picked boring women aw your life ya daft cunt! Ally smiles and gives me a big hug.

Foaahh … ah'm cunted here, ah feel like I'm shiting my soul out of every pore in my face. – Ah've goat tae dance through this one or ah'll sit cabbaged ay night … Nukes … help ays oan tae that flair, man …

– Ah'm blinded, man … blinded by the fuckin light … wis that no a song by some cunt … goat tae sit doon, Nukes groaned, a magnificent aura rising from him. Ah staggered towards the speakers.

– Aw Lloyd, man, stey here n spraff a bit, Ally says, his pupils getting blacker but his lids getting heavier.

– In a bit, Ally. Ah feel that disco vibe. Rock the disco tek, eh.

Ah leave Ally to dance with Amber and her mate Hazel, two definite Party Chicks by any classification, who look as deliciously cool and colourful as a couple of happy-hour cocktails perched temptingly on the bar of Old Orleans. After a shuffle, my legs get moving and I'm enjoying it all. More strange things start happening behind my genitals. Ah remember ah fired intae Amber at a party last year and looking at her made me wonder why ah hadnae done it again. Ah say to Amber first, – Listen, fancy hitting the bedroom for a meeting of, minds and the other bits?

– No, I'm no into sex with you. Ah fancy firing right intae Ally later on, he looks so fucking gorgeous.

– Yeah, yeah, yeah, ah smile, and ah look over at Ally with his Tenerife tan and have to admit that the cunt does look, eh, a wee bitty more than presentable; mind you, every cunt does on E. He's gesturing over and I'm waving back at him. A big white

Not a whitey, though heartbeat, perspiration and heating have all definitely increased. Hit the Volvic. Can you feel it, crew!

– Fucking good tape, Ambs … make ays a copy … is it Slam? Is it?

She closes her eyes and then opens them briefly and nods at me seriously, – Jist a Yip Yap mixed tape, eh.

Whoa, yes to fuck …

– I'm up for it, Haze says to me.

– Eh?

– A shag, like. That's what you were talking to Ambs aboot, eh. You and me, then. The bedroom.

Ah was going to get round to asking her before ah goat diverted by … let's just see … before ah was diverted by Amber's KB; whoa ya fucker am ah in touch with my feelings or what, but it's all right and ah shout: – Hey Ally, ah'm sexually jealous of you, and he pouts and comes over and gives me a hug and Amber does too so ah should feel good but ah feel a bit of a cunt for making them feel bad because ah discover that I'm no really sexually jealous of Ally who's a smashing lad as Gordon McQueen on Scotsport would say but only he's no oan it now it's that Gerry McNee gadge that gets tae say it now, and the other radge who writes aboot the fitba n aw that's on it as well, but as they boys would say: ah wish him every success, etc., etc.

– Amber's saying she's intae firing intae ye, ah tell Ally.

Amber smiles and pushes me in the chest. Ally turns to me and says, – The important thing, man, is that ah love Amber, he wraps his arm around her. – What happens sexually … that's just detail. The important thing is, man, that ah love everybody that ah know in this room. And ah know everybody! Except these boys, he points to the crusties who are skinning up in the corner. But ah'd love these cunts as well if ah knew them. Ninety per cent of people are loveable, man, once ye get tae ken them … if they believe in themselves enough …: if they love and respect themselves, eh …

Ah feel ma face opening up like a tin ay sardines as ah give Ally a smile and then ah turn to Haze and say, – Let's go for it …

In the bedroom Hazel struggles out of her kit and ah get out of mine and we're under the duvet. It's too hot to be under the duvet but this in case any cunt comes in, which they will. We've got the tongues working hard and I probably taste very salty and sweaty cause she does. It takes me yonks tae get an erection, but that doesnae bother ays because I'm mair intae the touching oan E than the penetration. She's gaun pretty radge though and ah manage tae bring her off using my fingers. Ah'm just lying their watching her orgasm like ah was watching her score for Hibs. We'll just play that one back again, Archie … I want it tae happen for her seven times. After a while, though, ah start to feel something happen and ah have tae stop and get out and rummage through my jeans.

– What is it? She asks, – I've got a condom here …

– Naw, it's the nitrate like, the poppers. Ah find the bottle. It's got soas ah don't get anything out of the shagging now without the amyl nitrate. Es are mair sensual than sexual, but you've got to have the nitrate though, man, no really an optional extra, now really as essential as a cock or a fanny like.

So well, so well, we're still playing skin games and this is so good cause I'm still rushing and the tactile sensitivity has been increased a mere tenfold by the ecky and our skins are so sensitive it's like we can just reach inside each other and caress all those internal bits and pieces and we work ourselves round into the sixty-nine and as ah start licking and she does there's no way that I, at any rate, am no going to come quickly so we break off and ah get on top and inside her and then she's on top of me and then I'm on top of her and then she's on top of me, but it's a bit too much theatrics from her, ah suspect; could be wrong, perhaps she's just inexperienced because she must only be about eighteen or something when I'm thirty fucking one which is possibly too old to be carrying on like this when ah could be married to a nice fat lady in a nice suburban house with children and a steady job where ah have urgent reports to write informing senior management that unless certain action is taken the organisation could suffer, but it's me and Purple Haze here together, fuck sake

and now it's getting better, more relaxed, soulful. It's getting good …

… it's fine fine fine and Haze and ah spill fluids in and over each other and I'm sticking the amyl nitrate up her nose and mines and we're holding onto that high crashing wave of an orgasm together

WHOA HO HO

HO HO

HO

OOOHHHHHOOOOOOOOOOOOOOHHHHHHHHHHHHHHHH

OOOOOOOOOOOOOOOOOOOOOOOOHHHHHHHHHHHHHH
HHH!!!!!!!!!!!!!!!!!!!!!

Ah like the after-feeling with my heart pumping from orgasm and nitrate. It's barry feeling ma body readjust, ma heartbeat slow doon.

– That was brilliant! Hazel says.

– It was ... ah try tae find the words, – fruity. A full, fruit-flavoured one.

Ah wonder if anyone will be up for cocktails at Old Orleans later today or tomorrow night, or is it now tonight?

We talk for a bit, and then join the others. It's really weird how you can be so intimate with someone you dinnae really ken on E. Ah dinnae really ken Hazel, but you can have a barry ride oaf ay a stranger oan Ecky. It takes a long time tae get that intimate oan straight street. Ye huv tae build up tae it, eh.

Ally's right over to me. – That wee Hazel, a total wee doll. Dirty cunt man, you, eh. Fuck sake, Lloyd, ah wish ah wis sixteen now and had aw this. Punk and that, that was shite compared tae this ...

Ah look at him and then look around the room, – But ye have got it, ya daft cunt, just like you had punk, just ye'll have the next thing that comes along, cause you refuse tae grow up. Ye just like tae have yir cake n eat it. It's the only fuckin way, man.

– Nae point in huvin yir cake if ye cannae fuckin well scran it back, eh, no?

– This is brilliant ... how wis Tenerife by the way? Ye never really telt ays.

– Ace, man. Better than Ibiza. Ah'm no jokin. Ye should've come, Lloyd. You'd have lapped it up.

– Ah really wanted tae, Ally, but the hireys fucked it but, eh. Cannae save, that's ma problem. What aboot John Bogweed last week? How wis that?

– John Bigheid? Shite.

– Aye.

– Happens though, eh.

– Aye ... jist nivir goat intae the stuff eh wis playin ... mind you, some ay it wis awright ... you're a dirty cunt ...

– Ah know, ah know. You should fire intae Amber. She's up fir ye, man.

– Fuck Lloyd, man, ah cannae be bothered shaggin Amber. I've started tae feel bad aboot chasin wee dolls, fillin thir heids wi shite and knobbing them, then runnin like fuck until the weekend, man. Ah feel like ah'm between fourteen and sixteen years auld again, when it was just a shag tae try and get it over wi as soon as possible. Headin straight back tae the first stage ay sexual development, me, eh, man.

– Ah aye, what's the next stage?

– Ye take your time, gie the lassie a good feel, try to get her tae come, find clitoris, try oral sex … that wis me fae aboot sixteen tae aboot eighteen. Then eftir that, fae aboot eighteen tae aboot twenty one, it wis eywis positions wi me. Dae it different weys, try different approaches like doggy style, on chairs, up the erse and aw that sort of stuff, sort ay sexual gymnastics. The next stage was tae find a lassie and try tae tune intae each other's internal rhythms. Make music thegither. The thing is, Lloyd, ah think ah've passed that stage and ah'm headin back in the full circle when ah want tae go forward.

– Maybe yuv jist covered everything, ah venture.

– Naw, he snaps, – no way. Ah want that kind ay psychic communion, gittin right inside each other's nut, like astral flight and that. He presses his forefinger onto my head. – And that period is now until I find it. Never had it, man. Had the internal rhythms, but no the joining ay the souls. Never even came close. The eckies help, but the only way you can get the joining ay the souls is if you let her into your head and she lets you into hers, at the same time. It's communication, man. You can't get that with any Party Chick, even when you're both E'd up. It has to be love. That's what ah'm really lookin for, Lloyd: love.

Ah smile into his big eyes and say, – Yir a fuckin sexual philosopher, Mister Boyle.

– Naw ah'm no jokin. Ah'm lookin for love.

– Maybe that's what we're all really looking for, Ally.

– The thing is Lloyd, man, mibee ye cannae look fir it. Mibee it hus tae find you.

– Aye, but until ye do, ye want a fuckin good ride but, eh.

★

Later on, Amber tearfully tells me that Ally's rejected her and won't sleep with her cause he doesnae love her as a lover, just as a pal. Nukes is in the kitchen with us and he just throws his hands up as if this is aw too heavy and says, – Ah'm away … see yis … But ah notice that the cunt has left wi this lassie, and this is the cue for everybody to head off but ah stay back and try to explain Ally's stance to Amber and Hazel and do some lines of coke with her and we watch the sun come up and discuss everything. Hazel goes through to bed but Amber wants to stay up talking. Eventually, though, she falls asleep on the couch. Ah go through to another bedroom and get a quilt and put it over her. She looks peaceful. She needs a boyfriend: a nice young guy who'll look after her and let her look after him. Ah think about getting intae bed with Hazel and crashing but ah could feel the distance growing between us with the MDMA running down in our bodies. Ah head hame and although I'm not religious ah pray for a boyfriend for Amber and a special girlfriend each for Ally and me. I'm not religious but ah just like the idea ay friends hoping for good things for each other; like the idea of all this goodwill floating around in psychic space.

Back hame ah neck two eggs and wash them down with a bottle of Becks. Ah stagger tae bed where a strange, disturbed sleep descends on me. Ah'm in Cunt City's familiar district of Shag-You-Up-The-Fuckin-Hole.

part one

The Over-whelming Love Of Ecstasy

1 Heather

You're typing up that report using the mainframe's word-processing package and Brian Case, *Mister* Case, is leering around and says: — How's the light of my life today? What you want to say is that I'm not the light of your life, or if I am you seriously need to get one, you sad, demented creep, but you need the job and you don't need the hassle so you just smile and keep typing your data onto the screen.

Only it hurts inside.

It hurts inside because you are called something you aren't, seen in a way you aren't. That's why it hurts.

On the way home I stop off in a pub. This bar in the East Port. The last two weeks I've glanced in here, trying to pluck up the courage to go in. Looking at all the drinkers, hearing the noise, the odd raucous laugh, smelling the smoke. When I eventually walked through the door I thought it would be a powerful cathartic moment. But I don't even realise I'm at the bar until I'm asking an old guy with a lined face for a gin and tonic. What am I doing here?

I never go into

I never

Because Liz asked me to come. Liz. She isn't even here yet.

It seems like it's all men here in the bar this dinner-time, even though they've done it up to make it more trendy. One prick looks at me like I'm soliciting. Here. In the East Port Bar. Dunfermline. Here! It would be laughable. It should be laughable. Things just aren't funny now, though. I've laughed for too long. Laughed when I didn't know why I was laughing.

Liz comes in. I get another gin and tonic for me with the one I get for her. Liz and I. Still friends, despite being assigned to different offices. Official reason: beneficial to our career development to have the opportunity to work with different people in different teams in different areas. The opportunity to increase our skillsbase. This was a power our union recently negotiated for the bosses to have: increased flexibility. The opportunity to input data into a different machine in a different office. The real reason we were moved, of course, is that we got on together and had a good time and they don't like people to be *too* happy at work.

Liz is older than me. She chain-smokes and drinks loads of gin. I live with Hugh, *in a house*, but I *live* for my laughs with Liz. And Marie, my best pal Marie.

2 Lloyd

My head is a bit fucked; basically cause ah took a couple ay jellies tae come doon. Stupidity and sleaze, that's what it is. Schemie windows. Ah look at the world through schemie windows. The phone rings by the bed. Nukes is on the other end of the line.

– Lloyd … it's me.

– Nukes. Awright. Recovered fae last night, or wis it this mornin? Ah cannae git gaun, man. Took a couple ay these fuckin jellies tae come doon …

– Tell ays aboot it. Ye gaun tae the fitba?

– Naw … ah fancy a pint.

– Ah'm intae seein what the view's like fae the new stands, eh.

– Fuck the new stands up the hole, man.

– They look awright but … fuckin better than the Jambo's shite.

– Aye, cheap B&Q flatpack rubbish. Gary MacKay knocked them up when thir wis nae fitba oan Sky one night. Dinnae ken if ah could sit in the one place for ninety minutes but, Nukes …

– Awright then chavvy, we'll keep oor options open …

– Sound.

– Right, see ye in The Windsor in half an hour. Dinnae phone up Ally but. If ah hear that cunt spraffin oan again aboot how good Jon Digweed wis the other week, or aboot how brilliant Tenerife is, ah'll throw the cunt in front ay a bus.

– Right … that chancin cunt telt me Digweed wis shite.

– The cunt sais the same aboot Tony Humphries. Eh eywis starts the night by saying everything's shite. Later oan ye hear um tell some cunt it wis no bad and then, by the end ay the night, aw eh kin talk aboot is how brilliant it wis.

Ah take a shower and try tae get moving. These fuckin jellies:

never again. Ah stagger out up the Walk tae meet Nukes. We go off on the pish. We take a couple ay jellies each to save money. Nukes had a sound argument: — Ye get the same effect with a couple ay jellies and four pints that you would get fae thirty pints. Why gie they brewer cunts the money and waste time?

The afternoon dissolves into a sludgy evening. — Ah'm fucked, man, ah say to Nukes. Ah drift off intae the City Of The Cunted, Noddyland, and get shaken back intae Planet Leith by the barman. He's saying something but ah can't make out what it is. Ah wobble along out the door. Ah can hear Nukes singing Hibs songs but ah can't see the cunt. Ah dinnae ken whair we are, we seem tae be up the toon. Ah hear people laughing at me, sort of posh voices. Then I'm in this taxi and I'm in another pub in Leith. Ah hear a guy shouting at me, — That was the cunt that shagged his sister, and ah tried to say something but ah was too drunk, and ah hear another guy saying, — Naw, he's Lloyd Buist, Vaughan Buist's brother, eh mate. You're thinkin ay the other Lloyd, Lloyd Beattie that boy's name wis.

— Dinnae tell ays thirs two fuckin Lloyd's in Leith, one guy sais.

Next thing ah know is that I'm talking to ma mate Woodsy, whae ah havenae seen in yonks, and he's gaun oan about God, drink and E. He takes me back to his and ah crash.

3 Heather

Hugh's home. He works later than I do. He has a more responsible position. He's responsible. What is he responsible for? — Good day? he smiles, briefly breaking off from whistling the Dire Straits song 'Money For Nothing'.

— Yeah, ah say, — No bad. What do you want for tea? I should have got something ready before this. I just couldn't be bothered.

I've spent over an hour doing my nails: clipping, filing, painting, it all takes time. Time just sort of flies past.

— Whatever there is, he says, switching on the news.

— Eh, scrambled egg on toast okay?

— Great.

I go through to make the eggs. — How was your day? I shout.

— Not bad, I hear his voice coming through from the next room, — Jenny and I did a presentation for the area management team on zoning. It seemed to be well received, he stuck his head round the door, — I think we'll persuade them.

— Nice one, I say, trying to fuse enthusiasm into my tone.

Hugh and I left university at the same time and went to work for different local authorities. He's now the manager of a building society and I'm exactly where I was six years ago.

It's nobody's fault but my own.

If I loved him, it wouldn't be so bad. I once thought I did. He was what I thought a rebel was: working-class, into student politics. What a lot of fucking nonsense.

— I'm going out tonight, I tell him.

— Oh … he says.

— With Liz. From my work. Now that we work in different offices

we never get a chance to see each other. I'm just going round to hers.
Probably get a takeaway and a bottle of wine.

    – There's a good film on Two tonight, he says.

    – Oh aye?

    – *Wall Street*. Michael Douglas.

    – Oh right. I said to Liz but.

    – Oh yeah. I see.

    – Fine then.

    – Fine.

Fine. I meet Liz in MacDonald's, then we're back in the East Port Bar
and we've downed some gins and then it's a taxi out to Kelty and to
the club. – What ye daein gaun oot tae Kelty, girls? Only hoors n
miners come fae Kelty, the taxi driver tells us.

    – Hi! Enough ay that, neebs! Ah come fae Kelty! Liz says.

    – What pit is it ye worked at, hen? the driver asks, before dropping
us off in the club car-park.

We got in and found seats in the corner. There was a huge
mirrored ball in the centre of the dance-floor. Liz cast her eye over to
a table near the bar.

    – That's ma ex, she said, – Davie. Good-lookin felly, eh? She
nodded over at a guy concentrating on his bingo card. He was soon
making his way towards us.

I nodded at Liz's remark with as much enthusiasm as I could
muster, but I wasn't really in full agreement. You could tell that
Davie's looks had once been there, but that impression was more to
do with his flirty confidence than any physical tasties the ravages of
time and drink had left over. He gazed over at me and smiled almost
moronically. There was something though.

    – It was the blue eyes ah fell fir, Liz said, as Davie came through the
crowd and sat beside us.

    – How ye doin, hen? And who's this lovely young lady?

    – This is Heather fae the work.

    – Hello, I said.

    – Glad to make your acquaintance, Heather. And can I get you
lovely ladies a drink?

– Two G&Ts would go down well, Liz said.

– As good as done, Davie smiled, heading for the bar.

Davie not so much played to the strength of his big blue eyes, as put all his eggs into the one seductive bucket. Soon his playing around with his gaze made him look more than vaguely cretinous.

– The trouble wis, Liz confirmed my suspicions as he went up to the toilet, – thir wisnae that much gaun oan behind those eyes.

4 Lloyd

Ah woke up on Woodsy's couch feeling shitey. Ah was sick, with a dentist-drill headache and my lip was burst and swollen and ah had like a nasty smudged bit of purple black mascara under my right eye. This reminded me why ah took Class As instead of alcohol. Ah mind ay Nukes and me paggering. Fuck knows whether it was wi each other or some other fucker. Given the slightness of my wounds it was probably some other fucker cause Nukes is a hard cunt and would have done me a lot more damage.

— You fucked it up goodstyle last night, eh? Woodsy said, bringing me a cup of tea.

— Aye, ah said, still too out off it to feel too apologetic, — Nukes n me hit the satellite tellies and went for it. Ended up in some brawl.

— Youse cunts are fuckin crazy. Alcohol's Satan's instrument, man. As fir jellies … well, it's no often that ah agree wi that poofy wee Tory cunt on the telly … but fuckin hell, man, ah expect such behaviour fae Nukes, him being a cashie n that, but ah thought you'd have a wee bit mair savvy, Lloyd.

— Aw Woodsy, man, ah pleaded. That cunt Woodsy was still on this religion kick. He'd kept at it, mind you, it was last summer when it began. The cunt had claimed to have seen God after two Supermarios and two snowballs at the outdoor Rezurrection. We dumped him in the Garage Room tae chill, he seemed tae be overheating badly. Ah stuck a Volvic in his hand and left him to the pink elephants. Wrong really, but ah was so fucking up and the light show was so phenomenal in the main tent that ah wanted tae get back to the action. Two maternalish Party Chicks kept an indulgent eye on him.

The careplan fucked up when Woodsy's queasy attack necessitated him leaving the Party Chicks and heading for the chemical bogs to converse with the big aluminium telephone. It was in one of those putrid traps that he met the Big Chief.

The worst thing was that God apparently told him that Ecstasy was His gift to those in the know, who then had the duty to spread the word. He apparently instructed Woodsy to set up a Rave Gospel club.

Now ah didnae ken whether or no Woodsy's head had fried, or he was on some self-important control kick; perhaps a Koresh-style scam to access as many Party Chicks as required. Are you receiving me, girls? Are you really ready to receive me, and all that head-fucking schissee, shit, merde, shite. Whatever, he was picking the wrong drug for a control freak. The only person you can control on E is yourself. Koresh wouldn't have lasted five minutes if he had his posse E'd in Waco. Cut the fuckin religious shit, Davey ma man, we came to dance ...

— Listen, Lloyd, you still goat they Technics decks at yours?

— Aye, bit thir Shaun's like. Jist till eh comes back fae Thailand, eh.

Shaun was gaunny be away for a year, but if he had any sense he'd stey away for good, and Shaun was a sharp cunt. He'd teamed up with this guy from Lancashire called The Crow, and they had made a small fortune screwing rich cunt's hooses. They had wisely decided tae call it quits before they did that one job too many and hit the trail to Thailand via Goa. Nice for them and nice for me as ah inherited the decks and Shaun's record collection which boasted some ice-cool soul rarities.

— Ye must be gitting quite good oan them, eh?

— Awright, aye, ah lied. Ah'd only been looking after the decks for a couple of months. Ah had nae sense ay timing, nae motor skills and no a great deal ay vinyl. Ah had wanted tae practise oan them mair, but ah had been doing some joinery work on the side with my mate Drewsy and ah was daein quite a bit ay dealing for The Poisonous Cunt.

— Look, Lloyd, ah've goat this gig organised at the Reck-Tangle

Club in Pilton. Ah want you oan the bill. You first, then me. What
dae ye think?

— When's this?

— Next month. The fourteenth. It's a while likes.

— Sound. Count ays in.

Ah was shite on the decks but ah reasoned that a deadline would
force ays tae get my act thegither. Ah wisnae so chuffed when
Woodsy telt me he wanted samplings of hymns and gospel music
mixed intae techno, house, garage and ambient stuff, but ah was still
up for it.

Anyway, ah decided tae spend a lot of time at home with the
decks. A lot ay my mates, especially Nukes, Ally and Amber, were
pretty supportive. They came round for a blow, and often brought
dance records they'd borrowed. Ah started going tae a few clubs
straight to watch the DJs and see what they did. My favourite was
Craig Smith, the Edinburgh DJ at Solefusion, who always seemed to
be having loads of fun with what he was doing. Too many seemed
po-faced cunts with no spirit, and it showed in the Richard
Millhouse. Ye cannae gie other cunts enjoyment if you cannae enjoy
it yourself.

One afternoon ah was settling down to a bit of Richard Nixon when
the door went. Ah had the music on low, but ah still thought it was
the yuppie cunts across the landing who complained about anything
and everything.

Ah opened the door and before me stood auld Mrs McKenzie
from doonstairs. — Soup, she spat out, her face screwed up.

Ah remembered. Ah had forgotten to go to the supermarket to get
ingredients for a pot of soup. Ah always make a big pot on a Thursday
before the weekend ay abuse starts so ah know I've got something
nutritious in if I'm too fucked or skint tae dae anything else. Ah take
auld Mrs McKenzie some doon in a tupperware bowl. She's a nice
auld cunt, but what started off as a one-off gesture of goodwill has
now evolved into custom and practice and it's starting tae fracture ma
tits tae pieces.

— Sorry, Mrs Mack, no had a chance tae make it yit eh no.

– Aye … ah jist thought … soup … the laddie upstairs usually brings doon a bowl ay soup oan a Thursday … ah wis jist tellin Hector. Soup … ah wis jist sayin tae Hector the other day. Soup. The laddie up the stairs. Soup.

– Aye, ah'll be makin it in a bit.

– Soup soup soup … ah thought we'd be gittin some soup.

– It's aw in hand, Mrs Mack, ah kin assure ye ay that.

– Soup …

– THE SOUP ISN'T READY YET MISSUS MCKENZIE. WHEN I'VE MADE IT, WHICH WILL BE LATER ON TODAY, I SHALL BRING SOME DOWN TO YOU. OKAY?

– Soup. Later on.

– THAT'S IT, MISSUS MCKENZIE. SOUP. LATER ON.

Ah must have been making a racket cause the Straight-Peg woman across the way comes tae her door to investigate the noise. – Are you okay, Mrs McKenzie? Did the noise from that music disturb you too? she asks the auld dear, the fuckin self-centred manipulative soulless cunt.

– The soup's comin, Mrs Mack said, cheerful and appeased as she moved painstakingly slowly along the landing and down the stairs.

Ah went back inside, wrapped it on the Richard and headed oot tae the shops tae get the ingredients for the soup. As ah left there was a message on the answer-machine. It was a long rambling statement fae Nukes that actually said nothing except that he had his hoose raided by the polis.

5 Heather

As if.

As if the physical proximity can make up for the emotional distance.

He's holding me tightly, but there's no love or tenderness in it, just desperation. Perhaps it's to do with the realisation that I'm slipping away from him, slipping away from this world he wants me to inhabit: his world, which is not our shared world.

It's not our shared world cause I'm his, his property and he won't relinquish it easily. I'm a source of comfort, a teddy bear for a grown-up wee boy. Only they'd never see him as that and if they did see through the mind-shaking immaturity of this supposedly successful man, they'd only find it endearing, like I once did. Only I don't now, because it's sad and pathetic.

He's a fucking retard.

What does he get out of acting like that?

He thrives while I'm dying inside.

He should be dying too, but he's not.

He's not because he has me to do it for him.

What do I want? Love is not enough. It has to do with being in love. I love my mother, my father. I don't want another mummy and daddy. I used to. I used to by default because I didn't know what I really wanted.

I don't want to be protected. Hugh protects.

I used to need that too.

But Hugh, I've been growing up inside, growing up more than you want me to. You used to tell me that I had to grow up. You'd fear me if you saw who I really was. I think you already do. That's why you're holding on, holding on for dear life.

Dying inside.

Growing up inside.

How do you reconcile them?

6 Lloyd

When ah got back from the supermarket with the soup ingredients, ah was just in the door when the bell behind me sounded tersely. It was The Poisonous Cunt and she was in tow with The Victim whose coupon was fixed in a nervous, tense stare which even my most open smile couldn't break down.

The Victim was a chronic fuck-up. People like her always seemed to hang out with The Poisonous Cunt. In turn, she kept their self-esteem low and made sure that they stayed in psychic immiseration. She was a curator of dead souls. It concerned me that ah seemed tae be spending more time with The Poisonous Cunt; we just turned each other onto suppliers of drugs, and good deals. Ah had once shagged The Victim, when ah was coked up ah bullshitted her intae bed one night … intae bed, my arse, it was actually onto the flair, the flair behind the couch where Ally was shagging this lassie he'd met at Pure. Anyway, The Victim gave ays hassle for weeks after, with phone calls, at clubs, etc. She had a tendency to put up with anything, and was into any form of attention. That was why she eywis ended up in abusive relationships.

– Diddly dit dit dee, two ladies, ah sang at them with a cheerfulness ah didnae feel as ah ushered them in, only to be met with frost. The Poisonous Cunt rolled her bottom lip downwards like an inverted red carpet. She had that fatigued, irritated air of a young woman who had seen more than she should but had not yet seen what she wanted, and had just about decided to wrap it rather than look further.

– Wait here, she snapped at The Victim who began to softly bubble. Ah went over tae do a bit of token stagey comforting, but The Poisonous Cunt wrenched my arm and pulled me into the kitchen, shutting the door behind us and lowering her voice so much that ah could only see her lips move.

– Eh? ah asked her.

– She's fucked up.

– What's new? ah shrugged, but ah don't think The Poisonous Cunt heard ays.

– She's deluding herself, ah told that to her, she said, sucking on a fag and contorting her face in a mask of hateful contempt. – You're fuckin well livin in a fool's paradise, hen, ah said tae her, Lloyd. But she widnae listen. Now she's getting it aw back. And who's the first one she comes runnin tae?

– Right … right … ah nodded as empathetically as ah could, loading my food from the shopping bag into the cupboard and fridge.

– She misses fuckin periods aw the time and goes through this 'I'm up the stick' shite. Ah felt like saying to her: you cannae get up the stick when he's shagging you up the arse, but ah didnae. Ah felt like saying tae her: the reason you always miss periods is because you're fucked up in the heid, hen; your life's a mess and if you're that fucked in the heid it's bound tae tell on yir body.

– Ah see, ah see … her and Bobby again …

The Victim's current principal exploiter was a crazy biker guy called Bobby who ah'd known for years. Bobby had a split personality. One side of him was pure evil, the other completely cuntish.

– But ah bit ma tongue. Thing is, Lloyd, he came roond and started playin mind games wi her. Solo wis just fuckin laughin, so we had tae get oot. We just want tae sit here and chill for a bit until that bastard Bobby goes.

– Look, that's sound by me, but ye'll huv tae dae it alaine, eh. Ah'm meetin this boy whaes supposed tae have some ay they pink champagnes, the speedballs, ken?

– Git me five … naw, six … she rasped, rummaging through her bag for her purse.

– That's if ehs goat thum likes, ah said, taking her money. Ah wasnae gaunnae try and score, ah was just going to my brothers for a scran. It wasnae just because it didnae sound cool enough tae tell The

Poisonous Cunt that; it was because she was a nasty, nosey bastard and ah didnae want her kennin too much aboot ays.

Ah left them to it, clocking The Victim's arse in her black stretch leggings before ah left, both strangely pleased and disappointed no tae feel any reaction whatsoever.

Ah took the bus at the foot ay the Walk tae ma brother Vaughan's. Ah was a bit late. When ah got there, ah had to ring for ages. Vaughan was out and Fiona, my sister-in-law, was in the back playing with my niece, Grace, who was two and a bit of nutter, like two year aulds are.

– Lloyd! ah thought it was you. Come in, come in.

Ah clocked that Vaughan had been at the decorating but ah didnae say anything. The hoose was furnished in tasteless Habitat country-style, ridiculous in a suburban semi. That was Vaughan and Fiona. Ah love them in a strange way – a tense, dutiful love – but you cannae say nowt tae cunts like that about taste. It just isnae an issue with them. It comes oot the page ay a catalogue.

Ah asked Fiona if ah could use the phone and she took the hint and took Grace out into the gairdin. Ah called Nukes. – What's the story? ah asked him.

– That's me finished wi the cashies and the collies. Ah'm a marked man now, Lloyd. Polis doon here the other night accusin ays ay sorts ay things, man. Well oot ay order.

– Ye git charged?

– Naw, but it shit ays up. Some ay the boys say no tae worry, but fuck that, man. Ah'm daein a bit ah dealin and that could be three fuckin years oot ma life jist for a bit ay swedgin at the fitba.

– Ah wis gaunnae ask if you could punt some stuff fir ays n aw ...

– No way. Low profile for a while, that's me.

– Awright then. Come doon fir a blow next week but, eh.

– Awright.

– Cheers, Nukes ... eh, ye mind ay what happened the other night? Did we git intae some bother?

– Ye dinnae want tae ken, Lloyd.

– Nukes ...

The line clicked dead.

That was me para as fuck, but no as para as Nukes. Something was bugging the cunt bigtime. Ah knew that Nukes wasnae so intae the casuals these days, but he still got it together for the odd big swedge. Ah could never understand the attraction, but he swore by the rush. If he's kent by the polis, though, that's bad news; when you're holding just a few drugs for you and your mates, they call you a dealer. He was being sensible, n ah resolved that ah was going tae try tae take it easy n aw for a bit.

– Like the new colour? Fiona asks.

Grace climbed up on me and tried to push my eyeball out of its socket. Ah removed her hand before she could go for my other eye, the one that was bruised. – Aye, it's sound. Very relaxing. Ah wis jist gaunnae say, ah lied. – Ye must have been keepin Vaughan busy, eh, no? Where is eh?

Grace climbed down and ran over to Fiona and wrapped herself around her leg.

– Three guesses, Fiona smiled in the kind of way that changed her from being a young housewife into a shag.

– The boolin? ah asked.

– Right first time, she nodded wearily. – He said to tell you to meet him doon thair for a pint. The dinner'll no be ready till five.

– Sound … ah said. It wisnae really sound. Ah would rather have stayed with Fiona and Grace than listened to Vaughan's shite. – … eh, but maybe I'll jist chill here for a bit.

– Lloyd, I've got loads to do. I don't want you under my feet, one bairn's enough, she smirked.

– Thanks a lot, ah laughed, pretending at being hurt. We continued with this ritual. It was pathetic and dull, but it often gave me a strange, queasy feeling of exhilaration to talk bland shite with people and not worry about being a smart cunt simply because you were linked in some way to each other. It was a wild trip.

Too much ay this shite can fuck a cunt's heid but, and after a while ah decided ah'd better go and see Vaughan.

It was a pretty glorious summer's evening when ah got out in the street. Ah found myself with a strange spring in my step. Of course, it was Thursday. Last weekend's drugs had been well and truly processed by now, the toxins discharged: sweated, shat and pished out; the hangover finito; the psychological self-loathing waning as the chemistry of the brain de-fucked itself and the fatigue sinking into the past as the old adrenalin pump starts slowly getting back into gear in preparation for the next round ay abuse. This feeling, when you've cracked the depressive hangover and the body and mind is starting to fire up again, is second only to coming up on a good E.

At the club, Vaughan's playing bools with this old cunt. He nods at me, and the auld cunt looks up with a slightly tetchy stare and ah realise that I've broken his concentration by casting my shadow over his line of vision. Steeling himself, the auld codger lets the bool roll, roll, roll and I'm thinking he's gone too far out, but naw, the wily auld cunt kens the score because the bool does a Brazilian spin, that's what it does, a fuckin Brazilian spin, and it comes back like a fuckin boomerang and slips like a surreptitious queue-jumper in behind Vaughan's massed lines of defence, rolling up to the jack and sneaking it away.

Ah cheer the auld gadge for that shot. Vaughan has his last one but ah decide no tae watch it but to go in and get some drinks. Ah discover I've a wrap of speed in my pocket, left over from fuck knows when. Ah take it to the bog, and chop it out into some lines on the cistern. If I'm gaunny have to talk bools ah might as well fuckin go for it in a big way … Ah come out, charged up to fuck. Ah remember this gear, dabbing away at it the other week. It's much better to snort though, this stuff.

– Didnae stay for the climax, Vaughan says, looking deflated. – Could have done wi yir support fir that last shot thair.

– Sorry, Vaughan, ah wis burstin fir a tropical fish, eh. Did ye git it?

– Naw, eh wis miles oot! The auld cunt roars. The auld cunt is dressed in white slacks, a blue open-necked shirt and has a sunhat on.

Ah slap the auld cunt on the back, – Nice one there, mate! Brilliant shot by the way, that wee spinner that nicked it at the end. Ah'm Lloyd, Vaughan's brother.

– Aye Lloyd, ah'm Eric, he extends his hand and gies ays a crushing masonic grip, – ye play the bools yersel?

– Naw, Eric, naw ah dinnae, mate; it's no really ma scene, ken. Ah mean ah'm no knockin the game n that, a great game … ah mean ah wis chillin oot the other day watchin that Richard Corsie gadge oan the box … he used tae be wi the Post, did eh no? That boy kens how tae fling a bool …

Fuck me, this Lou Reed is hitting the mark quickstyle.

– Eh, what yis wantin? Vaughan shouts, a wee bit embarrassed at ma ranting.

– Naw naw naw, ah'll git them. Three lager, is it no?

– Poof's pish, Eric scoffs, – make mine Special.

– A special drink for a special victory, eh, Eric, ah smile. The auld cunt gie ays one back. – Yuv goat Vaughan's puss seekint here right enough!

– Aye, right, Vaughan goes, – are you gaunnae git them in, or what?

Ah hit the bar and the guy behind says that you have to have a tray to get served, and ah joke that I've got enough to carry as it is and he says something short like house rules, but a wee cunt in the queue hands me one anyway. I've forgotten about all the daft fuckin rules they have in places like this, the Brylcreemed cunts wi their blazers wi the club badges on them and how at closing time there's mair falling masonry than when the Luftwaffe bombed Coventry cathedral … and now I'm back at my seat.

– Cheers, boys! ah say, raising my pint, – Tell ye what, Eric, ah knew that you had the bools after seeing ye in action there. This gadge has bools, ah telt maself. That Brazilian spin, man! Whoa, ya cunt that ye fuckin well are!

– Aye, said Eric, smugly, – it wis a wee thing ah thought ah'd try. Ah said tae masel, Vaughan's marshalled his defences well, but, ah thought, try a wee sneaky one roond the backdoor, and it just might come off.

– Aye, it wis a good shot, Vaughan conceded.

– It wis fuckin ace, ah told him. – You've heard of total fitba, the Dutch invented it, right? Well this man here, ah nodded towards

Eric, – is total bools. You could've went for the blast there, Eric, tried that Premier League style huffing and puffing but naw, a bit ay class, a bit ay art.

The pint was drained. Vaughan hit the bar.

This was always a thing with Vaughan when he met me. He had a sense of duty, of the responsibilities ay a married man and a parent, so that whenever he did have an allocated time he would try tae squeeze as many units of alcohol into it as he possibly could. And he could drink. Thank fuck it was draught Becks ah was on. Ah wouldnae touch any Scottish shite, especially McEwan's lager, the vile toxic pish that it is, for anything. The pints kept flowing and this speed was still digging in, and ah was almost hyperventilating. The thing is, it was like auld Eric got dragged in by the vibe, by the exuberance, and it was like the auld bastard had snorted a few lines n aw.

After a quick draining of the next pint he came back wi some mair beers, wi nips as chasers.

– Fuckin hell! ah said, – Expect the unexpected wi this man, eh?

– Aye, too right, Vaughan smiled. Vaughan was looking at us both with a big, indulgent those-are-mad-cunts-but-I-love-them smile. It made me feel close to him.

– Ye should go up n see Ma n Dad, Vaughan told me.

– Aye, ah guiltily conceded, – ah've been meanin tae drop by this tape ah made up for them. Motown, eh.

– Good. They'll appreciate that.

– Aye, Marvin, Smokey, Aretha n aw that, ah said, then promptly changed the subject, turnin tae Eric, – Listen, Eric, that stunt you pulled wi the bools, ah began.

– Aye, Eric cut in, – fair took the wind oot ay Vaughan here's sails, that's if ye dinnae mind ays sayin like, Vaughan! Eric laughed. – Expect the unexpected!

– Do-do-do-do, do-do-do-do, ah start the Twilight Zone theme tune, then ah think of something, – Listen, Eric, your second name isnae Cantona, by any chance, is it?

– Eh naw, Stewart, he said.

– It's just that there wis a Cantonaesque quality aboot that final shot thair, ah began giggling, a real dose ay the Flight Lieutenants, and Eric did too, – it fair blew fuckin Vaughan Ryan's Express right out the water …

– Aye … awright then, ya cunts, Vaughan sulked.

– Ooh ah, Cantona, ah started, and Eric joined in. A few groups of drinkers and auld couples looked over at us.

Encouraged, auld Eric and ah were up doing the can-can: na, na na, na na na na na na na na, na, na na, na na na na na na …

– Hey, come oan now, that's enough. Thir's folk here tryin tae enjoy a drink, a mumpy cunt with a blazer and badge moans.

– Aye, well nae herm done! auld Eric shouts back, then says in lower voice tae us, but still enough for every cunt tae hear, – What's his fuckin problem?

– C'moan Eric … Vaughan goes, – Lloyd's no a member here.

– Aye, well, the laddie's been signed in. Signed in as a guest. It's aw bona fide. Wir no daein herm. Like ah sais, nae herm done, Eric shook his heid.

– Procedures have been observed, eh, Eric, ah smirk.

– The situation's completely bona fide, Eric confirms stoically.

– Ah think a certain Monsieur Vaughan Buist may be smarting over a recent sporting setback, n'est-ce pas, Monsieur Cantona? He ees, ow you say, ay leetal peesed off.

– Je suis une booler, Eric cackles.

– It's no that, Lloyd, Vaughan mumps, – Aw ah'm tryin tae say is thit you're no a member here. Yir a guest. Yir the responsibility ay the people that bring ye. That's aw ah'm tryin tae say.

– Aye … bit nae herm done … mumbles Eric.

– It's jist like that club you go tae, Lloyd. That place up at The Venue. What's that club called?

– The Pure.

– Aye, right. It's like if you're at The Pure n ah wis tae come up n you were tae sign ays in …

– As ma guest, ah snorted, laughing uncontrollably at the thought. Ah heard auld Eric start as well. It got soas we were gaunnae peg oot.

– As your guest … Vaughan had started now. Ah thought: this is me fucked. Flight Lieutenant Biggles, hovering over the grim metropolis of Cunt City … Auld Eric started wheezing, as Vaughan carried on, – as the guest of one's brother Lloyd at the exclusive club in town he frequents …

We were interrupted by a choking sound as auld Eric boaked thin beer-sick ower the table. The humpty cunt with the blazer and badge was right ower to him and grabbed up his pint. – That's it! Oot, c'moan! Oot!

Vaughan grabbed the pint back. – That's no fuckin well it at aw, Tommy.

– Aye it bloody well is! That's it, the humpty cunt snapped.

– Dinnae fuckin well come ower tae this table n say that's it, Vaughan said, – cause that's no it at aw.

Ah slapped Eric on the back and helped the auld cunt to his feet and through to the lavvy. – It's a sair ficht, right enough, ah caught him gasp between mouthfuls of sick as he spewed up into the bog pan.

– Aye, Eric, yir awright, man. Nae danger, ah said encouragingly. Ah felt like ah was at Rez, talking Woodsy down when he had his freak-out, but here ah was with a daft auld cunt in a bowling club.

We got Eric hame. It was an auld hoose where the door led straight oantae the main road. We propped him against it and rang the bell and moved away. A woman answered and pulled him in and slammed the door shut. Ah heard the sound of blows and Eric's screams from behind the door, – Dinnae, Betty … ah'm sorry, Betty … dinnae hit ays again …

Then we went back tae Vaughan's. The meal was a bit dried oot, and Fiona wisnae pleased at our state. Ah didnae want tae eat anything, but ah scranned with fake enthusiasm.

Ah felt heavy and embarrassed and ah left early, opting tae walk doon tae the port. As ah was coming doon Leith Walk, ah saw The Poisonous Cunt on the other side. Ah crossed over.

– Where ye gaun? ah asked.

– Just gaun back tae yours. Ah phoned Solo and he wanted ays tae pick up some stuff for him. You're pished!

– A bit, aye.

– Did ye git the speedballs?

Ah looked at her for a bit. – Naw … ah didnae see the boy, eh. Ah ran intae some cunt, eh no. Ah had a sudden twinge of fear. – Whaire's The Victim?

– Still at yours.

– Fuck!

– What is it?

– The Victim's bulimic! She'll clean oot aw that fuckin shoppin! Ye shouldnae huv left her oan her ain!

We hurried back to find that The Victim had eaten and vomited up the three raw cauliflowers ah had earmarked for Mrs McKenzie's soup.

Ah had to hit the Asians for some rotting overpriced ingredients – but fair enough ah suppose as the cunts've pulled ays oot a hole wi bevvy and skins many times – and then it took me ages, half pished, tae make the soup. The Poisonous Cunt had some tabs ay acid which she gave me in lieu of cash the scabby hoor owed ays. – Go lightly wi this stuff, Lloyd, it's the fucking business.

She played around on the decks with the phones for a while. Ah had to admit it, The Poisonous Cunt wisnae that bad, she seemed to have a good feel for it. Ah noted that she had a ring through her navel, exposed as it was by her short T-shirt. – Cool ring, ah shouted at her, and she gave me the thumbs-up and did a strange wee dance and flashed me a weird, ugly smile. If a Hollywood special effects department had been able tae reproduce that rictus grin it would have made several careers.

The Victim sat and sobbed at the TV, chain-smoking. The only thing she said to me was, – Any cigarettes, Lloyd … in a breathless, hoarse voice. Eventually they left and ah took the tupperware bowl down to Mrs McKenzie. Ah was heading through to Glasgow for the weekend to see some mates there. Ah was looking forward to it, fucked off as ah was wi Edinburgh. The thing was that ah had said tae ma mate Drewsy that I'd help him out the morn's morning which ah wisnae really up for but it wid be cash in hand and ah needed hireys for the weekend.

7 Heather

Happy families.

Me and Hugh and my Mum and my Dad. My Dad and Hugh are talking politics. My Dad's saying that he's for the NHS while Hugh's saying that we need to build a:

– ... responsibility-orientated society. That's why people should be free to choose the sort of health care and education they want.

– That's just Tory rubbish, my dad says.

– I think we have to face facts – that old-style socialism, as we used to perceive it, is long dead. It's now about appeasing different interest groups in a more diffused society; about taking what's best from both traditional right and left philosophies.

– Well, I'm afraid I'll always be a Labour man ...

– I'm Labour as well, always have been, says Hugh.

– You're New Labour, though, Hugh, I say. My mum looks disapprovingly at me.

Hugh looks a bit startled. – What?

– You're New Labour. Tony Blair Labour. Which is the same as Tory, only Major's probably further left than Blair. Blair's just a snidier version of Michael Portillo, which is why he'll do better than Portillo will ever do.

– I think it's a wee bit more sophisticated than that, Heather, Hugh says.

– No, I don't think it is. What's Labour planning to do for working-class people in this country if they get back in? Nothing.

– Heather ... Hugh says wearily.

– Well, I'm afraid I'll always vote Labour, my dad says.

– Labour and Tory are now both exactly the same, I tell them.

Hugh rolls his eyes in the direction of my mother as if to apologise for my behaviour. We agree in silence to change the subject and my dad says, – It wouldnae do if we all had the same opinions, would it?

The rest of the evening is pretty uneventful. Outside, in the car as we leave, Hugh says to me, – Somebody was a bit bolshy this evening.

– All I did was to say what I believe to be true. Why such a big deal?

– I wasn't making a big deal. You were. There was no need to be so combative.

– I wasn't being combative.

– I think you were a little, honey, he smiles, shaking his head. He looks that kind of wee-boy way and I want to kill him because of the horrible tenderness I feel inside towards him. – You're some broad, baby, he then says in an American gangster accent, and squeezes my leg. I'm happy to seethe inwardly as the tenderness evaporates.

8 Lloyd

Drewsy and me are in this Gumleyland ghetto. Ah think it's Carrick Knowe but it could be Colinton Mains. Ah was fucked and hungover in the van. – It's just a skirtin job, Lloyd. That and new doors. Take nae time at aw, he telt ays.

Drewsy always seems to be smiling because he has laughing eyes and Coke-bottle glasses. The thing is that he is a very happy cunt and gives off a good vibe. Ah worked with him ages ago out at Livingston in a sweatshop where we built house-panels, and since he went tae graft for himself he always puts a bit of casual my way if he can; which was champion the fuckin wonderhoarse fir the Double L. Oh. Y. D.

At the house, the boy, a Mr Moir, makes us a cup ay tea. – Anything you need, lads, just give's a shout. I'll be in the garden, he told us cheerfully.

Anywey, wir knockin oaf the rooms finestyle, and I'm starting tae feel better, looking ahead tae the night oot wi the weedgie cunts. Drewsy and me are in this room which is like a young lassie's bedroom. There's a big poster ay the boy fae Oasis oan one waw, one ay the gadge fae Primal Scream and one fae the dude oot ay Blur oan the other. Close tae the bed, though, is the boy oot ay Take That, him that went and left. There's a few tapes thair n aw. Ah pit oan Blur's *Parklife*, cause ah quite like the title track where ye hear the boy that wis in *Quadrophenia* spraffin away. That wis a fuckin good film.

Ah start singing along as ah rip oot the old skirting-board.

– Hey! Phoah … look at this! Drewsy shouts. He's rummaging through the lassie's chest ay drawers and ah know which one he's looking for. He locates the underwear drawer pretty sharpish, pulling a pair ay panties oot and sniffing at the crotch. – Wish tae fuck ah could find the dirty laundry basket, he laughs, then, suddenly inspired, goes out into the hallway and opens a few presses. There's nothing there though – Bastard. Still, some nice wee panties here, eh?

– Fuckin hell, man, ah'm totally in love wi this wee chick, ah tell him, hudin up a pair ay scanties tae the light and trying to mentally visualise a nice fuckin hologram tae fit intae them. – How auld dae ye reckon she is?

– Ah'd say between fourteen and sixteen, Drewsy smiles.

– What a fuckin ice-cool wee bird, ah say, looking through the spot-on-sexy collection of undies. I take out Blur and put on Oasis who are giving it laldy and ah don't really like bands being mair ay a club sort ay cunt but ah decide that I'm up for this. Ah go back to my skirtings but Drewsy's still intrigued.

Ah look up and jump as Drewsy's dancing around tae the music, but he's goat a pair ay the lassie's knickers stretched ower his heid and his glesses oan toap. At that point ah at first think then I definitely know that I'm hearing something from outside and before ah can shout tae Drewsy the door opens and it's the guy, Mr Moir, standing there, in front of Drewsy who's dancing away. – What's going on! What are you doing? That's … that's …

Poor Drewsy pulls the pants off his heid. – Eh, sorry, Mr Moir … jist huvin a wee joke, eh. Ha ha ha, he says adding a playful, stage laugh.

– Is that your idea of humour? Going through someone's personal belongings? Acting like an animal in my daughter's underpants!

It was that bit that got me. Ah started laughing uncontrollably. Ah had the Flight Lieutenant Biggles in a big way. Ah was contorting like ah was having a fit and ah could feel my face reddening. – Heagh heagh heagh heagh …

– And what are you sniggering at? He turned to me, – You think that's fuckin funny! This … fuckin sick imbecile rummaging through my daughter's personal items!

– Sorry … Drewsy weakly lisped, before ah could speak.

– Sorry? Fuckin sorry are ye! Have you got children? Eh?

– Aye, ah've got two laddies, Drewsy said.

– And you think that's the way a father should behave?

– I've said I'm sorry. It was a stupid thing tae dae. We were just having a laugh. Now we can stand here and discuss how faithers should behave or me and my mate can get on and finish the job. Either way, you get billed. What's it to be?

Ah thought Drewsy was cool, but the cunt Moir didnae think so.
– Take your tools and leave. I'll pay ye for the work that you've done. You should think yourself lucky you aren't getting reported!

We tidied up, the cunt coming back in and moaning at us occasionally, oblivious tae the fact that he was carrying his daughter's underpants around with him, clenched tightly in his hand.

Drewsy and me hit the pub. – Sorry ah couldnae tip ye oaf in time, Drewsy. It wis the music. Ah never heard the sneaky cunt. One minute nae sign, the next the cunt wis standin over ays watchin you daein yir wee dance.

– One ay they things, Lloyd, Drewsy smiled. – Good fuckin laugh though, eh. Did ye see the cunt's face?

– Did ye see yours?

– Right enough! he exploded with laughter.

Drewsy peyed ays and we drank up. Ah got a taxi up tae Haymarket and got oan the train tae Soapdodge City. When ah got off at Queen Street ah took a taxi up tae Stevo's flat in the West End, travelling the same distance as in the Edinburgh taxi but for about a third of the price. It reminded me what cunts Edinburgh taxi drivers were. Ah wis nearly fuckin well cleaned oot already. Ah would have tae try tae flog they shitey E's ay The Poisonous Cunt's.

Claire, Amanda and Siffsy were at Stevo's and they were all getting togged up. – What the fuck's this fashion parade fir, man? ah bleated nervously, checking the inadequacy ay ma ain togs.

– Wir no gaun tae the Sub Club now, cause Roger Sanchez is on at the Tunnel, Claire said.

– Fuckin hell … ah whinged.

– You're awright, Stevo said.

– Ye think so?

– Aw aye, Claire nodded.

Siffsy kept buttin in and oot ay the front room, treatin it like a fuckin catwalk. He wis takin ages. – Ah don't know about they shoes n strides wi this toap, eh said.

– Naw, ah said, – the strides dinnae really go wi the toap, eh no.

– Ah cannae no wear the toap though, man. Sixty-five bar oot ay X-ile. Thing is, if ah wear they broon strides they'll clash wi the shoes.

– We need tae go, said Claire rising, – c'moan.

Amanda and Stevo followed her lead. Ah couldnae get it together to stand up, it was a cracker ay a couch, you just sank doon intae it.

– Hud oan a minute! Siffsy begged.

– Get tae fuck, Stevo shook his head. – C'moan, Lloyd, ya fuckin east-coast poof. Ye fit?

– Aye, ah said, rising.

– Ah'll no be a minute … Siffsy pleaded.

– See ye in the next life, Stevo said, exiting, as we followed. Siffsy came behind feeling self-conscious about the Gordon Rae's.

His embarrassment evaporated at the Tunnel. They Es Stevo had got were shit-hot, much better than the crap I'd brought through if the truth be telt. Roger S was on fine form and we were well away with it when we headed back to Stevo's the next morning. Siffsy started tae get self-conscious again as the E ran down, and fucked off hame tae get changed. Ah dropped one of The Poisonous Cunt's 'business' acids back at the gaff on the proviso that if her eckies were shite then her acids wouldnae be too hot either.

Ah took out my plastic bag of Es from doon my baws. – These are shite, ah said holding them up to the light. Ah'll never fuckin well sell these. Ah stuck them down on the table.

None of the poofy Weedgie cunts were into daein trips. Stevo stuck on the telly while Amanda and Claire started spliff-building.

The acid wasn't up to much at first. Then it kicked up. Then it kicked up some mair.

9 Heather

I don't want a baby.

Hugh's ready. He's got the wife, the job, the house, the car. There's something missing. He thinks it's a baby. He doesn't have a great deal of imagination.

We don't really communicate so I can't actually tell him that I don't want a baby. We talk all right, talk in that strange language we've evolved for the purposes of avoiding communication. That non-language we've created. Perhaps it's a sign that civilisation is regressing. Something is anyway. Something is.

The only good thing about this is that Hugh can't actually tell me that he wants us to have a child. All he can do is smile at little kids when we're out, make a fuss of the nieces and nephews he never had any time for before. If only he could say: I want a baby.

If only he could say that so that I could say: no, I don't want one.

NO.

NO.

I don't want a baby. I want a life. A life of my own.

Now his fingers have gone to my cunt. It's like a child trying to get into a jar of sweets. There's no sensuality to it, it's just a ritual. I feel a sick tension. Now he's trying to get his prick inside me, forcing his way through my dry, tight, tense walls. He's grunting. He always grunts. I remember when I first slept with him at university. My friend Marie asked, – What's he like?

– Not bad, I said, – bit of a grunter.

She laughed loud and long at that. She meant what was he like *as a person*.

I used to think like that a lot. I was sassy, in my own quiet way. They all said it. That was what I was like. I'm not like that now. But I am. I am in here.

My mother always said that I was lucky to have found someone like Hugh. Someone ambitious. Someone who could provide. – He'll be a provider that one, she told me, as I held up Hugh's sparkler for her inspection, – Just like your father.

If Hugh provides everything, what do I have left?

Nurture.

Nurture Hughey-wooey.

Nurture Baby-waby of Hughy-wooey.

Nurture resentment.

– … Ohh … you sexy fuck … he gasps, shooting his load inside me and moving off me and collapsing into a deep slumber. Sexy Fuck. That's what he calls me, me underneath him like a piece of meat, gripping the bedclothes with tension.

Sexy Fuck.

I habitually leave *Cosmo* open strategically on the coffee table and watch Hugh squint at and then recoil from its headlines:

> **the vaginal and clitoral orgasm**
> **is your partner good in bed?**
> **how's your sex life?**
> **does size really matter?**
> **improve your sex life**

I used to browse through *Woman's Own*. A degree in English Literature, a worthless qualification, yes, but worth more than a browse through *Woman's Own*. Hugh used to ask – Why do you read that muck, honey? in a voice part contempt, part patronising approval.

Does this captain of local industry in Dunfermline realise that he's sailing the ship of our relationship onto the rocks of oblivion? Does he realise the effect he's having on his esteemed wife, Heather Thomson, also known in some select circles as Sexy Fuck? No, he's looking the other way.

His toxic sperm is inside me, trying to batter through into my egg. Thank heavens for little pills. I find my clit and, dreaming of a mystery lover, rub deliciously.

It happens.

As Hugh slumbers deeply, it happens. I become Sexy Fuck.

10 Lloyd

There is a ringing in my ears and ah hear some cunt say something which sounds a little like 'perhaps they'll understand the truth someday of why things remain different' in an accent which is reminiscent of The Crow's: not quite Manc, a bit more small-town East Lancs.

Who said that? Ah start to panic because it's goat nae context and because nobody could have said it. There are were are were four of us in the room: me, yes, I'm here, and there's Stevo, who is sitting watching the golf or rather watching the blue arse of this guy who may or may not be a golfer; Claire, lying on the couch laughing loudly and talking about why people in the catering game make crap shags (fatigue through unsocial hours and alcohol-induced impotence ah think she concluded – a bit unfairly, I'm thinking, but well, fuck it); and Amanda is here too, eating strawberries with me.

We're eating strawberries and cream cheese.

The best approach is to slice the strawberry, kind of cross-sectioning it. This reveals an aspect of the fruit we seldom see. Aye right ye are, ya daft cunt. Then just enjoy the reverb of the red and white and watch the brown carpet in the room change into polished, speckled-marble floor tiles and extend luxuriously into infinity and doing this, just indulging the whim ah see myself moving away from Amanda and Claire on the couch and Stevo, who's still watching the golf and I'm screaming: PHOAHH YA CUNT THAT YE ARE FUCK THIS MAN and ah drop the strawberry and the room assumes something approximating its normal dimensions and they look round at me and Stevo puckers his lips which look like huge strawberries and Claire laughs even more loudly causing me to emit gasping, fractured, machine-gun laughter and now Amanda's at it too and I'm going: – All hands on deck! These are good fuckin trips, ah'm off ma fuckin tits here, man …

– You've got the Flight Lieutenants in a big way there, Lloyd, Stevo laughs.

It's true. Ah have.

To calm down ah start on the master-chef preparation for the strawberries which becomes something of an urgent mission in my head. This is not because I'm para or fuck all like that, but because there is a vacuum, a space in my head, which will be filled with bad thoughts if ah don't busy busy chop chop these strawbs and the trick is to daintily use this sharp knife to stab some cunt

Eh

No no no fuck off the trick is to why did ah say that no no no bad thoughts cannae be explained, that makes them worse, they just have to be ignored because what you do with the knife is to remove the white bit of the strawberries and fill the resulting hole with cream cheese with a knob of cream cheese with the cream of knob cheese of what

Fuck

Ah don't know if I'm thinking this or saying it or both at the same time, but you can sometimes say one thing while thinking another. So if I'm saying this, actually saying this out loud, what am ah thinking? Eh? Ah ha!

– Listen, wis ah gaun oan aboot the strawberries, ah mean was ah talkin oot loud aboot it? ah ask.

– You were thinking out loud, Stevo says to me.

Thinking. That's what ah was doing, but wis ah thinkin out loud? Cunts are fuckin well trying to wind me up but it takes more than a wee tab ay LSD to knock auld Lloyd Buist here out of his fuckin stride ah will tell you that for nothing matey of the seven seas. – Thinking out loud, ah said or thought.

Ah said, because Claire says, – Drug psychosis, Lloyd, that's what it is. The first sign.

Ah just laugh and keep repeating: – Drug psychosis drug psychosis drug psychosis

– Fine by us you eatin aw the strawberries by the by, Lloyd, Amanda says.

Ah look at the punnet and sure tae fuck the remnants of strawberries are in evidence, husks n that, but examples of the fruit in its complete state are conspicuous by their absence. Greedy guts, Lloyd, I think to myself.

– Greedy guts Lloyd, Claire says.

– Fuckin hell, Claire, ah wis jist thinkin they words ... it's like telepathy ... or did ah say thum ... this acid is fuckin really mad n the strawberries, ah've eaten aw the strawberries ...

Ah start to panic a little bit. What's got me is that with the strawberries being consumed I've lost my means of space-and-time travel. The strawberries were my space craft/time machine; no that's too simple, too crass, delete that line of thought and start again: the strawberries were my means of transportation from this dimension or state into another. Without strawberries I'm condemned to live in their fucking world which is no good at all because without hallucinations of a visual and auditory nature, acid is pretty crap; ah mean you might as well just be pished out of your face beery and bleary, giving profits to the brewers and the Tory Party which you do everytime you raise a glass of that shite to your lips but without the hallucinations the only advantage you had with the old acceeeed was the Flight Lieutenants which is still better than bevvy because you just looked a moosey-faced cunt sitting drinking the depressant called alcohol so fuck that that was it for me it was STRAW-BERRIES ...

– Ah'm away doon tae the deli fir mair ay they strawberries, eh, ah announced. Something in Claire's face made me laugh. Ah took a chronic attack of the Flight Lieutenants.

– You mind yirsel, trippin like that, Claire said.

– Aye, watch, Amanda nodded.

– Mad gaun oot like that, Stevo turned his attention from the golfer's blue arse.

– Naw man, it's sound, ah said. – Ah feel great.

Ah do. It's barry tae ken that people actually care about me. Not enough tae stop me fae gaun oot or to say 'I'll chum ye' but that just could be paranoia. Ah said ah wanted to be alone did I say

Ah wanted tae be

Ah do a pish before ah go. Ah hate pishing on acid because you never feel like you're finished and the distortion of time makes you think you've been pishing longer than you have and it gets boring and the next thing ah know is that I'm fed up with this pish and I'm putting my cock away before it's actually finished, well, it's *finished* but I've not really shaken it out but fuck me I'm no wearing jeans I'm wearing flannels it would not be so fuckin bad with denims but with flannels I'll have a map of South America or Africa on my groin unless ah take some positive fuckin action which ah do stuffing bog paper down my keks. My keks. Stuffing. Accusations fly. J'accuse. Fuck off. It's Lloyd Buist.

Lloyd Buist is my name, no Lloyd Beattie. B.U.I.S.T. Another bad attack of the Flight Lieutenants. Breathe easy …

Imagine getting me, Lloyd Buist, *me*, confused with Lloyd Beattie, the cunt that was rumoured to have shagged his wee sister. Ah huvnae even got a fuckin wee sister. I rest ma fuckin case, your honour; your judge, jury and executioner psychopath who begins every Leith pub conversation with: Ah mind ah you. You wir the dirty cunt that …

Ah mean, how the fuck can you get us mixed up? Yes, we both live in Leith, and are similar ages. Granted, our given name is Lloyd … indeed an uncommon name for Leith. Okay, myself and the other Lloyd both have the first initial B in our surnames. Oh, I suppose there is one other area of similarity, your honour; okay, it's time to come clean: we both shagged our sisters. What can I say? Keep it in the family. No waste of time with long chat-up lines and Bacardi's. Just, hi sis, awright? Up for a shag? Eh? Aye? Sound. Well, in my case it was some other cunt's sister. Awright? Awright, ya cunts? The rock opera I'm composing about Lloyd Beattie, the other Lloyd:

> In his hometown, Lloyd sits and waits
> Lloyd masturbates
>
> From his bedroom window
> Lloyd looks down and out
> Lloyd looks out and down
> Aint nuthin out there but town.

That is fuckin shite cause it's too personal cause it's about me, or as ah was as a young teenager and this is supposed to be about Lloyd Beattie and ah have to try and understand the complexities which led Lloyd Beattie into this incestuous affair with his sister cause these things dinnae just fuckin happen, no just like that, but hud oan the now ... if Lloyd B. Numero Uno whom ah must call The Non-Wee-Sister-Shagging Lloyd, i.e.: my good self, sat and wanked as a bored sexually repressed fourteen-year-old in his bedroom in Leith, what was Lloyd Numero Two doing; he who did, or was said to have, knobbed his junior femme sibling? Probably the same as Lloyd One, the same as aw Leith fourteen-year-aulds at the time. But he didnae jist wank the dirty cunt, he took it a stage further involving a wee lassie who was just twelve at the time they said, a mess for the social workers, relatively speaking ...

But ah am fuck all like that freak, we share a name ... that's aw ... take it easy, it's this fuckin acid. Back through to my friends to say proper bye-byes before ah finally, for good, once and for all, head for the deli.

– Ah never shagged my wee sister, ah tell them back in the front room.

– You've no got a wee sister tae shag, Stevo says, – if you did you probably would have though.

Ah think about this. Then something queasy moves in my stomach. I've had fuck all to eat in a couple of days bar Ecstasy, amphetamine sulphate and acid. Ah had one Lucozade Isotonic drink though, and a bit of a pear that Amanda had and of course, the cream cheese and the STRAWBERRIES. Time to go.

Ah left the flat and bounced, yes bounced down the Great Western

Road. Lloyd Buist, ah keep telling myself. It seemed important to remember. Leith. A party refugee. The most oppressed kind. Fight for the right to party; fuck diverting your energies into frivolous nonsense like food and jobs and the likes. Boring, boring fuckin boring. Party refugee Lloyd, stranded in Glasgow's West End. Ah was lost in France, in love. Naw naw ya daft cunt. You are just on a simple message. A simple fuckin message

– Awright, big man!

Two young guys are beside me, breathing heavily and looking around, not meeting my eyes as they swivel their heads. It's these boys ... Robert and Richard, from that Maryhill posse. Ah keep running into these boys, at the Metro, the Forum, Rezurrection, The Pure, The Arches, The Sub Club ... big Slam punters, naw Terry n Jason ... Industria ... – Awright, boys!

Their faces look distorted, and they are already moving away from me with great haste.

– Sorry, big man, cannae stoap, wi did a wee dine and dash ... yuv goat tae fir fuck sake, know what ah mean, big man ... ah mean ye cannae gie up the clubbin n that jist tae eat ... Robert gasps out running backwards like a referee. That's a good skill.

– That's it, boys! That's fuckin right! Good skills, Roberto! Good skills, Roberto my son! Ah shout encouragingly as they bomb off down the road. Ah turn around and this huge juggernaut is bearing down on me and ah tense up ready cause this mad cunt is gaunnae swing for me, going to attack the innocent Lloyd of Leith displaced person unaccustomed to your Weedgie ways but naw he's off doon the road in hot pursuit of Richard and Robert who are heading towards the Underground at Kelvin Bridge and the bloated alcoholic will never capture the younger fitter men because their bodies are honed by dance and Ecstasy; these boys are as fit as fuck and the more weighty, beefy fellow (he's no that fat) realises this and gives up. Our heroes escape, leaving their breathless pursuer panting heavily with his hands on his hips.

I'm laughing. The boy's coming ower tae me but ah cannae stop. Flight Lieutenant Biggles is the name. – Where dae these cunts stey! he sort ay gasps and snaps. It's like Lloyd of Leith, a good boy, a decent, hardworking Edinburgh merchant-school lad who plays squash and loves nothing better than attending big rugby internationals at Murrayfield is being lumped alongside Ricardo and Roberto, two schemies from a Weedgie slum.

This is a bit like being accused of shagging the sister ah don't have.

– Eh? Ah think ah manage tae cough out.

– These cunts are your fuckin mates. Where dae they fuckin stay?

– Fuck off, ah say, turning away. Then ah feel his airm on my shooder. He's gaunnae hit ays. No. He's no gaunnae let ays go. That is worse. Violence in the form of blows ah can take, but the idea of being constrained, no fuckin way ... ah punch him, in the chest, what a place to punch any cunt, but ah didnae want to really punch him, just get him tae let go, and that's nae good cause as any wideo will tell you, you either punch some cunt or you dinnae and silly wee halfway-house slaps and pushes just make you look a cunt so ah start *really* punching the boy but it feels like I'm punching a mattress and he's shouting: – Phone the polis! Phone the polis! This man's ran out of my restaurant without paying, and I'm screaming: – Lit go ya cunt it wisnae fuckin me, and punching at the cunt but ah feel like rubber and I'm out of breath and he keeps a grip, his face aw screwed up and determined through its fear and apprehension

and

and a polisman is beside us. He's pulled us apart.

– What's this? he asks.

Ah've got four trips in my flannels. My poakits. The wee poakit, the compartment. Ah feel them. The cunt is saying: – This guy's mates ran up a food and drinks bill for nearly a hundred and twenty pound and then did a runner! I'm fishing out those wee squares of impregnated paper.

– This true? the polisman turned tae me and asked.

– How the fuck dae ah ken, eh, ah mean, ah jist sees they two guys runnin doon the road. Ah recognised one ay them vaguely fae the Sub Club so ah jist lets ontae the boy. Then this cunt here, ah nods at the restaurateur, – he's eftir the two boys. Then he comes back and grabs a hud ay me.

The polisman turns back tae the restaurateur. Ah get the trips between my forefinger and thumb and ah swallow the lot, silly fuckin cunt; ah could have left them, the polis would never find them wouldnae search me anywey I've done nowt wrong but ah swallowed the fuckin lot when ah could've even fuckin flung them away. No thinkin straight ...

> They called the child Lloyd Beattie
> the cunt grew up a right wee sweetie

Lloyd One calling Lloyd Two, can you hear me Lloyd Two? Can you hear me Lloyd Two? Can you hear

am I floating

The beefy bastard is not amused. – These cunts robbed me! Ah'm strugglin tae make this business pay n they fuckin wee toerags ...

A few people had stopped to witness the commotion. Ah became aware of them for the first time when a woman whae'd been watchin us said: – You jist grabbed that laddie! Jist grabbed um! It wisnae anything tae dae wi the laddie ...

– That's right, ah said, nodding at the cop.

– This true? asked the polisman.

– Aye, ah suppose, says the beefy restaurateur, looking aw fuckin sheepish as well he might because he tampered unjustly with one Lloyd Buist from Leith who is a waster and has set himself up in opposition to the fascist British state but who now to his extreme embarrassment finds one of its law enforcement officers taking his side and ticking off the capitalist businessman who tried to apprehend said Leith man.

Another woman says, – The likes ah you have goat enough bloody money as it is!

– That's fuckin men fir ye. Money, money, money, that's aw they think aboot, another one, the one that took my part, laughs.

– That n thir hole, the other woman said. Then she looks at the restaurateur and gives him a dismissive sneer.

The guy looks at her, but she's sort of staring him down and starts to say something then thinks better of it.

The cop rolls his eyes in a manner obviously meant to indicate exasperation but which seems a camp, theatrical gesture. – Look, says our lawman, looking bored, – we can play this by the rules which means I'll huv yis both doon the station n charged wi breach. He raises his eyebrows in a what's-it-to-be manner at the restaurateur who looks like he's shiting himself.

– Aw c'moan … geez a brek, the restaurant guy appeals.

– You were out of order, pal, the cop lectures, pointing at the guy, – attempting to restrain this man when the culprits were in fact two other men. You admit that this man wasn't even in your restaurant?

– Aye, the guy said. He looks quite ashamed.

– Too right, ah goes. Cheeky bastard. Innocent passer-by me, eh, I said to the cop. He looks like Noddy.

He turns to address me, adopting that formal Officer-Of-The-Law mode, – And you, goes the polis, – you're out of your face. Ah dunno what the fuck you're on, and right now ah've goat far too much on tae be bothered. Any fuckin mair lip fae you and ah will be bothered. So shut it. He looks back to the restaurateur. – I want details from you, about the other two guys.

The guy makes a statement and gives the polis descriptions of the youths, as they say. Then we're made to shake hands, like we were bairns in a school playground. Ah think about taking exception to this patronising behaviour, but it feels strangely good to be magnanimous and ah can see the bruises and swelling coming up on the side of the poor cunt's face and ah was a bit out of order hitting the boy like that, poor cunt was upset at being ripped off and only trying tae get justice but wisnae thinking straight in his emotional state when he apprehended said Leith man. Then the lawman gets into his car and departs, leaving us looking at each other. The women have gone up the road.

– Embarrassment that, eh! The guy laughs.

Ah said fuck all; ah just shrugged at the cunt.

– Sorry, mate … ah mean, ye could've goat me intae bother thair. If ye'd pressed charges like. Ah appreciate it.

Get *him* intae fuckin bother … – Listen, ya daft bastard, ah wis trippin oot ay face n when that polis wanker came ah hud tae swallow some mair trips ah wis haudin. In aboot one minute ah'm gaunnae be totally cunted here!

– Fuck … acid … ah've no done acid for years … he said, then: – Listen, mate, come along the road wi me. Tae the restuarant. Sit doon for a bit.

– If ye goat drink thair, aye.

He nodded.

– Ye see the only thing ah can dae is have a good bevvy. It's the only way ye can control a trip: force doon as much alcohol as possible. It's a depressant, ken.

– Aye, awright. Ah've goat drink in the restaurant. I'd take ye for a beer in a boozer, but ah've goat tae get back and prepare for the night. Seturday night, the busiest time n that.

Ahm in nae position tae refuse. The trips hit me like a slap in the face from a wet fish. Loads of wee explosions go off simultaneously in ma heid and ah realise that ah can see nothing at all, just a big golden light and some obscure objects swirling around me out of reach. – Fuckin hell … man, ah'm gaunnae die dinnae let ays walk intae that road …

– S'awright, mate, ah've goat ye here …

The guy's holding me again, this time I'm keeping a grip on him, even though he looks like that fuckin dinosaur in Jurassic Park, one ay they nippy wee cunts which, awright, are wee by dinosaur standards, no as big as the T.Rex; T.Rex, now there was a cunt: – Ah love to boogie on a Saturday night … mind that cunt T.Rex?

– S'awright, mate, wir jist alang the road … wir jist alang here … jist cause ah've goat a restaurant though, pal, it disnae mean tae say that ah'm some big rich bastard who's hud it aw handed tae them oan a silver plate. Ah'm jist like they boys, they pals of yours. Stealin fae thir ain kind! That's what that wis. That's the thing that disgusts me the maist. Ah mean tae say, ah'm fae Yoker, ye know Yoker? Ah'm a red sandstone boy, me.

He's fuckin rabbiting oan a load ay shite and I'm fuckin blind and my breathing is fucked oh no don't think about fuckin breathing no no no bad trip hopeless when ye fuckin think aboot the breathing most bad trips happen when you think about the breathing

but

but we're different from say dolphins, because these daft cunts have tae think consciously about each breath they take when they come up for air and that. Fuck that fir a game ay sodgirs the poor cunts.

No me but, no Lloyd Buist. A human with a superior breathing mechanism, safe from the acid. You didnae have to think aboot the breathing, it just happened. Yes!

What if

What if, but, no no no but what if no no no a staggering trip; me now flying off into space seeing the Buist body: a deserted shell being dragged along to the mass murderer pervert restaurateur's lair, this body being folded over a table with lubricants applied to the arsehole and penetration achieved just as the victim's carotid artery is severed with a kitchen knife. The blood is expertly drained off to be collected into a bucket to make black pudding and the body is systematically dismembered following being pumped with Yoker semen and that night in the trendy West End eating house the unsuspecting Weedgies sit spraffing unaware that instead of feasting on their usual dead rats they are munching the remains of Lloyd A. Buist, an unattractive divorcee of the parish of Leith, integrated into the City of Edinburgh in nineteen canteen, naw naw hud on, nineteen twenty cause ah ken my history and it's enough tae make yir hearts go ooh la la ah fancy a shag cause ah just saw something or someone gorgeous really fuckin gorgeous pass my line of trance-vision up here in the clouds but yeah, they took Leith into Edinburgh in spite of a popular plebiscite that rejected the merger by a ratio of something like seven billion to one but aye, they did it anyway because these stupid schemie cunts ken fuck all and they need a good benign central authority to tell them what is in their interest and that's how Leith has fuckin thrived ever since then ha ha ha like fuck … except for a few incoming yuppies but obviously the story of Leith had broader implications

– Ah've known hard times n aw, that's aw ah'm sayin, says my mate Red Sandstone Boy, as I snap back into my body with a shuddering jolt.

Ah still seem to be just breathing oot. There's nae sense of breathing in and if the breathing mechanism is part of the subconscious which it has to be, is that no precisely what the acid fucks up?

Precisely Holmes. That means you are up shit creek, you daft cunt. – Ha ha ha ha ha ha ha ha ha ha ha ha ha ha ha ha ha ha ha ha ha ha ha ha ha ha ha ha ha ha ha ha ha ha ha ha ha ha ha ha ha ha ha ha Flight Lieutenant Biggles reporting for duty, Sir. Biggles, old man, don't stand so bloody close to me and put away that weapon while I'm talking to you. Did ah tell ye that your breathing is rather laboured, it's aw fuck fuck fuck fuck

– Take it easy, mate, here we are.

No breathing.

no no no think of a Garden of Eden type scene where there are loads of sultry naked women lounging around and all of a sudden who should be here but Lloyd but the faces ah can't get the fuckin faces right n what if these cruel bastards in the research labs were to give dolphins LSD? I'll fuckin well bet it's been done before the cruel cunts. Amanda's showed me that stuff she gets stuff through the post that goes oan aboot what these cunts dae tae cats and dugs and mice and rabbits but that's nowt; that would be real cruelty: giein a dolphin LSD.

We are not now moving. Moving now not. Now we are not moving. We are somewhere else. Somewhere enclosed.

— What's the fuckin score?

— Take it easy there, yir hyperventilatin ... I'll get ye a wee bevvy.

— Whair the fuck is this?

— Stay cool, mate, it's ma restaurant. Gringo's. Gringo's Mexican Cantina. Hodge Street. This is the kitchen.

— Ah ken this place. Ah came here once. Barry cocktails. With ma then girlfriend. We drank cocktails. Ah love cocktails. Want one want one want one want one ... oh excuse me, mate, ah'm fuckin trippin oot ay ma box here. PHOAH! Yuh cunt ye! Aye ... my ex-girlfriend. Her name was Stella and she was nice. We didnae love each other but, eh no, mate. It's nae good unless there's real love thair ken? Ye cannae settle for second best. What aboot the cocktails though, mate? Eh?

— S'okay pal. I'll make ye one. What is it ye want?

— A Long Island Iced Tea would be nice.

Nice. Ah keep saying that word, thinking that word. Nice.

So the boy starts mixin the cocktails and I'm in this kitchen and it's all flying away fae me but he's still going on about being a red sandstone boy who doesnae care aboot money ...

— ... a red sandstone boy. It's no that ah'm a money grabber and ah know that plenty people are starvin and homeless in Glasgow, bit that's the fuckin Government's fault, no mine. Ah'm tryin tae make a fuckin livin. Ah cannae feed aw the poor, this isnae a soup kitchen. Ye know how much they fuckin criminals at the council charge in rates for this place?

— Naw ...

The boy should start a militant community group in Yoker and call it Red Sandstone. It sounds okay. Red Sandstone.

— It's no that ah'm a Tory, far fuckin from it, says Red. — Mind you, that council's jist a fuckin Tory council under another name; that's what that is. Is it the same in Edinburgh?

This is too fuckin radge. — Eh, aye, Edinburgh. Leith. Lloyd. Ah nivir, ah mean, no the one that shagged ehs sister, that wis a different Lloyd ... nice cocktail, mate ...

A Long Island Iced Tea.

The cocktail is fuckin reverberating like anything. It's gaunnae explode ...

– Cheers. Aye, see if ah wis votin fir any cunt, which ah'm no, ah'd vote SNP ... naw, ah widnae, ah tell ye whae ah wid vote for if ah wis votin fir anybody now; mind that boy that got sent tae the jail for no peyin his poll tax?

This cocktail is the wrong one. Ah need a strawberry something, Strawberry, a Strawberry Daiquiri.

– What wis the boy's name?

– Strawberry Daiquiri.

– Naw ... the boy that got sent tae the jail for no peyin his poll tax. The Militant boy.

Ah need strawberries ... – A Strawberry Daiquiri, mate ... that would dae me fine.

– Strawberry Daiquiri ... aye, sure. Finish that Iced Tea first though, eh! Ah'll just have a wee beer this time, a San Miguel, naw, too heavy, maybe jist a Sol.

– Nae Becks, mate?

– Naw, jist Sol.

Red Sandstone gets up from the seat opposite me to fix the drinks and it's like a volcano exploding and fuck this, the roof is falling doon ... not, ha ha ha fooled myself there, but the window has gone, that's fuckin defo.

– Sorry, ma man, nae strawberries. It'll huv tae be a Lime Daiquiri.

Nae fuckin strawberries ... what a fuckin load ay shite, man ... nae fuckin strawberries right enough the cunt goes so ah goes – Sound man, sound. And eh, thanks fir lookin eftir ays.

– Naw, ah sortay feel bad about it, you takin aw they trips n that. How ye feelin?

– Sound.

– Cause as ah say, ah'm jist tryin tae make a livin. But these guys, they're jist rubbish. They've goat the money tae go oot tae fuckin clubs aw night, but they steal food fae the likes of me. That's fuckin out of order.

– Naw, man, naw; ah admire they boys ... they know that the

game isnae fuckin straight. They know that there's a Government fill ay dull, boring bastards who gie the likes ay us fuck all and they expect ye tae be as miserable as they are. What they hate is when yir no, in spite ay aw thair fuckin efforts. What these cunts fail tae understand is that drug and club money is not a fuckin luxury. It's a fuckin essential.

– How can ye say that?

– Because we are social, collective fucking animals and we need to be together and have a good time. It's a basic state of being alive. A basic fuckin right. These Government cunts, because they're power junkies, they are just incapable of having a good fuckin time so they want everybody else tae feel guilty, tae stey in wee boxes and devote their worthless lives tae rearing the next generation of factory fodder or sodgers or dole moles for the state. It's these boys' duty as human fuckin beings tae go oot clubbin and partying wi their friends. Now, they need tae eat from time to time, it's obviously important, but it's less important than having a good fuckin time.

– Ye cannae admire people like that. That's jist rubbish, thon.

– Ah *do* admire the guys. Massive respect from Lloyd here; Leith's Lloyd, the one that never shagged his sister: massive respect tae they boys Richard and Robert fae Glesgie … dear auld Glesca toon …

– Thought you said ye didnae know them? Red Sandstone's hurt face pouts out at me surrounded by a cacophony of clattering sounds and throbbing, pulsating lights …

– Ah know them as Richard and Robert; that's it, mate. I've blethered wi the boys, in chill-oot zones n that. That's as far as it goes … listen, ah'm fucked. Ah could be dying. Ah need tae get ma heid doon or something or another Sol …

The Sol and the Daiquiri and the Long Island Iced Tea are empty and ah cannae remember who drank them surely ah never ah mean

The boy goes to make up some of the tables in the front dining area. Ah climb across the sink, through some dirty dishes and just slide like an eel out of the open window, falling onto some binliners stacked with rubbish and rolling into a dry drain in this concreted back court. Ah try tae stand up, but ah cannae, so ah just crawl towards this green gate. Ah just know ah have to go, to keep moving, but I've ripped my flannels and torn my knee and ah can see the flesh wound pulsating like an opened-up strawberry and now I'm on my feet which is strange because ah can't recall ever standing up and I'm on a busy main road which is maybe the Great Western or maybe Byre's or maybe Dumbarton and I can't see where I'm going and it should be home but that cannae surely tae fuck that cannae mean Stevo's flat.

The sun rises up above the tenements. I'm just gaunnae fly intae it.

Ah shout tae some people in the street, two lassies. Ah tell them, – The sun, I'm just up for flyin right intae it.

They say nothing, and they don't even notice as ah fly right up out of this world and its trivial, banal oppressions, right into that big fuckin golden bastard in the sky.

11 Heather

I suppose what attracted me to Hugh was his sense of commitment. As a student he had a tremendous sense of commitment. This changed, evolved, as he might say, through the years. How did Hugh's commitment change?

Name: Student Hugh.
Committed to: the liberation of working people from the horrors of capitalism.

Name: Jobless Graduate Hugh.
Committed to: fighting to maintain jobs for working people but to changing the system.

Name: First-rung-on-the-ladder Professional Employee Hugh.
Committed to: defending and improving the services working people are entitled to.

Name: Supervisor Hugh.
Committed to: optimising the quality of services for the users of the services.

Name: Public Sector Manager Hugh.
Committed to: excellence in service delivery through increased cost efficiency and cost effectiveness. (This meant redundancy for many of the working people who provided these services, but if it was to the benefit of the great many who used them, then it was a price worth paying.)

Name: Private Sector Manager Hugh.
Committed to: maximising profit through cost efficiency, resource effectiveness and expanding into new markets.

— But we've moved a little since nineteen-eighty-four, Heather, he'd smile from behind his *Independent*.

Only the innocent have been changed to protect the names. For Hugh, the 'final analysis' became the 'bottom line'. There is significance in the semantics. The banal slogans of revolution and resistance became the even more banal ones of business efficiency, accountancy and sport; bottom lines, moving goalposts, covering bases, level playing fields …

Along the way our dreams crumbled. The slogans of revolution may have been naive, but at least we were going for something big, something important. Now our sights are set so low. It's not good enough for me. It's all right for some; they're welcome to it. It's just not enough for me.

It's not enough because I'm twenty-seven nearly, and I haven't had a fucking orgasm in four years. For those four years he's fired his wallpaper paste into me, consuming me as I lie thinking about consuming.

As he fucks me I make out my lists:

                              sugar
                              jam
                              bread
                              milk
                              beans
                              rice
                              herbs
                              pizzas
                              wine
                              tomatoes
                              onions
                              green peppers

 … then I did something truly visionary: I stopped consuming for its
own sake.

The fat started to fall from my body. It started to fall from my
brain. Everything was lighter. Fantasising about getting fucked
properly was the start. Then about telling them all to fuck off and die.
It was the books I starting reading. It was the music I started listening
to. It was the television I started watching. I found myself thinking
again. I tried to stop because it was only causing pain. I couldn't.

When all this is in your head it has to come out into your life. If it
doesn't, you get crushed. I'm not going to get crushed.

12 Lloyd

It took ays a while tae get back fae Soapdodge City. Acid, man, fuck that, never again, never until the next time at any rate. When ah get back, The Poisonous Cunt's coming oot ay ma stair. – Where have you been? she says accusingly. The Poisonous Cunt is getting too fuckin possessive taewards me.

– Glasgow, ah tell her.

– What for? she asks.

– Slam night on the Renfrew Ferry, eh, ah lie. Ah don't want The Poisonous Cunt knowing my MO …

– What was it like?

– Awright, aye, ah goes.

– Ah've got some mair ay they Doves for you to punt, but they're back at mines, she says.

Great. Mair crap Es tae sell. Ma reputation will soon be so bad that people'll rather buy their chemicals fae Scottish and Newcastle Breweries. Ah left the other ones in Glasgow wi Stevo, who wasnae too hopeful, but who said that he would see what he could do.

– Right. Ah'll come up the night, ah tell her. Ah just want to get in and make myself a cup of tea and a spliff. Then ah realise that I've left my blow in Soapdodge City, with those Es. – Have you got any blow? Ah need a fucking blow. Ah'm exhausted after that trip. My jaw feels like it's been broken. Ah need tae mellow out. Even some fuckin jellies wid dae ays. Ah need some thing. Ah need, full fuckin stop.

– Aye. Ah've got black and soapbar, she says.

– Right then, I'll chum you back to yours.

We get up to The Poisonous Cunt's and Solo is in, as well as a couple of mates called Monts and Jasco. Ah was embarrassed as Solo started talking tae ays. Ah couldnae make oot a word ay it. It sounded like he was forcing his syllables out slowly through his nose. As The Poisonous Cunt went to the kitchen to stick on the kettle and get some blow, Monts stood behind Solo with a smirk on his face and pushed out one cheek with his tongue, in the cocksucker gesture. He and Jasco were like nothing more than two vultures circling over a large wounded animal. Ah found it sad, and ah felt sorry for Solo. It reminded ays ay a piece ay film ay Muhummad Ali ah'd seen oan telly, stricken from his articulate buoyancy by Parkinson's, probably brought on by the fight game. The Poisonous Cunt, when she came in, reminded me of Don King, manipulation screaming through a smile of searing delight.

– You gaunnae take that gear doon tae Abdab for ays then? she enquired.

– Aye, ah told her. Abdab was an old mate ay mine down in Newcastle. The Poisonous Cunt was sorting him out with some shite and ah was delivering. It was a Paddy Crerand ah didnae feel like running. Ah only agreed to do it to see Abdab and his Geordie mates and have a night oot doon thair. Ah always liked Newcastle. Geordies are just Scots who can't blame the English for them being fucked up, the poor cunts.

Jasco starts giein ays a hard time. Ehs normally a cool cunt but ehs been a bit nippy lately. Too much freebasin gaun oan wi the cunt. – Listen, Lloyd, if ah've goat a heidache ah'll take some paracetamol.

– Eh? ah goes.

– And if ah've goat a bad stomach ah'll take some bicarb soda.

Ah'm a wee bit too slow oan the uptake the day tae suss oot the cunt's game.

– Git oaf eh's case, Jasco ya cunt, Monts sais.

– Naw, listen, Jasco continued, – the point is, ah didnae huv a heidache or a sair stomach the other night. Naw. What ah wanted was tae git oaf my tits oan Ecstasy. So why did this cunt sell ays paracetamol and bicarb? He pointed at me.

– Moan tae fuck, Jasco, ah said defensively, – they wirnae brilliant Es, granted, and ah telt ye that fae the off, but they wirnae *that* shite. I kept it light cause it was like Jasco was in the mood where he couldnae decide whether or no he was bein serious or havin a jokey wee wind-up.

— Did fuck all fir me, man, he moaned.

— Hundred and twenty milligrams ay MDMA in them, the boy telt me, The Poisonous Cunt said.

That was bullshit. You were lucky if there was fifty mills in those Doves. You had to neck them two at a time for any buzz at aw.

— Aye, right, Jasco said.

— Fuckin wis. Rinty got them fae Holland, The Poisonous Cunt maintained. It was cool, her getting involved, because it stopped Jasco nippin at me.

— In ays fuckin dreams the cunt did. Scottish fitba clubs have spent longer in Europe than any pills youse cunts have been puntin, he grumbled at her.

Ah knew that the conversation would go on and on like this aw night and ah shot the craw as soon as it was possible. When ah got oot intae the street, ah saw this boy and bird gaun doon the road thegither, obviously really intae each other, no oan drugs or nowt. Ah thought, when wis the last time ah wis ever like that wi a lassie, withoot bein aw eckied up? In a fuckin previous life, that's when. Ah kicked a stane and it bounced up and rattled, but didnae brek, the windscreen ay a parked car.

part two

The Over-whelming Ecstasy Of Love

13 Heather

He's going to say something. Brian Case. Something like he says every other morning. He's going to say something creepy. *Mister* Case. What am I going to do? I'm going to smile like I do every morning. Like I have a spoon stuck in my mouth. Smile. Smile, when you feel like you're being stripped naked, exposed, held up for ridicule. No. I'm over-reacting. I have to take responsibility for how I react. I have to train myself to not physically react that way, to not physically cringe inside. To *not* do that. It's my fault. I must control how I react.

– How's the light of my life today? Case's usual question.

I prepare to mouth my usual answer: fine, but something happens.
– What makes you think I'm the light of your life?

Fuck. What am I saying? I can't say this ... why can't I? Yes I can. I can say anything really. If he makes a strange, inappropriate comment I can ask for him to expand, to tell me what the fuck he actually means. What lies behind that comment?

– Well, seeing you every day certainly brightens up my life.

Try as I may, I can't stop the bad Heather talking. She's only been thinking before. Now she's started talking. I'm schizophrenic and the bad Heather's taking over ... – That's strange really, I mean the sheer imbalance of it all. Seeing you every day has absolutely no positive impact on my life whatsoever.

The significant moment; when something I couldn't say becomes something I can not say. My rebellion has moved from inside my head to into my world. Yes! No! Yes! Fuck.

– Oh, he says hurt, it's not pretend hurt this time, this wretched thing is actually genuinely hurt, – it's like that, is it?

– I'm not sure what *that* is, I tell him, – it's like I see it and like I feel it.

– Listen, he says with an air of concerned confidentiality, – if anything's wrong you can talk to me about it. You don't have to bite my head off you know. I'm not all bad, he says simperingly.

– How good or bad you are has nothing to do wi me. That's for you to think about. Nothing's wrong with me. In fact, it couldnae be more right.

– Well, you're just acting a little strange …

I maintain a calm air, – Look, your behaviour towards me has been based on an assumption you've made that I actually care about how you think I look. It's nothing to do with anything. You're my manager in the organisation, an organisation which is concerned with getting the job done rather than aesthetics or sexuality or whatever. It's none of my business and I don't intend to make it my business, but if how I look brightens up your life in the manner you suggest, I'd take a long hard look at myself and ask how much of a life I had.

– Oh, well thanks for putting me in the picture, he sulks, – I was just trying to be friendly.

– Yeah, well it's me who is apologising. This is nothing to do with you. By acquiescing to your childish and boring behaviour I gave you the tacit impression I approved of it, which was wrong of me. I'm sorry for that, I really am.

He nods and looks a little bit bemused but then he smiles bashfully and says, – Right … I'll just get on then.

He smiles bashfully. *Mister* Case. Jesus Christ!

I sit back at my computer and feel euphoric. At lunchtime I stride into the East Port Bar and reward myself with a gin and tonic. I sit by myself, but I don't feel alone.

I feel really high and happy that afternoon and when I get home Hugh has left a message on the machine: Honey, I'll be a bit late tonight. Jenny and I are working on another presentation for the team.

14 Lloyd

Ah'd had a good one wi Abdab doon in Newcastle, but ah wis fucked. He'd gied ays mair than a few grams ay coke for The Poisonous Cunt and the packet burned a hole in ma poakit oan the bus up. It was come-doon para stuff but ah kept thinking aboot Nukes and half-expecting the DS tae come oan the bus at every stoap. It didnae happen. Ah goat hame and made some soup.

Later on that night ah went up tae Tribal wi Ally. Ah was just wanting tae crash but the cunt insisted that ah came along. Ah even had tae take a couple of my ain Es which was bad news. This batch were different again, like Ketamine or something. Ah was pure cunted, ah couldnae dance. Ah sat in chill-out and Ally spraffed with me. – How you feelin, Lloyd?

– Fucked, ah sais.

– You should try some ay that crystal meth ah've got back at the hoose. Didnae even fuckin well blink eftir ah'd snorted that. Ah hud a fuckin hard-on man for three days, eh. Ah wis gaunnae abandon this quest fir love n brek ma vows and bell Amber tae come roond n sit oan ma face. Didnae want tae fuck wi her heid even mair man though, eh.

– She in the night?

– Aye, she's upstairs. Her and that Hazel and Jasco. Jasco's been knobbin that Hazel, he observed with rueful bitterness, blowing air out through his teeth and pushing his hair back, – Ah might have tae move in thair masel, man.

Amber didnae take long to locate me. She relieved Ally, letting him have a spell upstairs on the floor. – Ye dinnae huv tae sit wi ays, ah slurred. – ah'm awright. Jist a bit cunted …

— Sawright, she snapped, holding my hand in hers, before thoughtfully adding, — aw aye, that Veronica wis lookin for you.

As usual, it took ays a second or two to work out who she meant, then it hit me. Veronica was the tasteless nickname some people occasionally gave tae The Poisonous Cunt.

— Is she in here the night? ah asked with some apprehension, checking Amber's watch tae see if we could make the curfew at Sublime or Sativa if it was a yes.

— Naw, this wis earlier at the City Cafe, eh.

Thank fuck. Ah took another pill and Ally, Amber and this young guy called Colin came back tae mine. Ah tried a shift oan the decks but ah was too fucked tae dae anything. This gig would be comin up soon n aw. We hud tae turn it doon cause the yuppie scum acroas the landin whae shouldnae be in Leith in the first place complained aboot the noise and ah didnae want the polis roond eftir what was gaun oan wi Nukes. It was a bit embarrassing as Amber was trying tae get intae Ally and this young Colin cunt was trying tae get intae her. If ah had a wee bit mair sexual ambivalence and energy, ah'd have tried to get intae the young guy just tae wind every cunt up even mair. Eventually, he went, then Ally did too and ah wanted Amber tae but she sat up all night playing music. Ah was cunted, ah telt her that ah was fir crashin. When ah woke up in the morning she was at the other end ay the bed, her feet in my face.

— How you doin, Lloyd? Amber asked.

She was pulling her trousers on, looking dead young with her make-up faded and ah was feeling a bit like some paedophile cunt, aye right ye are ya dirty wee fuckin stoat-the-baw cunt that ye are.

— Fine, ah goes.

— Dinnae look fine tae me. Your feet are boggin, by the way.

— It's good ay ye tae say so. That's real mates for ye. Ye want a coffee?

— Aye … sound. Dinnae go aw huffy but, eh, Lloyd. Everybody's feet smell eftir a night ay kickin it in trainers.

— Ah ken that. Take yours for instance. Fuckin mingin, they wir, ah say, rising to make the coffee, as she gies ays a long, contemptuous scowl.

Ah was feeling pretty ropey. The coffee wisnae daein it for me. Ah had tae see The Poisonous Cunt. Ah hud no tae see The Poisonous Cunt. This was getting oot ay hand. Ally had left some ay that crystal meth and ah was intae giein it a go. Ah needed a hit ay something before gaun tae that place. – Ye want a snort ay this? ah asked Amber.

– Nup, widnae touch it.

– That's sensible, ah said, chopping up a couple of lines.

– You're mental, Lloyd. What dae ye dae that fir?

– Dinnae ken. There's something missing in ma life. Ah'm an auld cunt now, compared tae you at any rate, and I've never really been in love. That's fuckin sad, ah telt her, snortin the lines. They are rough and fiery as fuck on my nasal lining.

Amber said, – Aw Lloyd … and gave me a hug and ah wished that ah could be in love with her but I'm no, so nae sense in kiddin oan aye cause that's shite fir every cunt and aw yi'll get is a ride oot ay it and a ride is never worth a good friendship.

She left just as my head blew apart.

15 Heather

The doctor has given me Prozac. Hugh agrees that I should take the Prozac.

– You've been a bit down in the dumps and this will help to tide you over, the doctor told me. Or was it Hugh who said that? I can't remember. It was them both.

Tide me over what?

– I'll see, I tell Hugh, – I don't like the idea of taking drugs in that way, becoming dependent on them. You hear so much about it.

I'm late. Late again for my work. I can't get out of bed.

– Hu–neh–eh ... the doctors are professionals. They know what they're doing, he tells me, as he swings his bag full of golf clubs over his shoulder. He's on a day off on flexi-time today. – God, I'd better go. Billy-boy'll be wondering where I've got to. We're on tee at Pitreavie today, just cause I slaughtered him last week at Canmore. That's Bill, Hugh shrugs. – Maybe we'll nip round to his and Moll's later, eh? Hugh kisses me and departs, – Bye, Honey.

I phone my pal Marie. She tells me to take the day off work sick and get the train over to Haymarket Station in Edinburgh. She's going to take the day off as well. It seems the easiest thing in the world to just agree.

At Dunfermline station I wonder why there's only one train an hour into Edinburgh, when Inverkeithing down the road has three or four. Thankfully I've only fifteen minutes until it's due and then it's only ten minutes late which is pretty good going.

Marie and I go around the shops and then back to her place and sit and drink tea and blether all afternoon. She skins up a few joints and I feel giggly. I don't want to go home. I don't want to but I have to make a move to Haymarket Station.

– Stay here tonight. Let's go out. There's a club on in town. Let's get E'd up and go out, you and me, Marie says.

– I can't … I have to get back … Hugh … I hear myself bleat.

– He's old enough to look after himself for one night. C'mon. Let's do it. You've got Prozac, that's brilliant. We can take them after the Es. They prolong the effects of the Ecstasy while destroying the toxins in the MDMA which may or may not cause brain damage in later life. Therefore Prozac makes E completely safe.

– I don't know … I've never taken drugs in years. I've heard a lot about Ecstasy …

– Ninety per cent of it'll be bullshit. It kills you, but so does everything, every piece of food you ingest, every breath of air you take. It does you a lot less damage than the drink.

– Okay … but I don't want to hallucinate …

– It's no like acid, Heather. You'll just feel good about yourself and the rest of the world for a while. There's nothing wrong with that.

– Okay, I agreed tentatively.

Like a coward, I left a message for Hugh on the answer-phone at home. Then we went out to a pre-club bar and then onto the club. I felt a bit foolish dressed in the clothes Marie had looked out for me. She was the same size as I was and she and I used to swap clothes when we were students. When we dressed the same. When I looked at myself in the mirror, I felt like a clown in the clothes, the short skirt, the tight T-shirt. But they suited Marie, and we were the same age. At the club, I thought everybody would be staring at me, but nobody bothered. I was a bit bored at first. Marie hadn't let us drink in the pubs. It'll spoil the E, she told us. I craved a gin for my nerves.

I took the pill in the club. It came on strong at first and I felt a bit sick in the stomach. I felt a bit bad, though not as bad as I was making out to Marie. – You're making yourself feel bad by fighting it, Marie whispered, smiling at me. Then I felt it in my arms, through my body, up my back: a tingling, rushy sensation. I looked at Marie and she was beautiful. I'd always known that she was beautiful, but I had come, over the years, to look at her in terms of decline. I looked for signs of crow's feet, extra pounds, signs of greying. If I found or didn't find these it didn't matter. The point was that I had been looking for them in Marie, and by implication, in myself, and blinding myself as to how she, and I, really were in totality.

I went to go to the toilet to see myself in the mirror. I didn't seem to walk, but to float through within my own mystical aura. It was like I'd died and was moving through heaven. All those beautiful people were smiling and looking like I was feeling. The thing was, they didn't look any different, you just saw the joy in them. I looked at myself in the mirror. What I did not see was the stupid fucking wife of Hugh Thomson. She was gone.

– Hiya, this girl said to me, – havin a good one?

– Aye … it's absolutely unbelievable! Ah've never been so happy! It's ma first time eckied … I gasped.

She gave me a big hug. – That's really nice. There's nothing like the first time. It's always brilliant, but see the first time …

We talked for ages, and I remembered I had to get back to Marie. It was like I knew everybody though, all those strangers. We shared an insight and an intimacy that nobody who hadn't done this in this environment could ever know about. It was like we were all together in our own world, a world far away from hate and fear. I had let go of fear, that was all that had happened. I danced and the music was wonderful. People, strangers, were hugging me. Guys too, but not in a creepy way. When I thought of Hugh, I felt sorry for him. Sorry that he would never know this, sorry that he had effectively wasted his life. Sorry that he had lost me, which he certainly had now. We were finished. That stage of my life was over and done with.

I was taking the next day off work as well.

16 Lloyd

Ally was right about this stuff. It was true: ye dinnae even blink for days. Ah was soon surging with energy and thoughts. Ah couldnae blink. Ah tried, tried tae force a blink as ah sat oan the lavvy daein a shite. Then something happened: ah couldnae stop blinking. Ah felt sick and thought ah was gaunnae pass out. Ah hit the cold lino on the bathroom floor and felt better with my red throbbing face against it. The blinking stopped and ah was alert again.

The door went and it was a guy called Seeker. He stepped past me into the hallway. He held up a bag and then hooked it onto a small, metal set of scales he'd produced. – Ten grams, he said, – take a dab.

Ah did, though ah couldnae really tell the purity ay the coke from it, cause I'm no a big coke-heid, although it seemed better than Abdab's. Ah asked Seeker if ah could snort a line. He rolled his eyes impatiently, then he chopped out one each for us on the worktop in my kitchen. Ah felt that satisfying numbness but ah was so up on the meth that a poofy line ay toot would make nae real difference. That whole fuckin bag would make nae difference. Anyway, ah gave Seeker his dosh and he fucked off. He's a weird cunt that, no intae any scene, but every cunt kens him.

Ah hive aboot a fifth ay the gear and stick in an equivalent ay non-perfumed talc and mix it. Thir isnae much ay a difference.

In the hoose ah couldnae settle. Ah wis phonin every cunt up and spraffin shite. Ah hud a red phone bill n nae dosh tae pey it, so ah always just go for it at times like that. Ah kept thinking about how ah got involved with The Poisonous Cunt. It was a while back, basically for reasons of finance. I'd do deliveries for her and Solo, who was like her boyfriend or husband or something like that. Solo was a radge, but since he'd received that bad kicking from this other firm he had

never been such a potent force. He seemed slow, like sort of brain-damaged, after he was blootered unconscious. As Jasco once put it: –
They ambulance radges that scraped Solo oaf the pavement seem tae huv left a wee bit ay the perr cunt behind.

Ah must admit that ah wasnae particularly heart-broken, but while he was a bad bastard, ye eywis kent where ye stood wi Solo. The Poisonous Cunt was a different matter. Ah should have suspected the worst when ah belled her and she wouldnae come to the phone. The Victim telt me that ah 'wis tae come round'.

When ah got there the front room was mobbed out. In a corner The Victim sat quietly, looking out the window, her large black eyes tense and furtive, as if trying to anticipate fae where the next shattering blow was going to come into her life. Bobby was there, displaying a smile that dripped sinister contempt. Monts was there, totally wasted, too wasted to even speak to me, while ah picked out Paul Somerville, Spud Murphy and some other cunt ah vaguely recognised. Solo sat in his wheelchair in the corner. It was a fuckin hammer house ay horrors right enough.

– The Poisonous Cunt got off her tits last night, Bobby informed me. – Freebasing coke. She's oan a brutal bastard of a comedown. Ah dinnae envy ye, Lloyd.

Ah didnae need this shite. Ah was just here tae dae a bit ay delivering. Ah went through to the Poisonous Cunt's bedroom, tapping on the door first, and hearing a throaty rasp which might have been come or fuck off, but ah entered anyway.

The Poisonous Cunt was lying on her bed wearing a garish red tracksuit. The telly was on a table at the bottom of the bed. She was smoking hash. Her face was drained of colour, but her black hair looked well washed, had a kind of sheen to it. Her face, though, looked rough, scabby and dehydrated and its contrast with the health of her hair made her look like an old hag wearing a wig. She still had her most startling feature ah had long admired, her thick black eyebrows which joined in the middle, making her look like one of those type of Celtic fans who always look like Paul McStay. Under these brows she had narrow green eyes which were permanently in shadow and usually half-shut. Ah remember once when ah was eckied ah got an erection when ah saw her unshaved armpits visible in a white, sleeveless cotton top. Ah once had a wank about fucking her armpits, ah don't know why this should be, but sexuality's a weird cunt tae try and fathom oot. It caused me some angst for a while, well aboot two or three minutes. There was one particular time when ah was tripping in the chip shop at the fit ay the walk, unable to speak, unable to indicate what ah wanted, unable to think about anything but The Poisonous Cunt's armpits. It was Ally who had started me off about them. He was on acid at Glastonbury and he said in a posh voice: – That lashie Veronica: an awfay abundance ay hair that lashie … After that we couldn't keep our eyes off The Poisonous Cunt's armpits.

Her face twisted at me in ugly recognition, then into a cartoon of disapproval, and ah understood just then why it should really be totally impossible to fancy her.

The Poisonous Cunt shagging: what a thought right enough.

– Well? she snapped.

– Goat it likes, ah said, handing over the bag ay coke.

She tore into it like a predator having a frenzied feast, chopping and snorting, her face contorted the same way it was when ah once saw her rummaging for fag dowts in the contents of my rubbish bin, which she'd tipped out onto the newspaper when she'd run out of snout. Ah cursed her angrily that time, and she went timid as she rolled up a single skin of stale baccy.

It was the first and last time ah saw The Poisonous Cunt deferential.

It was Monts that had given her her nickname. He'd fucked her once and either wouldn't do again, or did do it but no tae her satisfaction, so she'd got the pre-vegetative Solo tae trash his coupon. – That Poisonous Cunt Veronica, he'd muttered bitterly when ah went to visit him in the hospital, his face wrapped in bandages.

– How ye feelin? ah asked. Ah was staring at her profile. Ah could see the ring in her navel where the top part ay her tracksuit had ridden up.

– Shite, she hissed, sucking on the cigarette.

– Dae some rocks, eh?

– Aye … she said, then she turned towards me, – ah'm feelin fuckin crap. Ah've goat bad PMT. The only thing that helps me whin ah'm like this is a good fuck. Ah willnae git one fae that fuckin cabbage through thair. That's aw ah want. A good fuck.

Ah realised that ah was looking straight into her eyes, then ah was tugging at her tracksuit bottoms. – Ah'm fuckin well up fir that …

– Lloyd! she laughed, helping me undress her.

Ah stuck my finger in The Poisonous Cunt's fanny, and it was dripping. She must've been touching herself or it was maybe the crack or something. Anyway, ah got on top of her and pushed my erection into her fanny. Ah was licking her craggy face like a demented dug wi a dry, chipped auld bone as ah pumped mechanically, enjoying her gasps and groans. She was biting my neck and shoulders, but the crystal meth had numbed my body and made it as stiff as a board and ah could have pumped all day. The Poisonous Cunt had orgasm after orgasm and ah showed nae signs ay coming. Ah stuck the poppers under her nose the final time and pushed my finger up her arsehole and she screamed like a fuckin banshee and ah expected everybody tae come ben the bedroom but nae cunt did. Ma heart was thrashing and ah was frightened ah'd just peg oot cause ah got that rapid blinking for a bit but ah managed tae control it. – That's it … that's enough … ah heard The Poisonous Cunt gasp as ah pulled out as stiff and tense as when ah had gone in.

Ah sat up on the bed trying to bend my stiff cock into a semi-comfy position in my jeans. It was like having a piece of wood or metal down your pants. You just wanted tae break it off and chuck it away. Ah shuddered at the thought of how high my blood pressure must be.

– That was fuckin mad … The Poisonous Cunt lay back and gasped.

Ah had tae lie with her until ah could hear the others go. Fortunately she fell into a deep sleep. Ah lay rigid, looking up at the ceiling and thinking aboot what the fuck ah was daein wi ma life. Ah reflected that ah should've fucked The Poisonous Cunt's airmpits while ah hud the chance. If ye huv tae dae something unsavoury that

yir gaunnae regret as soon as you've done it, then at least realising a
sexual fantasy would make it mair acceptable.

Eftir a bit ah went through tae the front room and noted that Solo
and Jasco were asleep oan the couch. Ah left and wandered for a
while through the city, ecky heads going to and coming from clubs
smiling, arm in arm; pish-faces staggering down the road groaning
songs and other cunts cocktailed oan aw sorts ay drugs.

17 Heather

My mind was buzzing as I wandered down Princes Street. Marie had had to stagger into her work at the Scottish Office later that morning, but no way for me. That morning I had, in her flat, picked up a book of Shelley's poems. I couldn't stop reading them, then Blake and Yeats. It's like my mind was in an overdrive for stimulus, I couldn't get enough.

I looked around an art shop in Hanover Street. I wanted to paint. That was what I wanted to do, buy a set of paints. Then I saw an HMV record store and went inside. I wanted to buy every record I saw and I drew the maximum amount of three hundred quid out of my cashline. I couldn't decide what to buy, so I ended up getting some house-music compilation CDs which were probably not that good but anything would be all right after Hugh's Dire Straits and U2 and Runrig.

I went into Waterstone's. I looked around and I bought Ian MacDonald's book on the Beatles and their music in the context of the sixties. There was a quote on the back about a guy who read the book then went out and bought the entire collection of Beatles' albums on CD. I did the same. Hugh didn't like the Beatles. How could you not like the Beatles?

I went for a coffee and thumbed through an *NME* which I hadn't bought for years and read an interview with a guy who used to be in Happy Mondays and had started a band called Black Grape. I then went back to HMV and bought their album, *It's Great When You're Straight … Yeah!*, just because the guy said he had taken loads of drugs.

I bought a few more books and got the train home. There was a message on the machine: – Honey, it's Hugh. Phone me at work.

I then came across a scribbled note in the kitchen:

You gave me a fright. I think you've been a bit selfish. Call me when
you're home.

Hugh

I crumpled the note up. Hugh's Dire Straits CD, *Brothers In Arms*,
was lying on the coffee table. He always played that. I particularly
hated the song Money For Nothing which is what he always sang. I
stuck on my Black Grape CD and put *Brothers In Arms* in the
microwave to prove that what people say about CDs being
indestructible is a lot of rubbish. Just to make doubly sure though, I
watched *Love Over Gold* obliterate in a similar manner.

Hugh is perturbed when he comes in. By this time my mood is
different. I feel run down, depressed. I had four Ecstasies the night
before, which Marie said was way too much for the first time. I didn't
want to stop, didn't want to come down. She warned me about the
comedown. It all seems hopeless.

And Hugh is perturbed.

– Seen the *Brothers In Arms* CD, Honey? Can't find it anywhere …
we got the music n the colour te- veeeehhhh

– No.

– … munneee for nothin … listen, why don't we go for a drive?

– I'm really tired, I tell him.

– Too much to drink at Marie's? What a pair! Seriously though,
Heather, if you're going to take days off work, well, that I can't
condone. I'd be a hypocrite if, after underlining the importance of a
good attendance record to my own employees, word was to get
around; and Dunfermline's not a big place, Heather, if people were
to say that my own wife was a slacker and that I was turning a blind
eye to it …

– I'm tired. I did drink a wee bit too much … I might go upstairs
for a lie down.

– A drive, he says, holding up the car keys and waving them at me
like I was a dog and the keys were the leash.

I can't argue with him. I'm feeling sick, dizzy, tired and washed out, just like I've gone through a cycle on the washing machine.

– I thought that a drive might help cheer us up a wee bit, he smiles, as he pulls the car out of the garage.

Next to him sits this woman with lank hair and dark circles under her eyes. I recognise her from somewhere.

I put on a pair of sunglasses from the glove compartment. Hugh frets disapprovingly.

– I'm ugly, I hear myself say in a small voice.

– You're tired, he says. – You should think about going part-time. It's the strain of being in an organisation that's rationalising. I know; it's the very same at our place. They're bound to feel it at your level of the organisation too. There's always a human cost, unfortunately. Can't make an omelette, eh? Bob Linklater's been off for two weeks now. Stress. Hugh turns to me and rolls his eyes. – Anyway, I'm sure in your case it's genuine. Some people just can't cut it in today's working environment. Sad but true. Anyway, we're doing okay so there's no need for you to martyr yourself at that place to prove some big point, Heather. You know that, don't you, Honey-bunch?

I take off the glasses and look at the white sick face staring back at me, reflected in the side window. My pores are opening up. There's a spot under my lip.

– ... take Alan Coleman's wife ... what's her name? She's a perfect case in point. I doubt whether she'd go back now if they paid her. We'd all like to be in that position, thank you very much! Iain Harker: never off the golf course since he took early retirement ...

A man of twenty-seven talking about early retirement.

– ... mind you, Alasdair and Jenny have turned that section around. It's a pity that one of them has to be disappointed when they eventually come to fill Iain's vacancy. The smart money's on Jenny now, though I suspect they'll go outside and bring in a fresh face to avoid one of them being let down ...

I wondered when Jenny was going to come into the conversation.

– Do you want to lick her cunt?

– ... because when all's said and done – and they're both professional – but if one's appointed and the other isn't ... sorry, Honey, what did you say?

– Do you think she's got the front? Jenny? Quite a shop-window post, stacks of PR, I recall you saying. I'm shivering: paralysing shivers are going through my body in a digitally precise rhythm of one every two seconds.

– God, yeah, I don't think I've ever worked with anyone more assertive, man or woman, Hugh smiles fondly to himself.

Are you fucking her have you been for four years I hope so for your sake cause surely you can't be fucking me that badly unless you're fuckin someone else … – Does she have a boyfriend? I ask.

– She's living with Colin Norman, Hugh says, trying and failing to make the words 'Colin Norman' not sound like 'child molester' or, worse, 'employee with below-average sickness record'.

But the drive is, of course, stage-managed. I know where we're heading. We pull into a familiar driveway.

– Bill and Moll said it was hunky-dory to pop round for a drink, Hugh explains.

– I … eh … I …

– Bill's been on about his office extension. I thought I'd check it out.

– We never see *my* friends!

– Honey-eh-eh … Bill and Moll *are* your friends! Remember!

– Marie … Karen … they were *your* friends as well.

– Well those were Uni friendships; all that student nonsense, Honey. The world moves on …

– I don't want to go in …

– What's wrong, Honey?

– I think I should go …

– Go? Go where? What are you on about? You mean you want to go home?

– No, I whisper, – I think I should go. Just go. For good, my voice has gone into nothing.

Go away from you, Hugh. You play squash but you're still getting a bit paunchy …

– That's the spirit, Honey! That's my girl! he says, springing out of the car.

Bill's in the doorway, ushering us in with pretended surprise. – It's the Thomson twins! How's the fair Heather? Looking gorgeous, as per usual!

– Hugh's jealous, I say, fingering a button on Bill's shirt distractedly, – he says that your extension is bigger than his. Is it?

– Ha ha ha, Bill laughs nervously and Hugh bounds on ahead and has pecked Moll, and now my coat is being tugged off my shoulders. I shudder and I start the shivering again, although it's warm in the house. There's a sort of buffet on the table in the living-room. – Come and try some of Moll's world-famous garlic dip, Bill says.

I feel at this point I should say to Moll: YOU SHOULDN'T HAVE GONE TO ANY TROUBLE, but I can't be bothered. I feel the words coming but there's too many of them and they've stuck in my mouth; I feel I'd have to physically pick them out using my fingers. Anyway, Hugh gets in first: – You shouldn't have gone to such trouble, he smiles at her. Such trouble. I see.

Moll's saying, – It's no trouble at all.

I'm sitting down, hunched forward, and I'm looking at Bill's flies. I decide that opening them and looking for his prick would be like opening a knotted binliner and rummaging through its contents: that fetid stench in your face as you grasped the limp, rotting banana.

– … so Tom Mason stipulated in the contract for the service agreement that we would have a penalty clause on a sliding-scale basis for late delivery which, suffice to say, fairly had the desired effect of concentrating our friend Mister Ross's mind somewhat …

– … sounds like our Tom, covering all bases, Bill says with sage affection.

– Of course, our pal Mark Ross was far from amused at this. Well, the shoe was on the other foot.

– Too damn right! Bill smiles, and Moll does too and it makes me want to shout at her: what the fuck are *you* smiling at, what the fuck is all this to do with *you*, when he adds, – Oh, by the way, I got the seasons.

– Excellent!

– The seasons? I ask. Frankie Valli … and the Four …

– I've got a couple of season tickets for myself and your good true-blue hubby at Ibrox, in the old stand.

– What?

– The football. Glasgow Rangers FC.

– Eh?

– It's a good day out, Hugh says sheepishly.

– But you support Dunfermline. You always supported Dunfermline! For some reason this makes me angry, I don't know why.
– You used to take me to East End Park ... when we were

I can't finish the sentence.

– Yeah, Honey ... but Dunfermline ... I mean, I never really *supported* them as such; they were just the local team. It's all changed now, though, there's no local teams. You have to get behind Scotland in Europe, a real Scottish success story. Besides, I've a lot of respect for David Murray and they know how to put a good corporate hospitality package together at Ibrox. The Pars ... well, that's a different world ... besides, I've always been a bit true-blue deep down.

– *You* supported Dunfermline. You and I went. I remember when they lost that cup final to Hibs at Hampden. You were heartbroken. You cried like a wee boy!

Moll smiles at this and Hugh looks edgy. – Darling, I don't really think Bill and Moll want to hear us arguing about football ... besides, you've never really taken an interest in the game before ... what's all this about?

What's all this about?

– Oh, nothing ... I wearily concede.

That has done it. A man who changes his women you can forgive, but a man who changes his teams ... that shows a lack of character. That's a man who has lost all sight of things that are important in life. I couldn't ever be with someone like that.

– And Moll's made a great spread! This lovely garlic dip!

– It was no trouble, Moll says.

– I'm really sorry, Moll, I've just no appetite, I say, nibbling at a piece of shortbread. I almost jump out of my body as Bill flies across towards me and sticks a plate on top of my tits.

– Whoops! Crumb police! Bill says, forcing a smile on his worried face.

– New carpet, Moll says apologetically.

– Yes, it's such a worry, I hear myself saying.

– Let's take a look at that office, Bill, Hugh says jumping with excitement.

It's time to go.

After a night where I died a thousand deaths, Bill says, – Hugh, I don't think Heather's too well. She's sweating and shaking.

– Have you got a touch of the flu, Heather? Moll asks.

– Yeah, Honey, I think we'd better get you off, Hugh nods.

When we get home I start to pack. Hugh doesn't even notice. We go to bed and I tell him I've got a headache.

– Oh, he says, then drifts off to sleep.

I'm still waking up when he's ready to go to work. He's in his suit and he's standing over me and I'm groggy and he's saying: – You should get ready for work, Heather. You're going to be late. C'mon, Honey, shake a leg. I'm counting on you!

With that, he departed.

So did I.

I left a note:

> Dear Hugh,
>
> Things haven't been right between us for a while.
> This is my fault, I put up with changes in you and
> our life over the years. These were incremental
> so I was a bit like the 'boiled frog' you talk about
> in your business management seminars. The
> environment changes so gradually, you put up with
> it unawares that it's all slipped away from you.
>
> No blaming, no regrets, it's just over. Take all the
> money, the house, goods, etc. I don't want to
> keep in touch with you as we've nothing in common
> so nothing but falseness or nastiness would be
> served by that, but no hard feelings on my part.
>
>   Heather

I suddenly feel a liberating surge of anger and write: PS: when we fucked over the last four years it was like rape for me; then I look at it and tear that bit off in a strip. I don't want to get into that. I just want it ended.

I took a taxi to the station and got a train to Haymarket and another taxi to Marie's in Gorgie. I'm thinking of records, books, clubs, drugs and fresh paint on canvas. I suppose boys as well. Boys. Not men. I've had enough of men. They are the biggest boys of all.

18 Lloyd

Ally isnae amused and Woodsy's the source of his irritation. – That cunt, man, thinks eh kin jist swan in here like the pre-heart-attack Graeme Souness oan high-grade cocaine spoutin the contents ay *Mixmag* like we used tae dae wi the *NME* when we were younger, and every cunt's meant tae say: Wow Woodsy, man, right on, ya cunt, wow man, and queue up tae suck oan his cheesy wee helmet. That. Will. Be. Fuckin. Right.

– He's bad enough now, wait till ye see the cunt once he actually gets his hole, Monts smirked.

– Thankfully, there isnae much chance ay that, man, Ally smiles, – that's what it's aboot, man, this arrogance. It's just defiance. He's no hud his fuckin hole in yonks. That fucks up any cunt's self-esteem. This ego-projection, man, is just the cunt's wey ay copin. Once he gets his hole, he'll actually calm doon. That's what aw this religion shite's aboot.

– Well ah hope eh does. Either that or ah hope he just gits so fuckin arrogant that he willnae even talk tae the likes ay us. Then it would be problem solved, Monts decides.

– Ah'd get a whip-round, man, thegither n pey fir a hoor tae dae the business oan the cunt, if it helped tae sort his heid oot, Ally said.

– Woodsy's awright, ah said. Ah was daein a gig wi him the morn so that obliged ays tae back the cunt up. – Ah mean, ah dinnae mind aw the referencing ay DJs n clubs aw the time. That's cool, save me buying *Mixmag* and *DJ* hearin that cunt recitin it tae ye. It's the religion shite ah cannae really git tae grips wi. Tell ye what though, man, ah respect the cunt for it.

– Fuck off, Lloyd, Ally says dismissively.

– Naw, ah thought it was a fad. Then ah read that book by that

cunt that writes aboot E whae wis sayin that he kens monks and
rabbis that take it tae get in touch wi thir spirituality.

– Lick on, dug's baws, Ally grins, – so man, you're tryin tae tell ays
that eh talked tae God at Rezurrection?

– Naw, what ah'm sayin is that the cunt thinks eh does, and eh
thinks it in good faith. So for him it's the same as it huvin happened.
Personally ah jist think that he wis pure cunted and went intae the
auld white room and had a hallucination, but he thinks it wis mair
thin that. Neither ay us kin prove the other cunt wrong so ah huv tae
accept that what the cunt says is real *fir him*.

– Shite. By that fuckin logic, man, some community-care cunt
could tell ye he believes that he's fuckin Hitler or Napoleon, and you
believe that?

– Naw … ah say, – it's no a question ay *believin* some cunt's reality
as they see it, it's a question ay *respectin* some cunt's reality as they see
it. Of course, that's as long as they dinnae hurt any other cunt.

– Declare a fuckin interest here but, Lloyd ya cunt: you're jist
backin the cunt cause ay the gig yir daein fir the guy, man. The
Rectangle. Pilton. A Tuesday eftirnoon! It'll be pony, Ally laughs.

– Sounds a wee bit dodgy right enough but, Lloyd, Monts laughs.

This bullshit is getting ays well nervy and hyper aboot this fuckin
gig.

19 Heather

We meet in the tea-room at the Carlton Hotel. My mother has that you've-been-a-big-disappointment-to-us-all expression on her face. Strange how I used to let it snap me right back into line. It still produces a strange, uncomfortable feeling in my chest and stomach: that framed, lined face with those strained, slightly terrorised eyes. Normally enough to put me back in my old place, but not now. I'm aware of the discomfort. Awareness is seventy per cent of the solution.

– Hugh came round last night, she says accusingly, leaving a long silence.

I almost start to speak. But no. Remember: do not be manipulated by other people's use of silences. Resist the temptation to fill in the gaps. Choose your words. Be assertive!

– He was broken-hearted, my mother goes on, – You work hard, he said. You give them everything. What do they want? What do they want? I just said, I'm damned if I know, Hugh. She's had everything, I told him. That's what's been the problem with you, you've had it all on a plate, young lady. Perhaps it's been our fault. We just wanted you to have all the things that we never had ...

My mother's voice has become low and even. The effect is surprisingly soothing and transcendental. I feel myself floating off, to all the places I wanted to go to, to all the things I wanted to see ... maybe there will be something for me ... good times ... love ...

– ... because we always felt that no sacrifice was too much. When you have children of your own you'll understand, Heather ... Heather, you're not even listening to me!

– I've heard it all before.

– I beg your pardon?

– I've heard all this. All my life. It means nothing. It's just a sad exercise in self-justification. You don't need to justify your lives to me; it's your affair. I'm not happy. Hugh, the life we have together, it's not what I want. That's not your fault … it's not his …

– I think you're being so selfish …

– Yeah, I suppose I am, if it means that I'm thinking about my own needs for the first time in my life …

– But we've always put your needs first!

– As you saw them, and I thank you and love you for that. I want an opportunity to stand on my own feet, without you or Dad or Hugh doing everything for me. It's not your fault, it's mine. I've capitulated for too long. I know I've hurt everyone and I'm sorry for that.

– You've become so hard, Heather … I don't know what's happened to you. If you knew how upset your father is …

She left shortly after this and I went back to the flat and cried. Then something happened to change everything. My dad called me up.

– Listen, I said, – if you're phoning to moan …

– No, not all, he said – I agree with what you're doing and I salute your courage. If you're not happy, there's no point in sticking around. You're still young enough to do what you want without getting yourself tied down. So many people just keep going, even when they're in a rut. You only get one life, you go ahead and lead it the way you want to. You'll always have our love and our support, I hope you know that. Your mum's upset, but she'll come round. Hugh's big enough to look after himself …

– Dad … you don't how much this means to me …

– Don't be daft. Just get on with your life. If you need anything … if you're short of cash …

– No … I'm fine …

– Well, if you need anything, you know where we are. All I ask is that you stay in touch.

– Of course I will … and thanks, Dad …

– Okay, darlin. You take care now.

I started to cry even more, because I realised that it had all been me. I had anticipated a reaction from the world which was nothing like the way it really responded. It wasn't going to condemn. It just didn't give a fuck.

That night I lay alone in bed in the flat and thought about sex.

Twenty-six years old.

Four previous lovers, before Hugh that is, but Hugh is now also previous, so it's five previous lovers before my current state of between lovers.

No. 1. Johnny Bishop

Tough, surly, sixteen. Another boy with nice looks playing at being James Dean. I remembered thinking that there was hidden tenderness in him that I could bring out. All the silly little macho arsehole did was to fuck too quickly and unimaginatively and pull out and leave me like I was the scene of a crime. He screwed me like he screwed the local shops; get in quickly with the minimum of fuss, then withdraw from the scene of the crime a.s.a.p.

No. 2. Alan Raeburn

Shy, reliable, dull. Johnny's antithesis. A cock so big it hurt, too much of a gentleman not to make it hurt just a little bit more. Left him when I went to St Andrew's University.

No. 3. Mark Duncan

A student wanker. Second year, a fuck-a-fresher exponent. A crap shag, or more like I was too pissed at the time to know the difference.

No. 4. Brian Liddell

Wonderful. It was all there. Sexually. I was still slightly worried about actually enjoying sex, about being seen to be such an easy lay, and I wouldn't let him go down on me for a long time. Once he did, he couldn't get his head out of my hands. Any boy who fucks that well at that age won't be just fucking one girl though, and he wasn't and I had my pride.

Then Hugh. Hugh Thomson. My Number Five. Did I love him? Yes. I can see him in the students' union bar, destroying reactionary arguments, destroying pints of lager. Everything always done with certainty. He made me feel safe with his certainties, until they changed to other certainties. Then I didn't feel safe with certainties any more. I just felt trapped by bullshit.

Now this.

Nothing.

Suspended animation. Suspended lack of animation.

So now I've done several things within four weeks which has radically changed my life. The first one was that I left Hugh and moved in with Marie: to my own room in her place in Gorgie. It was a cliché, but in order to find myself, I had to leave the thesis for the antithesis.

The second thing I did was to leave my job and apply to do a teacher-training course. I realised that I had £6,500 in the building society – not Hugh's, mine: my one little bastion of independence during our marriage. I had nothing to spend money on, as Hugh provided cash for everything. I was going to sign on the dole, but

Marie told me that there was little point as they would check that I had left of my own accord and I wouldn't get any benefit anyway. I was accepted on a course at Moray House; I didn't want to be a teacher but I did want to do *something*, and it was all I could think of.

The other thing I did which changed my life was to go to that club and take that Ecstasy. I'd do it again, but I had a lot to sort out in my head first.

Marie and I went to Ibiza for a fortnight. Marie shagged four guys while we were there. I shagged loads and took lots of Ecstasy ... no I didn't. I stayed in the hotel and cried my eyes out. I was depressed as fuck and terrified. There was no liberation for me. Marie swanned around the clubs and bars in San Antonio like she owned the place, a different young hunk with her every day. She lived nocturnally, coming back to our hotel room late in the morning looking really strange: not drunk, but tired, lucid, excited and positive. She listened a lot to me, let me talk about Hugh, about how I had loved him, about all our hopes and dreams and my aches inside. I left her and got an early flight back from Ibiza. She wanted to come back, but I told her no, I probably needed time alone to think. I'd fucked up enough of her break as it was.

– Don't worry, she said at the airport, – it was just a bit too much, too soon. The next time you'll enjoy it.

I went home, back to the flat in Gorgie. I kept up my reading. I would go to Thin's and Waterstone's during the day and read more. I sat in cafés. I hoped that the summer would end – anything to get me onto that course, to get me doing something to take my mind off Hugh. The thing was, I knew I would have to go through it. I knew that there was no turning back for me. This pain, this blockage, like a physical thing, it just wouldn't leave my chest. But there could be no going back. It just wasn't an option.

I don't know how he got my address, but he found me. It was just as well. It was one evening at six. I trembled when I saw it was him at the door. It was strange, but he had never been physically violent towards me, but all I could sense were his size and strength compared to me. That and the rage in his eyes. I only stopped trembling when he started talking. Thank God he started talking. This sad prick, he had learned nothing. As soon as he opened his mouth I could feel him shrink and me grow.

– I thought that you might have got this silly wee game out of your system by now, Heather. Then I got to thinking that you might be worried about the hurt you've caused everyone and be too ashamed to come home. Well, we've always talked things through. I admit that there's a lot I can't quite fathom about this at the moment, but you've made your little statement, so you should be happy now. I think it would be better if you just came home. What about it, Honey?

The thing was, he was serious. I had never been so grateful to anyone in my life as I was to Hugh at that moment. He showed me exactly how stupid I was to feel this way about him. The thing in my chest just evaporated. I felt brilliant: all high and giddy. I started to laugh; to laugh loudly in his stupid, ridiculous face. – Hugh … ha ha ha … look … ha ha ha ha ha ha … I think you should go home before you … ha ha ha … before you make an even bigger prick of yourself than you have already … ha ha ha … what a fucking wanker …

– Are you on something? he asked. He looked around the flat as if seeking confirmation.

– Ha ha ha ha … am I on something! Am I on something! I flew back last week a miserable wreck from fucking Ibiza! I should be on something! I should be E'd off my tits with Marie, shagging the first guy I set eyes on! Getting fucked properly!

– I'm going! he shouted, and left. In the stairwell, he rasped up at me, – You're off your head! You and your junkie pal. That fucking Marie bitch! Well, it's over! It's over!

– YOU FUCKIN WELL CATCH ON QUICK DON'T YE, YA STUPID FUCK! GET A FUCKIN LIFE FOR YOUR-SELF! AND LEARN HOW TO SHAG PROPERLY!

– YOU'RE FUCKIN WELL FRIGID! THAT'S YOUR PROBLEM! he shouts back.

– NO IT WAS YOUR FUCKIN PROBLEM! YOU HAVEN'T GOT FINGERS! YOU HAVEN'T GOT A TONGUE! YOU HAVEN'T GOT A SOUL! YOU HAVEN'T

GOT AN INTEREST IN ANYTHING BUT YOUR STUPID
FUCKIN BUILDING SOCIETY YOU POMPOUS LITTLE
PRICK! FOREPLAY! LOOK IT UP IN THE FUCKIN
DICTIONARY! FOREFUCKINGPLAY!

– FUCKING LESBO! STICK WITH MARIE, YOU
FUCKING DYKE!

– GET SHAGGED UP THE ARSE BY THAT OTHER
BORING PRICK, BILL! THAT'S WHAT YOU FUCKING
WELL WANT!

Mrs Cormack from across the landing comes out. – Sorry … I
heard a noise. I heard shouting.

– A bit of a lovers' tiff, I tell her.

– Aw well, the path ay true love, eh hen? she said, then she
whispered, – better off withoot them.

I gave her the thumbs up and went back in, already looking
forward to Marie returning. I was going to take every drug known to
the human race and shag anything that moved.

It was weird going out during the day and feeling free, feeling really
single. I got whistled at from those workies doing the pavement in
Dalry Road but instead of getting embarrassed as I would have done
a few years ago, or angry as I would have done the other day, I did
actually do as one stupid fucker in his silly death-moan of a voice
suggested and smy-yelled the-ehn. I then felt a little annoyed at
myself, because I didn't want to give those sad fucks their way, but it
was for me, because I was happy.

I found myself up Cockburn Street, not seriously cruising guys,
but sort of checking them out. I bought about four hundred quid's
worth of clothes and make-up. Most of my other clothes I stuffed
into binliners and took to the Cancer Research Shop.

Marie could tell there was a big change in me. The poor lassie was
totally fucked when she came back. – All I want to do is lie low for a
while, she moaned, – and I never want to see another pill or another
cock as long as I live.

– No way, I told her, – Tribal Funktion's on tonight.

– I think I liked you better as a housewife, she smiled.

20 Lloyd

Just talking aboot Woodsy got me nervous about the gig. The mair ah thought aboot it, the mair uncool it was. Woodsy was planning to have a rave at the Rectangle Club in Pilton (or Reck-Tangle as he'd put on the flyers) on a Tuesday afternoon. That was pretty fuckin weird in itself. Ah tried to get every cunt to come, but Ally said no way, just because of how he felt about Woodsy.

Amber and Nukes were up for it but, and Drewsy ran us down in the van. When we got there nae cunt was around except the hall caretaker. Woodsy already had his decks, mixer, amps and speakers set up. His gear was better than Shaun's so I wanted a shot before I started.

Woodsy came in a wee bit later with this minister cunt. – This is Reverend Brian McCarthy of East Pilton Parish Church. He's supporting the gig, Woodsy telt us. This straight-peg cunt in a dog-collar grins at us. Ah wondered if he was eckied.

Ah didnae huv long tae wait before findin oot cause Woodsy goes, – Ah've goat some fuckin good Es here, and handing one over to the Rev., urged him, – Neck it, Bri.

– I'm afraid I can't take ... *drugs* ... the poor cunt sais, looking horrified.

– Neck it, man, neck it and find the Lord, says Woodsy.

– Mr Woods, I can't condone drug-taking in my parish ...

– Aye, well, whaire's aw yir parishioners then, eh? Woodsy growled, – Yir church wisnae exactly stowed oot when ah wis doon last Sunday. Mine wis!

There were some wee kids and some mothers and toddlers

coming into the hall. – When's this rave startin then? a woman asked.

– In a wee minute, eh, Amber told her.

– It's great thit thir daein this for the bairns, another mother said.

The minister cunt walked away, leaving Woodsy shouting at him: – Fuckin hypocrite! You've nae spirituality! Dinnae fuckin tell ays otherwise! Satanic cunt in a cloth! Thirs nae church except the church ay the self! Thirs nae medium between man and god except MDMA! Fuckin scam artist!

– Shut it, Woodsy, ah sais, – c'moan, let's git started. A crowd were clocking the embarrassed minister leaving.

There were plenty young cunts coming in. – They should aw be at school, Amber went.

When ah got in ah'd noted that two hard bastards had got a table-tennis table out and had started playing in the middle ay the dance floor. Woodsy flipped when he saw them. – Hi! We've booked this! he snapped.

– You wantin a fuckin burst mooth, ya cunt? You're no fae here! one of the nutters snarled.

– The boy's right, Woodsy, this isnae your club, ah cut in, – thirs plenty room here. Youse dinnae mind us playin our sounds and huvin a bop, boys? Ah addressed this remark tae the hardest-lookin ay the two hard cunts.

– Dae whit yis like, eh, the probably hardest cunt replies.

Ah got up and started puttin on the tunes. At first ah wisnae really mixin, just sort ay playing the sounds like, but then ah started really gaun for it, tryin oot one or too things. It was shite, but ah was so intae it, every cunt was getting intae it tae. The mothers n toddlers were jumpin, the wee neds were rave-dancing wi each other and even the two hard cunts had stopped playin the t.t. and were going fir it. Woodsy's Es were all snapped up and Amber even managed to flog a few ay ma Doves. Ah necked a couple myself and swallowed a wee wrap ay that crystal meth. Within an hour, the place was fill tae the brim. At first ah didnae see the polis come in, but the guy pulled the plug oan us and broke it up, before perr auld Woodsy got a chance to dae anything.

Then ah went up to the toon tae this club that wis oan and then ah saw her.

21 Heather

I was at the club with Denise and Jane, two pals of Marie's who had become pals of mine in the time it takes for that first Ecstasy to flow through your body and for you to dance with them, hug them and sit up and cry with them about how you fucked everything up for the last few years. What you learn when people open up like this is that we are all basically the same and that all we have is each other. The politics of the last twenty years in Britain are liars' politics. The problem is we are ruled by the weak and the small-minded, who are too stupid to know that they are weak and small-minded.

In the club I'm sitting like this in the chill-out room, talking with Jane, and we're just coming up on an E. I know I'm going on, but I'm learning so much again, I'm feeling so much. This guy comes and sits beside us. He sees Jane and asks if it's anyone's seat. She says no.

He sits down and smiles at her and says, – Wasted, twiddling his finger against the side of his head.

– Yeah, us as well, she says.

– Ah'm Lloyd, he turns and shakes her hand.

– Jane.

He smiles at her and gives her a wee hug round her shoulders. Then he turns to look at me. He says nothing. His eyes are huge black pools. There's something going from his eyes to inside me, right deep inside of me. It's almost like I'm feeling my self reflected back at me. Eventually I clear my throat and say, – Heather.

Jane seemed to sense something happening and went upstairs to dance. Lloyd and I just sat and talked and joked. We blethered about everything: our lives, the world, the lot. Then after a bit, he said, – Listen, Heather, is it cool for me tae gie ye a hug, eh? Ah'd just like tae hold ye for a bit.

– Okay, I said. It had happened. Something. Something had happened.

We hugged for a long time. When I closed my eyes I was lost in his warmth and his smells. Then I felt like we were moving, floating away together. I felt his grip on me tighten and I responded. We were feeling it together. Then he suggested that we leave. He walked with his arm around me, tucking me close to him, occasionally brushing my hair from my face so that he could see my eyes.

We walked up Arthur's Seat and looked down on the city. It was getting cold and I only had on a light top, so he took off this warm zipper top and wrapped it carefully round me. We just talked a bit more and watched the sun come up. Then we walked home across the city, and I asked him in. We just sat in my room playing tapes and drinking tea. Then Marie and Jane came back.

We all just talked. I don't think I've ever been happier.

Later Lloyd got ready to go. I wanted him to stay. At the door he was stroking my arms as he told me, – That was mair than just a brilliant night. I'll gie ye a phone. There's a lot ah want tae talk tae ye aboot, cause ah really enjoyed that spraff last night. Gave me loads tae think about, in aw ways.

– Me too.

– Well, ah'll phone ye.

He kissed me on the mouth, then stood back. – Fuckin hell … he gasped, shaking his head. – Tro Heather, he said, moving down the stairs.

My pulse was racing so much. I wanted to get away. I ran through to my room and wrapped myself in my duvet.

– Whoahh! Marie said. I hadn't even realised that she was still sitting there in the room.

– What the fuck am I playing at? I laughed.

All day I was marking time until the phone went.

22 Lloyd

You can tell that something's cooking in the emotional stratosphere beyond the buzzes ay the drugs U4E ah when your personal behaviour starts to change. Since ah met her last week ah've started to shower every day and brush my teeth twice a day. Ah've also taken to wearing fresh pants and socks on a daily basis which is a killer at the launderette. Usually one pair ay Y's lasted during the week and the other pair did for the clubbing. Most crucially, ah've been scrubbing under the helmet meticulously. Even the flat looks different. No clean and tidy exactly, but better.

Nukes is up for a blaw. It's strange that Nukes is such a peaceable guy who would never think of ever getting intae bother outside the fitba. Saturday though, it's all different: a different Nukes comes out to play. But no now. He's taken a back seat oan everything since the polis clocked him. I'm a wee bit stoned. I'm really better talking tae Ally aboot affairs ay the heart, but Nukes is pretty cool.

– See, Nukes, ah'm no used tae this game, eh no? Ah mean ah've nivir really been in love before so ah dinnae ken whether or no it's real love, the chemicals or just some kind ay infatuation. There seems tae be something thair though, man, something deep, something spiritual …

– Cowped it yit? Nukes asks.

– Naw naw listen the now … sex isnae the issue here. We're talkin aboot love. Electricity, chemistry n aw that – but beyond that, cause that's sex, just the buzz. But ah dinnae ken what love is, man, likesay *being in love*.

– You wir mairried wir ye no?

– Aye, donkey's years ago, but ah didnae have a clue then. Ah wis only seventeen. Aw ah wanted was ma hole every night, that wis the reason tae git mairried.

– Good enough reason. Nowt wrong wi yir hole every night, eh.

– Aye, aw right, but ah soon discovered that, aye, sure, ah wanted it every night awright, but no offay the same lassie. That wis when the trouble started.

– Well that's mibbee it but, Lloyd. Mibbee you've jist found the definition ay true love: Love is when ye want yir hole every night, but offay the same lassie. There ye go. So did ye git yir hole offay this bird then?

– Listen, Nukes, thir's some lassies that ye git yir hole offay, and there's others that ye make love tae. Ken what ah mean?

– Ah ken that, ah ken that. Ah fuckin well make love tae them aw, ya cunt, ah just use the expression 'git yir hole' cause it's shorthand and sounds a bit less poofy, eh. So where did ye meet this bird?

– Up The Pure, eh. It wis her first time there.

– It's no a stoat-the-baw job, is it? That's your usual fuckin style, ya cunt!

– Like fuck, man, she's aboot twenty-six or some shite. She wis mairried tae this straight-peg, n she just fucked off and left him. She was oot wi her pal, jist her first or second time eckied like.

Nukes pits his hands up in front ay his face. – Whoah … slow doon thair gadgie … what ye fuckin well saying tae ays here? Ye meet this bird whae's oot fir the first time since she escaped this straight-peg, she's taken her first ever ecky, you're E'd up and yir talkin love? Sounds a wee bit like the chemical love tae me. Nowt wrong wi that, but see if it lasts the comedoon before ye start thinkin aboot churches, limos and receptions.

– Well, we'll see, ah say tae Nukes, noticing how different each ay his profiles is. One side ay his face is dead handsome, the other really geekish. The American-evening-television Nukes and the American-daytime-television Nukes. I'm tryin tae visualise Heather in her totality. All I can think about is eyes and face. It strikes me that ah dinnae even ken what her tits and arse are like: size, shape, form n aw that. It surprises me; ah always clock that sort ay thing first. My face seems never tae be more than a few feet fae hers when we're thegither. This is defo different, but it would be fuckin horrible tae die the now, just fuckin peg oot withoot ever huvin that total sense ay her.

– Tread warily, Lloyd, that's aw ah'm sayin, Nukes turns tae show off his good side, – Ye ken how easy it can be tae feel great aboot somebody when yir eckied up. Ah mind ay once a few ay us gaun through tae a Slam do oan the Renfrew Ferry. Ah wis jist comin up oan ma pill n Henzo comes runnin up tae ays sayin, fuckin battle stations here, ye cunt, the place is full ay Motherwell cashies. So ah looks over and sure enough, it's the whole Saturday Service crew, top boys n aw, groovin doon in a big wey. So ah turns tae Henzo an says: just fuckin chill ya tube. Every cunt's fuckin loved-up the night. They boys are sound. They're jist like us, eh; they'll take the fuckin buzz where they can find it. Disnae matter whether it's the house buzz wi the E or the swedge buzz wi the adrenalin, it's aw the same. So ah goes up tae this big cunt ah recognised and wi jist point at each other and laugh for a bit, then it's big hugs aw roond. He introduces ays tae the rest ay his crew and we're pertyin away thegither. He says tae me: this rush isnae quite as good as the swedge rush, but ye can get tae sleep easier eftir a few nights. Ah'm up fir days wi the swedge rush, cannae sleep or fuck all. That's us big mates, but jist wait till we're next at Fir Park. Nae quarter asked or given, eh.

– So what ye sayin?

– It's like at a rave we create a kind ay environment, and it isnae just the E – although it's maistly the E – that encourages that kind ay feelin. It's the whole vibe. But it doesnae transfer that well tae the ootside world. Oot thair, these cunts have created a different environment and that kind ay environment lends itself mair tae the swedge rush.

– Thing is but, ye could still find love, real love, in the club environment. It just helps people tae get thegither, tae open up mair and lose thir inhibitions. Nowt wrong wi that.

– Ah bit listen tae this. Sometimes the whole thing plays tricks oan ye. When yir eckied, every bird looks a fuckin doll. Ye want tae try the acid test: go oot wi her trippin the next day. See what she looks like then! Ah remember one night at Yip Yap ah pills this wee bird.

Fuckin tidy n aw, ah'm telling ye, man. So the emotions are sizzlin away and bein a romantic type ay cunt ah suggests a wee walk up Arthur's Seat tae watch the sun comin up, eh no?

– Bein E'd up oot yir face, ye mean.

– That's exactly the fuckin point but! If ah wis jist left tae ma ain devices ah wid huv said somethin like: fancy comin back tae ma place, ken? Bit naw, cause ah wis eckied ah acted in a different wey fae usual. Mind you, the thing is that now ah'm eywis eckied so that's become the fuckin normal wey ah do act! But anywey, what wis ah sayin?

– The bird, Arthur's Seat, ah reminds him.

– Aye, right … well, this bird thinks, cause she's E'd in aw, she's thinkin tae herself: this is a romantic cunt. So wir up oan Arthur's Seat and ah looks at her in the eye and says: ah really want tae make love tae ye now. She's up for it, so it's oaf wi the fuckin gear n we starts gaun for it, cowpin away, looking doon oan the city, fuckin great it wis. Thing is, about ten minutes intae it, ah started tae fell like shite. Ah goat aw that creepy, tense, sick wey; the comedoon's diggin in good style. They wir funny cunts fir that, they flatliners. Anyhow, aw ah wanted tae dae was tae blaw ma muck and git the fuck oot ay thair. That's what ah did, eh. The bird wisnae pleased, but there ye go, needs must. So ye have tae watch oot before ye call it love. It's just another form ay entertainment. See if the feelings transfer tae yir everyday life, then call it love. Love's no jist for weekenders.

– The thing is, Nukes, ah'm changin the keks everyday and cleanin under the helmet.

Nukes raised his eyebrows and smiled, – Must be love then, he said, then he added, – Oan your side, right enough. What's gaun oan wi her though, mate?

23 Heather

— Lloyd. You never really think that you'll be going out with someone with a name like that, I tell Marie.

Marie looks tired. She hates her job, and it's Tuesday. She's on the comedown and she's burnt out. She says she wants a life beyond the weekend but she can't resist its temptations. Besides, what's on offer during the nine-to-five weekday doesn't measure up. — Yeah, it's funny how it all works out, she moans distractedly.

— The thing about Lloyd is, I say, well aware that I'm boring her, exasperating her, perhaps even irritating the fuck out of her, but I can't stop, — is that he doesn't seem to want anything.

— Everybody wants something. Does he want you? she asks, forcing her attention on me. She's a wee sweetheart.

— I think so, I smile. This flat's in a real state. It must look even more horrible to Marie, her on that comedown. I'll give it a tidy later.

— When are you going to shag him? she asks, then says, — it's about time you got fucked properly.

— I don't know. I feel pretty strange around him. Very inexperienced and nervous.

— Well, that's exactly what you are, she tells me.

— I've been married for five years, I tell her.

— Exactly! If you've been with the same guy for five years who hasn't even been fucking you satisfactorily, then it's like being totally inexperienced. If the sex is just a meaningless ritual, if it means nothing and feels nothing, then it is nothing, and it's like never having had it. A lot of men are wankers cause they don't mind bad sex, but for a woman bad sex is far worse than no sex at all.

– What do you know about bad sex, Ms Shag-Artiste? I thought you always sought out the best?

– I know a lot more about it than you think. Remember back in our teens we used to joke about the smash-and-grab brigade? Well, they still exist. A few weeks ago I met this really cool-looking guy, a real hunk; about twenty-five, twenty-six. We're both on these really nice pills and there was a brilliant love vibe up at Yip Yap. Anyway, I got swept up in it all and ended up on Arthur's Seat with him. We got wrapped into each other, but he started to go all tense and funny and then just came inside me and got away as quick as he could. He wouldn't even wait for me. Left me there on top of the fucking hill. A fucking silly bastard in a jerkin walking his dog came past while I was sobbing my heart out. Watch out for this guy if it's a chemical romance. Go slow. Beware.

– You know, Lloyd played me this record the other day, by Marvin Gaye, one of his less well-known songs. It's called Piece of Clay. It was saying like, everybody wants someone to be their piece of clay, to mould them, you know. Lloyd doesn't seem like that. With Hugh, it was like he was moulding me right from the start. Everything I said or thought or did was circumscribed and controlled by his views, obsessions or ideologies, from revolutionary socialism to managerial career advance. There was always a struggle of some sort, identified by him of course, that dictated the pattern of our whole fucking lives. There was no time for us to just act like human beings. Lloyd, though, he's interested in me. He listens to me. He doesn't laugh or sneer or cut in or put down or counter-argue with what I say, or, if he does, at least I know he's heard me. I don't feel ridiculed or belittled or patronised when he challenges me.

– So Lloyd isn't Hugh. You're free, you're attracted to this guy who sounds a bit of a waster. Nae job, deals drugs, no ambition to do anything else, crackpot pals. That must seem a very tempting world after the one you've been in, Heather, but I wouldn't get too carried away by it all. It won't seem so glamorous after the passage of time. Just enjoy it as a trip. Don't give out so much. That's your trouble, you give out too much. Hold back something for you, Heather. Otherwise you'll find that they'll just keep taking. They'll take it all, girl. It's one thing winning freedom, it's another thing holding onto it.

— You're a cynical fuckin cow, hen.

— I'm trying to be realistic.

— Yeah, you're right. That's the big fucking problem. You're right.

24 Lloyd

It was just so beautiful, beyond anything ah could have imagined I'd ever feel. It was love no sex. Sex was just the starting motor; this was pure love action. Ah felt her essence, ah know ah did. Ah know she did too, ah know she got there like she'd never done in her life, cause she was greetin and hiding her face. She felt like she had never been that exposed before. Ah tried tae put my arm around her, but she pulled away. Ah suppose after her sexual problems with the guy she was married to, it was such a big emotional ordeal and she needed time to herself. Ah could dig that, thank fuck I'm a sensitive cunt. Okay, ah said to her softly, okay, I'll gie you some time oan yir ain. It sounded a bit fuckin daft but it was all ah could think of saying. Ah went through to the living-room and put on Scotsport: Hibs v. Aberdeen.

She was a bit distant and nippy eftir that, and she went back over tae hers. Ah suppose she just needed time tae git it sorted oot. Ah made up a Bobby Womack tape fae Shaun's collection and took it up tae ma Ma and Dad's.

25 Heather

It was a nightmare. Our first fucking time and it was a nightmare. The most horrible thing was that I was so close to getting there. I never got close with Hugh, so it didn't really bother me. I got close but I knew I wasn't going to, so I cried with frustration, and that selfish bastard Lloyd did fuck all except blow his load and roll over, then walk around with a stupid smile on his face all day, talking hippy bullshit and watching football on the telly.

I had to go.

26 Lloyd

This time it was even better than the first time, for me *and* for her. Ah didnae realise it, but ah fucked up big style the first time. She telt me how it felt for her. It was a bit ay a shock. Ah think it's because you always want to get the first one over, there's too much at stake when it's someone you're really intae. The first shag stands alongside yir fledgling relationship like a big question mark, when it's somebody you really care for, really love. Then once you get it oot the road you can settle down tae making love. Things like foreplay can come mair intae their ain. It's funny how there's nae embarrassment aboot stickin yir cock intae a strange lassie, but like licking and caressing her are a bit dodgy the first time. Ah should've got E'd up the first time ah made love tae Heather, eh. E makes it great for strangers, the barriers come down so that sex with a stranger on E is magnificent. See wi someone you love though, the barriers should be down anyway, so the chemicals shouldn't make any difference. Eh, no? This is what ah want tae discuss with Nukes when he comes up.

Ah make some tea and build a spliff and put on the video of the Orb, the one wi the Dolphins. Keep it psychoactive, there's sex things ah want tae confide in wi Nukes. The spliff is good for Edinburgh soapbar and Nukes is up at my door on cue. Ah've goat ma love tape oan: Marvin, Al Green, The Tops, Bobby Womack, The Isleys, Smokey, The Temptations, Otis, Aretha, Dionne and Dusty. It melts ma fuckin hert, man. Jist git that oan and apply it tae yir ain life n ye'd huv tae be a deid cunt no tae feel as emotional as fuck, eh no. Barry.

– Awright, ma man, Nukes smiles.

– Glad ye came ower, mate, thir was somethin ah wanted tae talk tae ye aboot.

– Aye?

– Ah jist wanted tae see if ye fancied comin up tae McDiarmid Park for the BP Youth game the moarn's night. Ally's takin the car, eh.

– Na, cannae be ersed. Snooker tourney doon the club, eh ... by the way, you cowped that bird yit, Lloyd?

Ah like Nukes, ah lap the cunt up, but see the day? The day ah wish it wis Ally or Amber that had come roond.

27 Heather

When I get home I can hardly keep the smile off my face.

– How was it then, Marie asks me, toking on a spliff.

I'm looking around the flat. It's a total wreckage. Ashtrays full, curtains still drawn, cassettes and records out of their boxes and sleeves. It's been some night round here. – Let me get me coat off first! I smiled.

– Fuck the coat, how was it? she insists.

– He's a total shag, I told her.

– Ms Cheesy Grin herself, Marie smiles.

– Well, darling, if you'd been sucking on a cheesy cock you'd have a cheesy grin too, I say to her.

– C'mon then, I want all the details.

– Well, he's hot on fingers and tongue stuff, once he relaxed and stopped trying to please me, stopped being so …

– Performative?

– Yeah, that's the word I was looking for.

– He didn't give you head …

I smiled and nod, curling my lips inwards and tremble in delicious recall.

– Heather! The second date!

– It wasn't the second date, it was the sixth date. It was the second shag, remember?

– Go on.

– I came bucketloads, woke up the whole of Leith. It was fucking marvellous. So good, in fact, I did it again. I could feel him right up in my stomach. It was weird, I thought it was because he was bigger than Hugh, but they looked about the same size. Then I realised that it was because Hugh had only been fucking me with half his cock, the poor bastard. I was just so tense with him I'd never open up properly. With Lloyd, though, he just opens me like he's peeling a fucking orange. What a wide-on I got ... you could've got a convoy of lorries up there.

– Lucky cow ... no, you deserve it, hen, you really do. I'm just jealous. I fucked a coke-head last night. It was good for him and shite for me. So fucking cold, she shook her head ruefully.

I went over to her and gave her a cuddle, – It's awright ... it's just one of those things ...

She rubbed my wrist, – Yeah, next time ...

28 Lloyd

Ah'm sittin wi Ally and ah'm telling him: – Ah've never been sae fuckin scared in ma puff, Ally. Mibbee huv tae chill on this relationship thing a bit. It's gittin too heavy.

Ally looks at ays and shakes his heid. – If you run fae this, Lloyd, make sure it's fir the right reasons. Ah see ye when yir wi her. Ah see how ye are. Dinnae deny it!

– Aye, but …

– Aye but nowt. Aye but dinnae you start actin the cunt unless thirs something ah dinnae ken. That's aw the fuckin aye buts you need tae listen tae. Dinnae be feared ah love, man, that's what they want. That's the wey they divide. Dinnae ever be feared ah love.

– Mibbe yir right, ah say. – Ye fancy daein some eggs?

29 Heather

The thing about Lloyd, though, was that he was never around during the week. It started to get to me. The weekends, it was great, we were E'd up and we made love a lot. It was big party. But he used to avoid seeing me during the week. One day I confronted him about it. I went round to his, and I didn't call him first.

When I got there the place was a tip. Worse than Marie's at its worst. – It's jist thit ah'm intae a different scene during the week, Heather. Ah know myself. Ah'm just no good company, he told me. He looked terrible: worn-out, tense; dark circles under his eyes.

– I see, I said to him. – You come out with all that bullshit about how you love me but you only want to be with me when you're high at the weekend. Great.

– It isnae like that.

– It is, I heard my voice rising, – You just sit here during the day, all depressed and bored. We only make love at the weekend, only when you're E'd up. You're a fake, Lloyd, an emotional and sexual fake. Don't touch what you can't emotionally afford. Don't lay claims to emotions you can't feel without drugs!

I'm feeling guilty at giving him such a hard time, because he looks in such distress, but I'm annoyed. I can't help it. I want it to move on. I want to be with him more. I need to.

– It's not fuckin false. When I'm E'd up it's like ah want to be. It's no like anything's been added to me, it's like it's been taken away fae me; aw the shite in the world that gets intae your heid. When I'm E'd up I'm my real self.

– So what are you just now then?

– I'm a fucking emotional wreckage, the waste product of a shitey world a bunch of cunts have set up for themselves at our expense, and the saddest thing of all is that they can't even enjoy it.

— And you are enjoying it?

— Maybe no now, but at least ah have my moments, unlike these cunts ...

— Yeah, weekends.

— Aye, right! Ah want it! Ah want that. Why the fuck shouldn't ah be able to have it!

— You should be able to have it. I want to give you it! I need you to give it to me! Listen, just dinnae phone me for a bit. You can't do without drugs, Lloyd. If you want to see me, do it without drugs.

He looked totally devastated, but he can't have been as devastated as I felt when my anger subsided and I got home. I waited for the phone to ring, jumping out of my skin every time I heard it.

But he never called and I couldn't bring myself to call him. Not then, and not later, not after I'd heard what they said at the party.

Marie and Jane and me at a party, and my blood running cold in the kitchen as I hear some guys talking about a guy named Lloyd from Leith and what he was supposed to have done and who with.

I couldn't call him.

Epilogue

I was dancing away at The Pure, kicking like fuck because Weatherall's up from London and he's moved it up seamlessly from ambient to a hard-edged techno dance-beat and the lasers have started and everybody is going crazy and through it all I can see him, jerking and twitching under the strobes and he's seen me and he comes over. He was wearing that top. The one he'd had on when we'd met. The one he put around me that night. – What do you want? I roar at him, not missing a beat.

– Ah want you, he said, – I'm in love with you, he's shouting in my ear.

Easy to say when you're fucking E'd up. But it got to me, and I tried not to show that I was moved, or that he looked so good to me. It had been three weeks. – Yeah, well tell me that on Monday morning, I smiled. It wasn't easy, cause I'm well E'd and feeling so much. I would never be fucked around by a guy again though. Never. The noise was getting to me. It had been so good, but Lloyd had turned it into a grating grind with the piece of shit his simple words implanted in my head.

– I'll be round, he shouted, smiling.

– I'll believe it when I see it, I said. Who the fuck did he think he was.

– Believe it, he said.

Oh Batman, my Dark Fucking Knight I do not think. – Well, I'm away to find Jane, I told him. I had to get away from him. I was on my trip, in my scene. He's a fucking freak, a fucking sad freak. I should have known. I should have been able to tell. Lloyd. Go. I moved to the front of the house. I was trying to get back into the music, thrashing, trying to forget Lloyd, to dance him out of my mind, to get back to where I'd been before he appeared. The crowd are going crazy. This mad guy's in front of Weatherall giving it loads and standing back and applauding as the man responds, taking it higher. I got really hot and breathless and had to stop for a bit. I moved through the mental crowd and hit the bar for some water. I saw Ally, Lloyd's mate. – What's Lloyd on tonight, then? I asked him. I shouldn't have asked him. I'm not interested in Lloyd.

– Nowt, Ally said. He was sweating like he had been really kicking it, – he's just had a couple ay drinks. Didnae want a pill, eh no. Sais eh wis gaunnae take six months oaf n aw that shite. Didnae want ehs perspective damaged, that was what the daft fucker sais. Listen, Heather, man, he says with an air of confidence, – hope yir no gaunnae make him intae a straight-peg, eh.

Lloyd is not E'd up. A thousand thoughts shoot through my head with the MDMA. Weatherall took it down and I started to feel a bit giddy.

– Listen, Ally, I want to ask ye something, I say, touching him lightly on the arm, – Something about Lloyd. I told him what I heard, at that party. All he did was to laugh loudly, slapping his legs before composing himself and telling me the real story.

I felt a bit daft after this. I fingered my second pill which I had taken from my bra and slipped into the watch pocket of my jeans. It was time. But no. I saw Lloyd talking to this guy and these lassies. I nodded to him and he came over. – You talking to anybody special? I asked him, shrinking inside from my own voice: catty, jealous, sarcastic.

He just smiled softly and kept his eyes focused on mine, – Ah am now, he said.

– Want to go? I asked.

I felt his arm slide around my waist and his wet lips make contact with my neck. He squeezed me, and I returned the embrace, standing on my tiptoes, feeling my tits flatten against his chest. After a while he broke off and swept the hair back from my face. – Let's get the coats, he smiled.

We turned our backs on the chaos and headed downstairs.